Shot

by

Kristin Durfee

Dedication

To all the women who came before me and held doors open so I could walk through them.

Acknowledgements

It's no small feat to bring a book to publication, and this one was no exception. I've probably spent more hours collectively writing and re-writing this novel than any other piece I've done and I'm indebted to those who helped me along the way.

To Sarah Penner, Bria Burton, and "Richie" Ritesh Chaube, thank you for early feedback that was instrumental in giving me the confidence to keep going and the suggestions to make things better.

Arielle Haughee, you helped me so much in getting my early pages in shape. Thank you for your wonderful expertise as always.

Jill Witty. I am not sure if this book would be in your hands if not for her. Her invaluable suggestions, while overwhelming at first, changed every aspect of this book for the better. I'd surely still be querying and pulling my hair out if not for your brilliance and graciousness in giving your time and thoughts to me. And to Ralph Walker and the entire 5AM Writers Club for bringing us together and cheering me on through this process.

Sarah Hendess, for talking old maps, railway lines, and all the exciting research Historical Fiction has to offer and for being my book signing buddy.

Jennifer Greeff, the cover you have done was exactly as I'd pictured it. Thank you for giving such a stunning outside to reflect all the work inside.

Claudia Fallon and the entire team at Wild Rose Press. Thank you for believing in my work and for the countless hours spent on edits to make it the best it could be.

And as always, thank you to my family and friends. Writing is a part of who I am and I'm so thankful to each of you for cheering me on, asking me what I'm working on, and being the best cheerleaders a girl could ask for.

Chapter One

New York City, December 1929

A crumpled body lay in a puddle of blood in front of Detective Johanna Kelly's worn leather shoes.

Bile rose in her throat. She took long pulls of the cold morning air to shove it back down. Her back hurt like hell, and she knew it wasn't lady-like to think that way, but hot damn, it pained her.

And that's how she knew she was in for it.

But it wasn't like she hadn't been through some hell before. Hadn't fought for every scrap she got and now, she was finally here and she probably had about six months before it would be taken from her.

The ticking clock mixed with the putrid smells of rotting trash in the cramped alley, and she couldn't hold it back anymore.

She turned and ran a few steps before puking her meager breakfast up in a pile of trash.

A wolf whistle rang out behind her.

"Can't quite hang; maybe you should go to the pickpocket squad," one of the officers hollered, to a chorus of laughter.

Kelly waved behind her back and flicked them off.

"Whoa, no need to use such language," another called.

She took a deep breath, then regretted it as she was

too close to the trash and typical New York smells to think that would help steady her. She placed her hands on her knees for a moment then turned toward the three officers.

These idiots in suits who made about a grand more than her for no other reason than an appendage between their legs. She'd run into a million of them in the six years she'd been on the detective force. But she didn't do this job for them. She did it for her husband and kids.

And the dead guy at her feet.

"Got a name?" Kelly asked the youngest officer standing nearby.

The kid shrugged. "Dunno. Didn't really wanna touch him."

The other two also stood back and Kelly shook her head. They made fun of her for yakking when they wouldn't even take a step toward the body.

Kelly's gaze roamed around the cramped alley, which smelled of piss and the finest rank the city had to offer. Raised doors on the ground next to both buildings led to the basements of the businesses on either side. Easy escape routes. Kill someone and slip away.

The blood pooling around the downed man made the stained pavement even darker, adding to the mosaic of Lord knows what went on in these dark corners. Instinct pulled Kelly's attention upward.

The fire escape railing six floors up was bent, hanging precariously like an unhinged door over the street. She could picture the events in her head. One too many beers after a long day. The trudge up all those flights of stairs to get to a cramped, roach-infested apartment. Leaning against the railing to help stretch an aching back. The squeak of the rusty metal moments before it gave way.

"Hey," Kelly called to the officers and pointed up. "You guys check that out?"

"Oh, shit. No," one of them said, then glanced at the other, who shrugged.

Kelly sighed.

Her hand may be forced, but yeah, maybe she could be done with all this ineptitude.

"Go knock on the door. See if anyone else is up there, but I doubt it." She stepped over the body and started walking away.

"Where you goin'?" the kid called after her, the group no longer laughing. "Oh, come on, Kelly, don't be like that."

"I work homicides. Bet you any amount of money this guy got drunk, leaned against the railing, and fell. Might wanna go after the super, but that's not my business."

She shrugged; surely another body would turn up and she'd have work to do, but in this moment, she enjoyed getting to cross this one off her mental list. She so rarely got to with all the roadblocks she faced. To find someone willing to talk to her. To help her either in the department or out. It was a nice change when she could do it all herself, at least while they still let her.

She strode away, her back aching as the new life grew inside her tired body.

Chapter Two

"Five. Four. Three. Two. One! Happy New Year!"

The band played Lombardo's "Auld Lang Syne" as people clinked glasses, hugged, and kissed. A woman grabbed Lawrence Henry by the lapels of his black tuxedo and kissed him full on the mouth. Before he was even able to say a word, she laughed and stumbled off, spilling Champagne on the marble floor of the ballroom.

Someone came up behind him and slapped him on the back. "Nineteen thirty is starting off pretty good already, huh, old chap?" Bobby said. "That market brouhaha will blow over soon too, you'll see. This year will be the tops!" He two-stepped away, carrying a green bottle as he wove through the crowd.

Lawrence made his way to the marble balcony in the back of the house. It overlooked the small patio and gardens, which lay covered in a thin layer of snow from the morning's flurries.

Light from inside poured over and illuminated the edges of what was left of this grand place. He remembered the huge grass field and woods that once was the view when he was a child, swallowed up and developed by the city's need for more space. The views disappearing as his father's pockets lined with money. Lawrence wondered how much longer the houses on this street would stand before someone decided their footprint was needed for something else.

Kids ran with sparklers, impervious to the cold. Couples swayed under the moonlight, clutching each other for warmth and company. The beat of the drum and high wail of the saxophone danced outside. The night was crisp and clear, his favorite kind, with the smell of snow in the air.

Nineteen thirty would be a good year. *His* year. He deserved it. For all he'd been through in his life, it was the least the universe could give him.

He'd only been back in New York for a few weeks, but already the city was wearing on him. It had all the bustle of Chicago, but without the hospitality. The twenty-four-seven of Miami, but without the warm weather and beautiful people.

But it was heads and tails better than Baltimore.

New York was drab and desperately trying to hold on to its importance in the world. Just like all those people inside. His father's friends, bankers, lawyers, the previous elite of the city, now pushed and prodded from their grand estates by the upcoming real estate moguls and gangsters who now ran the city. But they all pretended. Everyone inside the house behind him still lived as if they owned this place. As if the city was still theirs for the taking.

He'd show them.

Lawrence downed his glass. He had to admit, in all the places he'd been, no one could hold a candle to the free-flowing booze around here. Sure, other cities had it, but New York didn't care. It didn't flaunt it or hide it. It was just *there*. It made him tolerate the place just enough to stick around.

Voices swelled and fell around him, laughs cutting

through the muffled sounds. He shut his eyes and concentrated on his breathing. He let all the noise and energy fill him for the journey ahead—the possibility only a new year could bring.

This would be the one where he'd make his mark. He'd prove to his never-satisfied parents he could make a name for himself that was all his. He didn't need them; he would make it on his own. He *was* a worthy son. Charles wasn't the only one to be proud of in the family.

Charles. His brother, *younger* brother, received the coveted full Henry name. It was as if Lawrence's father—the previous Jr. upgraded to Charles H. Henry II—knew his firstborn would be a disappointment. Had he looked into Lawrence's newborn eyes and seen something even then? To risk the possibility this could be his only son, yet still skip the moniker and go with a less prestigious name?

This shouldn't be how the year started, with him standing in the cold alone, brooding over his family. Anger mixed with whiskey and the urge to smash his glass against the stone wall of the house bubbled in him. The music was so loud inside. No one was around. He let the heavy glass fly, the sound of it exploding against the wall barely registered through the drumbeat. He relaxed his shoulders and pushed a calming breath out of his nostrils. The tension settled to an acceptable amount.

He needed another drink. A step from the door and someone crashed into him. The ice-cold drink spilled on his crisp, white shirt, intensifying the shock of the collision. His fists balled automatically.

"Oh, shit!" the woman said, then her hand flew to

her mouth. "Pardon, I mean." She giggled and pulled out an embroidered mint green handkerchief to wipe up a spill much larger than the small cloth could handle.

He relaxed and grabbed her hand with his. "It's all right."

"No, no. I am so sorry."

Lawrence gazed down, his anger dissipating once he got a look at her. Her eyes drew him in, even partially shut by the booze. They were large and dark, pulling the memory of a deer from the back of his mind. He was transported to a time when he hunted off this very balcony with his father and brother. How his nerves got the better of him and his younger brother ended up having to take the shot for him. How is father beat on him as punishment for his weakness.

The woman's eyes appeared as if filled with ink, like you could fall in them and drown. She looked close to thirty and her hair was a few shades lighter than her pale skin under the moon. Gooseflesh broke out on her shapely arms as she struggled to dry him.

"I'm such a klutz. Please, send me the dry cleaning bill." She wobbled one step to the left.

Lawrence reached out to steady her. "Easy. Listen, let's go back inside. Someone broke a glass out here. I don't want you to cut yourself."

She smiled, white teeth beaming at him as puffs of air escaped her lips.

"I knew I shouldn't have come here," she whispered as they reentered the party.

"And why not, pray tell?"

She gestured to his shirt. "I don't drink much, and I guess the Champagne went straight to my head, just like Anna said it would."

"I'm Lawrence." He offered his hand.

She took it, allowing him to hold hers. "Ruth Smith," she said breathlessly.

He kissed the top of her hand. She turned her head away and her chest bloomed pink. Back in the light, the velvet on her royal blue dress was a bit discolored in places, the material rubbed from obvious years of use. No jewelry dripped from her neck or ears.

Lawrence pegged her as an outsider. A friend of a friend, something like that. He pictured her getting the invite to the party and then scrambling to find a suitable dress. Maybe borrowing one. An older sister? A trusted friend? He wondered how extensive her network was.

She looked back at him. "Well, I hope to see you again, Lawrence. Outside of this…" She gestured around them. "…ridiculous place."

"Ridiculous?" he asked, amused.

"Have you *seen* this place? Do they need this many butlers? And a live band? Every drop of booze in the tri-state area? It seems a bit pretentious to me."

Lawrence nodded, trying to keep his lips from smiling. Yes, definitely an outsider.

A woman rushed toward them, eyes wide and mouth agape. A look that could only mean she'd heard her friend's ramblings.

"Ruth, we have to scram." She tugged on Ruth's arm, but the woman made no attempt to leave.

"I'm all right," Ruth said.

"*Now*," the woman—presumably Anna—growled.

Ruth allowed herself to be dragged away. Lawrence waved and Ruth waved back, giggling. It wasn't until she was out of sight that Lawrence realized he still held the embroidered cloth in his hand.

Yes, he could use this.
Use her.
Maybe 1930 would be his year after all.

Chapter Three

Anna tugged on Ruth's arm so hard, she cried out in pain. Her friend did not loosen her grip, dragging her through the parlor and down the stairs to the coat check. Anna handed over their blue tickets, still not letting go of Ruth.

"What's wrong?" Ruth tried to wrench her arm back.

Anna took the coats from the man and shoved Ruth's toward her.

"Do you know who that was?" she asked. "Who you made a complete fool of yourself to?"

Ruth shook her head and tried to focus on the doubled vision of her friend.

Anna signed. "Lawrence," she whispered.

Ruth laughed. "I know, he introduced himself." She freed her arm and put on her coat.

"Lawrence *Henry*."

It took a moment to pass through the alcohol surrounding Ruth's brain. Her eyes widened. Oh God. Oh no.

Anna nodded. "Yeah, why do you think I dragged you out, you dolt?"

"I need to go back in there, find him, and apologize."

Anna shook her head. "Not a good idea. The best we can hope for is he'll forget all about it. Come on, let's get out of here."

They walked arm-in-arm, each a little unsteady and helping to hold the other one up. Women in silky dresses and men in tails pressed and jostled them as they pushed their way through Millionaire's Row and down Fifth Avenue. Ruth stared up at the Flatiron Building, her favorite in the whole city, and almost lost her balance. She started to pitch into the street, but then someone else bumped and righted her. She focused on her steps after that and tried to ignore the views. They moved through a more residential area and the large brownstones loomed on either side. The lights of clubs dotted the distance as people moved toward home or more festivities. Chatter about the new Times Square ball filtered into Ruth's ears, but she concentrated on Anna's cool arm and holding on to it.

It was the first time she'd been out in the city on New Year's. Normally, she'd stay home with her parents and sisters, counting down to the large clock in the kitchen before running out on the fire escape to bang pots and pans together. Even at twenty-nine, she loved the spectacle they made of it. They'd laugh and make bold promises and predictions for the following year.

When Anna invited her to the party after she'd become friendly with a Henry cousin, Ruth jumped at the chance. As she neared thirty, Ruth noticed the nervousness in her parents' eyes increased. One more day their daughter went without a prospect and closer to dying alone. A dreaded spinster.

At first, she scoffed at their worries. She was young, there was no rush. But as the years passed, their fear became her own. She watched as her classmates met men and got married. Date after failed date, set up by friends of friends of friends, yielding nothing but boring conversation over decadent dessert. The kicker was when her sister got engaged.

Her *younger* sister.

She attempted to go out more, really make an effort, but she had few friends left that weren't settling down, having kids, and becoming homemakers. Her frustration at not being chosen for such a life had intensified in the last six months. She began agreeing to most outings Anna suggested. Prohibition made Ruth nervous, so they only purveyed establishments with alcohol when Anna's husband could accompany them. While Prohibition was more a laughed-about suggestion in the city, there were still risks. All it took was a bored flatfoot in a bad mood. Then you could easily find yourself in the slammer and no amount of male protection could get her out of that mess.

Plus, that certainly wouldn't help her prospects, or job security.

She'd been at the department store for nearly ten years, working her way up from a lowly restocking girl to a floor manager. But this year would be her big break. If there could be one silver lining to not being wed, it was the blissful freedom to continue working much longer than her counterparts.

One of the buyers who did all the purchasing for the women's departments was retiring. Of course, to get married. Ruth decided this was her opportunity to give herself another avenue in life. If she wasn't getting any marriage proposals, she might as well fill the time that would have been spent cooking meals and caring for children by going to London and Paris fashion shows.

She'd interviewed for the position last week and was giddy with anticipation to find out if she landed the job.

Anna had worked with her for a year before transferring to the men's department. Ten months later, she quit after getting engaged to one of her regular customers, a high roller who traveled for work more than he was home.

When Ruth told her mother about the engagement, she'd been both excited and horrified.

"Then why are you staying in the women's department? Unless, oh Ruth…"

"Mother!" Ruth exclaimed.

"You know, Betsy Davis's daughter had a similar…affliction. But they were able to cure her of it! She went away for a few months and came back totally fine. She's married now with a child!" Her voice was shrill and hopeful.

Ruth groaned. "Mother, I am not a lesbian."

"Ruth!"

"I like my job and I'm sure if I'm meant to marry, I will."

Her mother had huffed, but it wasn't brought up again.

As they pushed their way through the throngs of people back to their apartments, Ruth couldn't help but feel a boozy conflict of emotions. She forgot to make a New Year's resolution, the first time ever. And which one should it be? Focus on her career and future, push harder and fight for better opportunities? Or find someone, settle down, and let this be her last single year? Instead, she resolved to simply go for it.

Though, what *it* was, she wasn't quite sure.

Chapter Four

Lawrence was disappointed Ruth got dragged away. Her confession about his family both amused and intrigued him. He was so used to people, women especially, fawning over him. Expecting his parent's money to shower upon them if they paid Lawrence a compliment. Those women were in it for one thing. That's not what he needed. The thought of being with someone so different was thrilling.

He made his way back through the house, catching glimpses of Ruth as she was pulled out of the door. He grabbed a martini from a silver tray as the butler held the door open for him, the man giving Lawrence a small wink Lawrence ignored. He had to focus.

After following the two women for a block, he lost sight of them, swallowed by the masses. He cursed himself, normally much better at this sort of thing. Must be all the drinks. He threw it in the trash. If his goal was his concentration this year, he'd have to work hard on tempering his vices.

This was too important.

He strolled a few paces before doubling back. Returning to the party seemed useless at this point. Being surrounded by happy, or faux-happy, partiers was the last way he wanted to spend the first moments of the New Year. It was funny how the clock striking midnight made everything feel possible. Like one second all hope was lost but in a single tick it all opened back up again. He decided to revel in it for a night. Then, he'd start making plans.

Yes. He'd make his own money. He didn't need his parents. Perhaps he'd even settle down, let some woman turn him respectable. Maybe Ruth. It would be a flawless irony. To bring home to his parents someone who could see through their charade. It would be the perfect revenge. That would show them.

Tomorrow he would call on Ruth. It would be easy enough to find out where she lived. The butlers would have kept records of all the invited guests. He'd track her down and invite her to dinner. The thrill made him ache for a card game, but they'd all already be well underway by now. He should have skipped the party and gone to one, but no. He wouldn't have met Ruth then. There was something about her that said she was his ticket out.

He needed to impress her, whether she expected it or not. While she may think the party too much, she also had to know by now who he was. It was obvious by the way her friend dragged her out she knew Ruth had put her foot in her mouth.

He'd need to take her someplace nice. Someplace expensive that he couldn't afford. Because if there's one thing he knew about having rich parents, it's that it meant shit to the bank account of their children. Especially if one of their children was named Lawrence.

When the older couple came out of through his parents' front gate, the thought entered his mind, as if it was buried there the whole time and burrowed its way out instead of in.

He followed them several blocks before they turned down an alley. They were easier to follow than Ruth and Anna had been. Lawrence reached into his pocket and cupped the wooden grip in his palm. He kept pace with them, making sure the clicks of his heels fell in line with the man's. They faced forward, but Lawrence recognized the man's greased dark hair and the woman's scandalously long gray locks. He didn't know their names, but knew they were friends of his parents.

Wealthy friends.

Halfway down the alley, they slowed, evidently realizing their error of direction and reversed, almost walking straight into Lawrence.

The man's face registered fear before recognition. "Lawrence!" he said, oblivious to the revolver.

"Oh, we got turned around," his wife added. "Glad we *ran* into you." Her laughter was high-pitched, puffs of hot air bursting into the freezing night. She pulled her fur coat tighter against the cold, the red of her dress trimming the exposed areas at her chest and wrists.

The neon lights across the street, plus the moon, bathed the dark alley in a pink glow. A glow that glittered off the woman's emerald and diamond necklace.

They tried to step forward, but Lawrence didn't move. The couple laughed awkwardly and moved single file, as if their side-by-side nature prevented their escape, not the armed man standing in front of them. Shouts and firecrackers littered the air, making it both quiet and loud in undulating waves.

"Lawrence, my dear boy," the man said, a glance at his watch a subtle indicator at his annoyance at their continued delay. "Won't you point us in the right direction?"

"I need you to give me your wallet." Lawrence's voice was steady as the gun he held.

The man stared at the gun for a second before he moved to stand between Lawrence and his wife. She wasn't so quick on the uptake and linked arms with him yet again.

"Lawrence…"

He squeezed the trigger without hesitation. The man gaped open-mouthed as his wife crumpled behind him, dragging him down slightly before he could jerk his arm away. The blood spilling from her chest blended into her dark red dress. His hands immediately shot into the air.

"Your wallet," Lawrence repeated.

This time, the man didn't hesitate. He reached into his jacket and pulled out a thick billfold with a silver clip. He pushed it into Lawrence's open left hand as he bent to tend to his motionless wife.

As the noises swelled again, Lawrence pressed the barrel against the man's head and pulled the trigger. The smell of gun smoke swirled in the air as flakes of snow fell to the ground.

Lawrence glanced back to the street, but no one noticed. No calls from the windows of fire escapes from above. He used the toe of his right shoe to push the man off his wife. Her necklace was spared of any blood. Lawrence carefully unclasped it and placed it in his pocket.

The green was the perfect color. It would look wonderful around Ruth's neck.

Chapter Five

Detective Kelly could barely see over her desk with the towers of papers surrounding her. She was about to pull another sheet toward her when one of the beat cops slapped another folder down.

"Boss wants you to go to the scene," he said, his voice hoarse with lack of sleep, too much drink, or a combination of the two.

The entire force had been working since the previous night, the uptick in crime expected on New Year's. Robberies. Looting. Drunks sobering up in the holding cells. Seventeen rapes. One murder.

Kelly flipped open the folder on her desk.

Make that three.

"Don't complain," the cop said. "You wanted this gig."

Her eyes flashed. "I didn't complain."

He shrugged and walked away, distributing files to the desk which surrounded her noticeably smaller one.

She read the hand-scrawled notes. A couple had been found in the morning by garbage men emptying the cans down the alley. She checked her watch. With how the city was running this morning, if she sprinted, she bet she could beat the coroner there to the bodies.

She arched to stretch her back, then grabbed her brown coat. It was of a dated cut and only had raccoon fur lining the collar and cuffs. What she wouldn't give for a full fox or mink coat to keep her warm against the elements. Maybe in ten years when those went out of fashion she'd be able to afford one.

Buttoning the jacket as high as it would go, she went out to brave the aftermath of too much celebrating.

The streets were littered with colorful disks of paper confetti and broken glass. She'd never understand the fine line between celebration and destruction. Most days the city toed the line, but not last night. No, it skipped rope with it, leaving a path of transgressions behind for folks to regret the next day. And for her to try to clean up.

When she got to the alley, two coppers were standing guard. They held up their hands.

"Ma'am, we're gonna need you to keep moving," one called to her.

She flashed her badge and forced herself not to take offense when they leaned in closer to inspect it before nodding.

"Guys here yet to pick up the bodies?" she asked.

They shook their heads.

"Nope," one said. "Fucking freezing and they just let us wait. Guess there's no rush since they're already on ice in this damn cold." As if for emphasis he blew into his hands and tucked them under each armpit.

Kelly made her way down the alley, noting that it wasn't particularly long but twice as wide as normal. Easily mistaken for a street if one was unfamiliar with the area. But what she didn't get was how no one saw anything.

Could the crime have been swallowed up by the melee?

The couple was older and impeccably dressed. Him in tails, and a top hat a few feet from him. Her in a red velvet dress topped with a brown fox fur coat. No jewelry. Maybe intentional. Probably not.

She didn't need to wait for the docs to get here to figure out how they died. His face was blown half off and her chest had a gaping hole. Blood in pools around them. Either the weapon was high-caliber, or the killer was close when he pulled the trigger. Maybe both.

She wasn't sure what it was inside of her that she could see a dead body and be moved to curiosity, not horror. It wasn't like she tortured cats as a kid or plucked the legs off bugs like the boys did, but she was always fascinated by death. Wanted to know what caused it, probably in a vain attempt to prevent it.

When her husband worked this beat, she'd ask him a million questions, but he never went into detail. He could stomach all this but still waited outside when their two children were born. Acted like birth was more alarming than death to witness. She'd never understand men.

And when he was shot and she changed his bandages right alongside changing diapers, he never commented on her resolve. When she leveraged his injury to move from the prison matron squad to his old department, arguing he was just as good as dead to them for all the money he could bring in, the board agreed with her. Nodded and patted themselves on the back for helping out a family who gave so much to them. Got to add her as a feather in their caps for how progressive they were, shoving that in the face of the LAPD and all the progress they made with female officers.

She gave two shits how she got there. It was where she wanted to be and she was damn good at the work. Let the boys at the station speculate. Let them whisper behind her back about her wheelchair-bound husband and wonder out loud if she went up the chain to "get her needs met". And when they found out she was pregnant? Heads would roll. She'd be shipped off and brushed away before any accusations, false as they were, could be made against her and her family.

It was a bitch to have a job you loved and were good at, but no one wanted you doing it. A damn bitch.

So she'd hunker down and work the last cases she'd probably ever get to, retire with a small pension and live out her days wondering what all she could have done in the world. Teetering between loving this baby fiercely and grieving that it would bring her professional end.

But not yet. She still had some time.

She looked around the alley, but nothing else seemed out of the ordinary. No thrown garbage cans or lids or other indications the couple tried to fight back. In her experience that meant they either were completely startled without the time to react, or they knew the person. She wasn't sure which one it was yet.

"Any idea who these two are?" Kelly called to the officer walking toward her.

A man in a lab coat pulling a rattling cart trailed him.

The officer's face was expressionless as he shook his head. "Wallet is missing. No one has reported anyone missing with a similar description, but it'll just be a matter of time. These two seem important. Someone'll be lookin' for them."

Kelly nodded and gave her information to the technician picking up the bodies. The man raised an eyebrow, but stuffed the card in his coat without comment.

"Usually I have the detectives help me lift on days when I'm shorthanded," the technician said.

"I can help." Kelly stepped forward, but the officer stopped her.

"I got this, ma'am."

She shrugged. Probably for the best anyway, but she hated the implication. As if she was weak. As if she hadn't subdued men twice her size in prison. There was no point hanging around anymore so she strode out of the alley, brain ticking through possibilities.

This wasn't the way she wanted to start the year. Probably her *last* year. Though she always knew she'd never solve all the open cases assigned to her, she still hoped for a bit more time. A few more chances.

The unsolved crimes which littered her past probably needed a death-bed confession to be solved. There were twelve. Not as high as some of the younger guys, even, but Kelly was acutely aware of each and every one of them.

And now, as she pulled her coat tight against the cold and returned to the station, she hoped in six months she wouldn't be leaving with lucky number thirteen left behind.

Chapter Six

Ruth teetered on a chair with three pins in her mouth as Suzy talked rapidly beneath her.

"The Henrys! I can't believe you went to the Henrys' for New Year's. I am just green with envy!"

"And made a fool of myself. You forget that part," Ruth mumbled through the pins.

She slipped the dress off the mannequin and gently handed it down to Suzy. They were quiet for a moment in acknowledgement of the beautiful piece held between them. The sequins rustled softly, like grass swaying in the wind as the garment shifted and moved.

It was beautiful, and chances were, would never be worn. Ruth could make herself cry if she thought too hard about all the waste around her. How fleeting the fashions were, how immediate their shoppers were, two days ago clamoring for *the* dress for all their fancy parties and today casting them aside as if the turn of the year doomed the clothes to uselessness.

And really, it did.

Sequined dresses were holiday-appropriate only. They all had to come down, to be replaced with the red, pink, and white garb of the impending Valentine's Day. The wedding dresses to lure those who exited the season with some new jewelry on their left ring finger. It was all a stark reminder to Ruth that she was still single. Whether or not she was all right with her current situation, she was aware of her aloneness as if it was a missing appendage. A ghostly feeling for what should be there.

They'd hung the dress on a hanger, zipped it in a black bag, and placed it on a rolling rack. The moment of silence passed. Ruth climbed back up on the chair and reached up to remove the accessories and hand them down.

Suzy was mid-sentence when she stopped talking. Ruth looked down, expecting her to be on her hands and knees looking for a missing earring, but instead the woman stood slack-jawed. Ruth followed her gaze and nearly tumbled off the chair.

Lawrence Henry walked toward them, a smile on his face and a single rose in his hand.

Ruth reached out for Suzy's arm to prevent herself from falling as she awkwardly stepped down. Lawrence rushed forward to help steady her. Suzy stood for a beat longer before she mumbled something about needing more hangers and scuttled away.

"Mr. Henry." Heat crept up her face and beads of perspiration formed on her scalp.

He shook his head. "Call me Lawrence, please. Here."

He thrust the flower at her, which she took and automatically smelled. Its fragrance was sweet, exactly how you'd want a rose to smell. She was about to ask where he got such a thing in the dead of winter, but stopped herself. A faint memory of a greenhouse off one of the sitting rooms entered her mind.

"This is beautiful. Thank you," she said, remembering her manners. "Is there something I can help you with?"

"Yes, I am looking for an outfit."

She nodded, gazing around the floor. "I am in the women's department, but I can show you to a gentleman that can help you."

He touched her arm and electricity coursed through her. She snapped her attention back to him.

"I am looking for a dress."

Yes, yes of course he was. Probably for his wife. She stole a quick glance at his hand. No ring. A girlfriend then. Ruth nodded at him and took a few steps back to the middle of the store when he stopped her.

"What about these?" He fingered the black bags on the rack.

"They are more of the New Year's dresses," she said, again feeling pity for the cast-off garments.

"Isn't it New Year's Day today?" His mouth formed a teasing half-smile.

She laughed. "As far as the fashion world is concerned." Ruth leaned forward and lowered her voice as if letting him in on a secret. "They may as well have been from last decade."

"Well, we can't have that, can we? Please take me to your newest arrivals."

Forty minutes later, a half-dozen dresses were lined up on a rack, their collective worth more than double her yearly salary. She lightly ran her hands over the smooth silk and lace as she presented the gowns for his inspection.

He looked at the dresses then gazed at her. "The green one."

It was stunning. Deep emerald, long sleeves, a high neck with a layered drop in the back. The silk flowed through her fingers like cool water.

"Will you try it on?" He stood right next to her.

The hairs on the back of her neck rose as she shivered. "Me?"

They were strictly forbidden from playing dress up and trying anything on unless they planned to purchase. But could she say no to a customer? She decided to take the risk. When else in her life would she wear something so magnificent, even if just for a moment?

Suzy giggled with her in the dressing room as she helped Ruth with the gown. "Wait!" She pulled Ruth's hair up, twisted it in a low bun and pinned it before opening the dressing room curtain.

Lawrence locked eyes with her as she glided forward. She fought the urge to cross her arms in front of herself, to cover the figure-revealing outfit. His look made her feel oddly naked and exposed.

Ruth caught her reflection in the mirror, but barely recognized herself. Suzy was right to put her hair up; it showed off her long neck and the open back. The silk draped on her as if custom made. Suddenly, she didn't mind Lawrence eying her up and down. She'd never felt so beautiful.

"Yes," Lawrence said a little smile on his face "That is the one."

"Good choice, Mr. Henry. We will wrap it right up for you right away," Suzy called, pulling Ruth back into the dressing room. "I thought that man would take a bite out of you," she whispered.

"Suzy," Ruth chided.

But Suzy held a finger up to her lips. "Just enjoy this for a moment. Take a deep breath and remember this feeling."

Ruth did as she was told, wanting to savor it for a beat longer, but Suzy was already unzipping her. Clad again in her plain black rayon dress and stockings, Ruth brought the expertly wrapped box to the checkout counter. As sad as she was to see the dress go, the commission she'd get would more than make up for it. She passed Lawrence his change along with the box.

As an afterthought, she slid the box back. "Would you like a bow?" she asked, remembering all the holiday ribbon they still had.

"What do you think?"

"I think it adds a nice touch."

"A bow it is then."

She took her time tying it, keeping him there for a few more moments. She wanted to say something, apologize for her behavior the night before, but was ultimately too embarrassed to bring it up. She'd never see him again anyway, so it probably didn't matter.

Finally, she'd delayed as long as she could. She walked around the counter and handed him the box, allowing her hands to touch his for the briefest of moments.

She guided him to the door. Just before he exited, he asked her to dinner.

She reflexively placed her hand over her chest. "Me?"

He laughed. "Yes. I'll pick you up at eight?"

She nodded.

"Wonderful. Here." He thrust the box into her hands. "Wear this." He winked and left.

A puff of cold air from the open door woke her from her daze.

Chapter Seven

Lawrence walked with a spring in his step, impressed with himself. He pegged Ruth being an easy mark, but this went better than he'd imagined. His brother was notoriously the smooth one in the family, impressing women and getting everyone to like him. Lawrence's heart thudded in his chest with the excitement of the entire dance he'd just pulled off.

As he watched Ruth gingerly touching the fabrics, trying to keep her gaze down as she twirled in the dress, then took longer than expected to wrap it up; he knew his ploy would work. She was expecting this as a gift for someone else. She would enjoy the moments of pretend, probably hang on to them for weeks to come, regale the other shop ladies about that time the rich man came in and she was able to try on dresses.

He knew what he was doing.

When he asked her to dinner, he knew she'd never say no. If he'd invited her when he first walked in, he was sure she would have turned him down. Apologize for her rudeness the night before and say she wasn't worthy of taking out. He'd have to try to convince her, but the whole ordeal would be tedious. Making her *want* it. That was the way to make it real. For her, at least.

He fingered Ruth's handkerchief in his pocket, unsure of where to go. He considered the Everyard

Bathhouse and walked a few steps in that direction, but then remembered with the holiday it would probably have more police presence. Anytime there was a big celebration, they kept a close eye on the few bathhouses in the area. Any excuse to try to rough up a few guys and slap them with some charges.

No. Not today.

He felt his pockets. They crinkled with what was left of the paper money from the couple. He checked his watch. Plenty of time.

He pushed open the door of the gambling parlor, filling it momentarily with light. Men sitting around tables brought their hands up to shield their eyes. The majority had most likely been here since last night. Betting from one year to the next.

Lawrence slapped a few twenties on the table and exchanged them for brightly colored chips.

The game was rowdy. Laughing and cursing as men trumped each other's hands. There were some knocked-over chairs and harsh words, but mostly it was a friendly game.

Lawrence was all business. He focused on each hand. Did the math, played the odds. Doubled his money. His heart raced in an entirely new way.

Three hours later, he was piping mad with himself. He owed the house twenty dollars. He should have walked away when he was ahead. He should *always* walk away when he's ahead, but he got too wrapped up. Felt too invincible. And now, here he was, an hour and change out from his date without any money.

He walked the ten blocks to his brother's place, nodding at the doorman before going up to the apartment.

Charles answered the door, surprise turning to delight in a flash. For all the faults of his parents, for the deep hurt they inflicted on him, their one saving grace was giving him Charles for a brother. Lawrence might be jealous of his brother's position, but he loved Charles as much as anyone.

"And to what do I owe this pleasure?" Charles pulled Lawrence into a crushing hug.

"I can't come visit my little brother and wish him a Happy New Year?"

"Ah, that you can always do. Please, come inside."

He moved over and motioned for Lawrence to enter. Lawrence declined his offer to take his coat.

"I can't stay long."

Lawrence looked around the apartment as he always did, sizing the place up. It was almost twice as large as his, the furnishings a tick or two of higher quality. No expense spared. But that didn't matter right now. All he was concerned with was a date in an hour's time that had to go well.

"I need some money." No point in dancing around the subject.

Charles laughed and shook his head. "I should have known. You don't do spontaneous visits."

"You won't believe what happened. Let me tell you this story—"

Charles held up a hand. "I don't need to hear your made-up story."

"It's not made up."

"Spare me," Charles said. "You couldn't ask Mother and Father while you were there last night? Why don't you ask them now? You disappeared without saying good-bye. I'm sure they'd like to know you are still alive."

"I don't need help from them, I don't need help from nobody," Lawrence said, anger building in him.

Here was his younger brother who got everything handed to him, and he couldn't pass a little of that on to Lawrence?

Charles sighed and reached into his wallet. He pulled out a hundred dollars and put the money in Lawrence's hand. "Here. Just tell me you aren't going to gamble it away."

"Never. This one is a sure bet." He winked.

"Aren't they all?"

Chapter Eight

A bag of clothing waited on Kelly's desk when she arrived in the morning.

"What's this?" she called to Peggy, the woman who answered the phones.

"Guy from the coroner's office dropped it off," Peggy hollered back. "Says it's the stuff from the couple."

Kelly brought the bag to an empty desk and spilled the contents. It smelled rank, the blood mixing with body odor to a scent that churned her already delicate stomach. She doubted the tech would have extended the same lack of courtesy to her male counterparts by not drying it all out first, but it wasn't worth fighting about.

There was nothing to the woman's dress other than fabric, no hidden pockets or paper pinned to it. The man's pants were also empty, but Kelly felt something stiff in the left side of the suit jacket. Folded in half, in thick cardstock leafed with gold lettering, was an invitation.

Mr. and Mrs. Charles Henry II, request the pleasure of your company as they celebrate the ringing in of the Year of Our Lord, nineteen-hundred-and-thirty. Ten p.m. Tails optional.

Blood on the top corner marred the stationary.

She went through the rest of the belongings. A set of keys on a gold key ring and some pocket change were in the coat, but still no identification.

The invitation was her only lead. She put on her coat and hoofed it across town.

A man in a butler's uniform greeted her after the second knock from the ornate brass ring on the door.

"The maids use the rear entrance." He started to shut the door in her face.

Kelly pulled out her badge and the man rolled his eyes. She knew she was a novelty, but the pushback still annoyed her, especially from working-class people. She considered herself on their side.

"Got a couple questions for the gentleman of the house, Mr. Charles Henry," she said, working to keep her voice even.

"The Second," the butler said, not moving.

"Sorry?"

"His name is Mr. Charles Henry the Second."

A step led to a small ledge by the door, forcing callers to be shorter than whoever was answering. It allowed the butler to literally look down on her, dressed in her skirt suit and worn-out low heels. Kelly sighed, not having the patience for the charade today but having few other options than to play the man's game.

"My mistake. Mr. Charles Henry, *the Second.* Is the gentleman home?" Kelly tried to look around the butler.

She hated coming to the homes of the rich. They were always the most important when they needed help, waltzing into the police station demanding to be seen right away, but would keep the coppers waiting anytime the tables were turned.

The butler stood aside. "You may wait in the parlor while I ask if he is receiving guests today."

"Much obliged," Kelly threw the butler her widest smile.

She paced the spacious room. A red oriental rug covered most of the parquet floors and a few velvet covered chairs and couches were pushed against the oak walls. Paintings of fields and country houses hung at various heights. A gold chandelier a half-size too large for the space towered over the room.

Twenty minutes later, the butler showed her to an office off a long corridor. She wondered if the staff ever got lost in this place. They'd only made two turns and she was already unsure if she could find her way out.

After another ten minutes, an older man entered, gesturing to Kelly to take the seat opposite a large, mahogany and cast-iron desk.

"You are not who I was expecting when my butler said a detective was here."

"Yes, I get that a lot. My name is Detective Johanna Kelly, New York Police Department, forty-fifth precinct."

Kelly reached her hand out and he grabbed the tips of her fingers, refusing to shake her hand properly. She had to let that slight go as well. "I appreciate your time, Mr. Henry, sir."

"What can I help you with?"

Kelly took a breath, unsure of how to bring this man into the wild-goose chase. Honesty was probably the best way.

"Mr. Henry, there was a couple murdered last night."

"Oh? And you think I did it?" he asked, a jesting tone to his voice. "You women and your crazy theories."

Let it go.

"No, sir. Nothing like that. They had an invitation to your party—"

"And?"

"All of their identification was stolen. I am hoping you may be able to shed some light on who they are. There have been no missing persons reports filed fitting their description." She paused, but Mr. Henry stayed silent. "The man and woman appear to be in their late sixties or early seventies. He had jet black hair, and was, of course, wearing tails. She had long gray hair and wore a dark red dress with long sleeves, fur coat over it."

Mr. Henry turned and pulled a braided rope which descended from the wall. Moments later the butler arrived.

"Would you please fetch Mrs. Henry?"

The man nodded and disappeared.

"I must confess I am not the most observant when it comes to the wears of women." He shrugged. "But my wife surely is. You know how that is." He gestured toward Kelly's wedding band.

Mrs. Henry entered and introductions were made. She was a mousy woman, down to her gray dress and gloves. Kelly wondered if this was some sort of new funeral-esque fashion. She never really stayed on top of such things.

Kelly explained why she was there and the descriptions of the ill-fated couple. Mrs. Henry placed a hand against her chest as she used the other to steady herself on her husband's desk.

"The Chanlers," she whispered.

"Chanlers?" Kelly repeated.

"Joy and Tobias. Oh dear. Oh, what a lovely couple. They have an older daughter, Clarice. Just got married. Oh, how terrible." Tears welled in her eyes.

"Was that the wedding with the terrible steak?" Mr. Henry asked. She didn't answer him.

"Mrs. Henry, I really appreciate the information. We are doing everything we can to try to catch who did this. Do either of you remember seeing them leave? If someone followed them?"

"No, it was a large party," Mrs. Henry said.

"And no one could have gotten in uninvited?" Kelly asked.

"Security is very strict," Mr. Henry said.

"Anyone you had to take off the list? Someone with…a status change?" she ventured.

"Unlike some circles, mine are smarter than to invest all in one place," he said. "The market crash may affect some, but not us."

"I see. Is there any way I could get a copy of the guest list?"

Mr. Henry puffed out a chuckle. "My dear, anyone who's anyone in the city was here. *There's* your guest list."

Chapter Nine

Ruth felt like she would throw up. From nerves or excitement, she didn't know yet. She flew around her room in a tizzy in her slip and stockings, trying to find a pair of gold hoop earrings her parents had gotten her for her eighteenth birthday.

Where were they?

As she looked around the space, inadequacy overwhelmed her. She didn't deserve this. He wasn't the match for her. Yes, she desperately wanted to get married. Have a family. But to this man? To this family?

She searched through her jewelry box for the twentieth time, sorting through cheap knock-offs. Fake jewels sparkling and faux metals slightly green with their deception. These weren't worthy of Lawrence. Of the dress.

It hung on her closet door frame, half-zipped in the bag. The fabric more luxurious and beautiful than she remembered, even though it had been mere hours since she'd gotten it. Somehow, it made the pale pink walls in her room look dingy and brought out the brown stain in her carpet.

The shoes that sat on the floor, appearing gold and pretty from far away, were really scuffed when seen up close. They wouldn't do, would they? She suspected Lawrence was the type to notice that sort of thing.

Other men she dated, no, but they weren't used to a certain quality of woman.

Maybe this wasn't a good idea after all. She wondered how she could get a message to Lawrence that she changed her mind. She was moments from a full-blown panic attack when her mother entered, holding up two gold hoops.

"Looking for these?"

Ruth almost burst into tears, the release of stress like a dam breaking.

Her mother enveloped her in a hug and rubbed her back. "Shh, shh. What's wrong?" she asked into Ruth's hair.

"I thought I lost them."

"Oh, I'm sorry," her mother said, pulling away from her. "I cleaned mine the other day and took yours as well. I must have forgotten to put them back. I thought maybe you'd want to wear them."

Ruth sniffled and nodded her head. She placed the hoops in her ears and sat at her vanity. Her room was small, just a bed, dresser, and vanity, but it held all she needed. But tonight, the walls closed in on her. She suddenly felt very old.

"Something else is wrong."

"I'm not sure if this date is a good idea."

"And why in heavens not? You said you met him at the New Year's party and he ran into you at work today and invited you out. Sounds like fate to me."

"Well…" She had glossed over the finer details. "It was his party. And I didn't so much run into him as he came in. I'm pretty sure specifically to ask me out tonight."

Her mother squealed in glee and clapped. "Oh,

Ruth, that's wonderful!" She paused in thought. "Wait, where did you say the party was again?"

"The Henrys'."

Her words hung in the air for a beat while her mother recovered.

"The Henrys'…"

Ruth sighed. "Yes, Mother. I have a date tonight with Lawrence Henry."

Her mother's hand flew to her chest. She stepped back and sat on Ruth's bed.

"Lawrence Henry," she breathed as if it were a holy name.

"Now you can see why I am so nervous. Maybe I'll cancel."

Her mother was beside her so quickly, Ruth shrank back momentarily in shock.

"You will do nothing of the sort," she said. "You are a beautiful girl. It's about time someone of caliber saw that."

"Mother," Ruth said, tired of the constant conversation of her worth as a woman tied to her worth to a man.

She pushed Ruth back and began gathering and pinning her hair. Ruth was silent, grateful for the intervention as she had no idea how she was going to wear it. Ten minutes later and her locks were a series of cascading curls.

Ruth reached up to hand to touch it and her mother slapped it away. Not lightly either.

"Now," she said. "Makeup."

She moved around Ruth and sorted through her cosmetic bag before rushing back to her room for her own. She dabbed cold cream and powder on her face until it looked flawless. Ruth sat motionless as her mother rimmed her eyes with kohl and darkened her lashes before painting her lips a fire red. If nothing else, at least she now looked the part.

"Thank you, Mother," Ruth said in awe of her abilities.

"What dress are you going to wear?" she asked.

Ruth gestured to the garment bag hanging on the back of her door.

"Ruth!" her mother exclaimed. "Ruth, did you *steal* that?" she whispered.

Ruth rolled her eyes. "No, Mother. You'll be even more thrilled to know he bought it for me."

If it weren't for the draw of the dress, Ruth was sure her mother would have fainted on the spot. She reached her hand out, but pulled it away.

"It's not a painting, Mother," Ruth said, getting up to join her.

"Ruth, it's stunning."

"I know. I'm thinking about returning it and pulling something out of my closet."

Mrs. Smith whirled to face her. "You simply *cannot*."

"Look at this dress, Mother. Look at how beautiful it is. Now look at me. This isn't me. I am not fancy enough." She pulled a cigarette from the gold case on her dresser. Her hands shook as she lit it.

Her mother plucked the stick from her mouth and crushed it in the ashtray.

"I *am* looking at you. And it doesn't matter what dress you wear, you will be stunning in it. But this." They both looked at the cascading fabric. "This dress is perfect."

"It's almost two weeks' wages…"

In one deft movement, her mother took the scissors from her vanity and cut the tag off. It floated to the floor and landed with a soft clink.

"Now," she said as she handed the shears back to Ruth. "Don't make me regret that."

Chapter Ten

"And then…" Lawrence leaned in conspiratorially. "The dog's leash got wrapped around her legs, sending her and all the packages sprawling right in the middle of Fifth Ave."

Ruth barked a loud laugh before covering her mouth and looked around the room. Lawrence stole a quick glance as well, but no one was looking at them in the dim dining room. Their booth was tucked away in the back.

"There's no way that is true," she said, a giggle still sparkling in her eyes.

Lawrence raised both hands, palms facing her. "I'm just telling you what I saw."

"So she refused to leave the dog outside?"

"Not even outside, in the car with the chauffeur."

"She had a driver?"

In that moment, the wonder of Lawrence's world was clear to him. As was that fact that he wanted to share it with Ruth. She'd looked stunning in the dress he bought her, but it was more than that. He hadn't laughed this much in a long time. At least not with a member of the opposite sex. He wasn't expecting to actually like her. Anger his parents, sure, start some talk around town about his mystery shop girl, yes. But to actually enjoy her company? He'd never considered it.

"Ruth." He dropped his voice to mock seriousness.

"She is one of the richest women in New York. Of course she has a driver."

Ruth sat back and Lawrence was worried for a moment he'd offended her. He made a mental note not to assume her knowledge of his lifestyle and that of the people in his circle again. Just when he was about to apologize, she broke into a wide grin.

"What?" Ruth shook her head. "All that money, all those people working for you, and you can still fall on your fanny in the middle of the street. I guess the fates even themselves out."

Now it was Lawrence's turn to stifle a laugh.

When the waiter came to clear their dinner plates, the side look he gave Ruth made it clear that he didn't recognize this beautiful woman, but Lawrence caught on a bit too late that Ruth should have been introduced when they sat down.

Driving the point home, the maître d' came over to their table to ask how everything was so far and top off Ruth's teacup with the Champagne sitting in the stand next to them.

"Monsieur," Lawrence said. "Please let me introduce you to Miss Ruth Smith."

The man leaned forward, took Ruth's hand, and kissed the top. "Miss Smith, it is a pleasure to meet you."

Ruth blushed and nodded her thanks to him.

"Now, don't get too impressed by Mr. Henry's stories here," he said, patting her hand and winking at Lawrence. "He's been known to spin a tale or two."

Ruth laughed and Lawrence smiled, but inside he boiled. Who was this man, this glorified servant, telling his date something negative about him? The cup he clutched shook, sloshing the liquid inside. The man must have noted Lawrence's shift in anger because he rushed to correct himself.

"I only jest," he said. "Mr. Henry here is a fine man from a fine family. You couldn't have chosen better company to share the first dinner of this wonderful New Year with." He dropped her hand and bowed in Lawrence's direction. "May I offer you some dessert? A gift for the happy couple."

Ruth beamed and bobbed her head. The man rushed off.

"I've never been offered free dessert before. He's right, I couldn't have done much better." She winked at him, and his anger softened.

The speakeasy was one of the finest in the city and Lawrence was proud to show his membership card at the door to get in. Ruth took the place in with wide eyes and remarked on how all the booze was served in tea and coffee cups to make it look inconspicuous. Lawrence had spent a great deal of money at this place since he'd arrived in New York, and it reasoned the staff here wanted to keep it that way.

Just then, a couple a few years older, sauntered up to their table. Lawrence was about to tell them to scram, but he didn't want Ruth to think less of him, so he smiled and exchanged pleasantries. It took a few seconds, but Lawrence finally recognized them. The man, Frank, was a partner at the firm his brother worked at and his wife, Ethel, was some sort of numbers girl at the bank.

"Great party last night," Ethel said.

"I'm surprised I am upright today!" Frank barked.

"Yes," Lawrence said. "Ruth and I had a wonderful

time as well."

The couple looked from Lawrence to Ruth, the latter finally being included in the exchange, and she introduced herself.

"And did you hear about the Chanlers?" Frank asked, lowering his voice.

Lawrence sat very still.

"Oh, it's terrible," Ethel jumped in. "*Murdered.*"

"That is terrible," Ruth said. "Lawrence, did you know them?"

Lawrence shrugged. "Friends of my parents, I believe."

"Robbery, they think. What is this world coming to?" Frank asked.

"And after such a fine party," Ethel said. "We are seeing all sorts of desperate people down at the bank, why, just the other day—"

At that moment, the waiter returned with two desserts. Lawrence thanked the couple for coming to say hello and turned his attention back to Ruth to make it clear that their conversation was over. He was grateful for the arrival of the food so he didn't have to ask the pair to bugger off and embarrass them.

When he looked up, Ruth stared as if she could see through the walls and all the way to Times Square.

"Ruth?"

"It's just so sad," she said. "And to think so soon after being in the same place as them. It easily could have been Anna and me…"

He took her hand. "Nonsense. You would have been more aware, safer. You and Anna would have been fine. Nothing bad would have or will happen. Understand?"

She nodded delicately wiped at her eyes. In a moment of inspiration, he lifted his cup.

"To their memory," he said.

She echoed his statement and they clinked the china.

"This looks delicious." The spoon hovered over a porcelain dish of Crème Brule.

They devoured the dessert, the custard thick and sweet. When the waiter brought the check over, Lawrence gave it a cursory glance before slipping all the money his brother gave him into the folio. His gut clenched at the exorbitant cost of the meal. He knew it was a necessary evil, but how long he could keep this charade up? Surely there were a few things he could sell or quick poker games he could jump into. He'd figure it out.

He poured them each the last of the Champagne, unwilling to let the expensive wine go to waste. "Let me tell you a story…"

She put her hand up, already laughing. "I'm so full. I don't think I can handle another funny tale."

He smiled. Yes, she might very well be worth keeping around a little while longer.

Chapter Eleven

When Ruth awoke the next morning, her entire body ached. She was grateful that it was Thursday, her day off, so she could roll over and go back to sleep. She didn't get in until after one a.m., making it two late nights in a row, something out of the ordinary for her. She knew she shouldn't have drunk so much Champagne, but it tasted so good and paired with the exquisite dinner so perfectly, she couldn't say no.

When the check came and Lawrence pulled out a giant billfold and pressed it into the folio without a mere glance, Ruth was flabbergasted. She couldn't remember a single time when money wasn't at the back of her mind. Anytime she shopped, went out with girlfriends, or was about to get a paycheck, it consumed her thoughts.

She gave what she could to her parents and saved the rest, determined one day to either travel the world or buy her children whatever they wanted. She wasn't sure what opportunity would show itself first.

But to live in a world where money just *was*. It seemed even with the ripple of the looming stock market crash, those in his circle didn't seem affected. They appeared to not fret about money or wonder where it would come from. An assumption they'd always have enough of it. The concept was so foreign to her. It became a delicious dream.

Lawrence. Her and Lawrence.

She had just about drifted back into sleep when her door banged open. Her older sister Della waddled into the room and collapsed on the bed in an exaggerated huff. She acted like she was about twenty months pregnant when really, she was only seven. Ruth covered her head with the pillow.

"I'm sleeping," she muttered, trying to sound groggy so her sister would leave her alone.

"You can sleep when you're dead." Della pulled away her pillow.

"Still pregnant?" Ruth teased.

Her sister mindlessly rubbed her belly. Ruth could just make out her silhouette in the filtered light through her shut curtains.

"I swear, I feel like it's been forever. I don't remember that with the other two. Robert thinks that means this one's a boy." She shifted again, her right hand hooking behind Ruth's bent knees. "Lord, I hope so, then I can be done with all this business."

Della was a year older than Ruth and already had two girls. Ruth thought again about her savings. She'd picture using it to buy something nice for her wedding day or a communion outfit for her firstborn. But even with Lawrence in the edges of the picture, Ruth still wondered if that future would ever happen for her.

Maybe she'd get the promotion. Pick up some beautiful things for herself in Europe. She'd be a spinster, but at least she'd be well-dressed.

"Really, sis." Ruth groaned. "It's my day off. Just let me sleep. I'm exhausted."

"Oh, I bet. But I'm here to find out all the details on *why* you are exhausted."

Ruth could picture it now. Della walking into their apartment and their mother immediately jumping into the new development on Ruth's love life. And in that moment, Ruth desired to keep it to herself. To not share how wonderful the dinner was, how much she laughed, how she felt like a million dollars in a dress that might as well have cost that much for her ability to afford it. Would saying it out loud take away some of its magic?

"It was just a date."

"Hogwash," her sister said.

Less than gracefully, she got up and opened the curtains, flooding the room with blinding light. Ruth raised her arm to shield her eyes until they could adjust.

"I need some romance in my life. Spill," she ordered.

Ruth sat up. "We had a lovely dinner, some drinks, and then came home."

Della raised her eyebrows. "The way Mom tells it, you met him at a lavish party and then he bought you a fancy dress before taking you out until after midnight."

"It was a New Year's party. And yes, he did buy me a dress."

Della looked around and spotted the garment bag hanging on Ruth's closet door frame. She pointed at it. "That?"

Ruth nodded.

Della sprung up and rushed to unzip the bag. She let out a soft gasp as she ran the silk through her fingers. She turned back to Ruth wide-eyed. "Well, I will say this, you just gave me motivation to stop eating ice cream every night so I can fit into this once the baby comes."

Ruth laughed. "Oh please, I bet you could fit into it

now." Her sister was always the petite one of the family even after having kids.

She sat back on the edge of the bed and took both of Ruth's hands. "Tell me everything."

Maybe it would be fun to let someone in on the secret.

Della shrieked when Ruth told her who the date was with, grateful her mother didn't spill all the beans.

"You are pulling my leg!"

Ruth shook her head. "He took me to Napoleon's."

"That fancy French speakeasy on Fifth?"

Ruth nodded. "We had an incredible dinner, Della," Ruth paused, enjoying the rapt attention. "I've never seen a bill so high in my life for food, even when we all went out to eat after your wedding. I couldn't believe it."

Della leaned forward and hugged Ruth. It was awkward, Della's belly only allowing the top half of the sisters to get close, but Ruth squeezed back just as hard.

"What was that for?" she asked when Della pulled away.

"I'm just so happy for you," her sister said, tears welling in her eyes. "You deserve this. I'm just so happy."

Ruth laughed. "I think your hormones are getting the best of you."

"I'm serious!" Della said, wiping her eyes. "You are such a wonderful person; it's about time that was noticed. And, let me be frank, out of just about anyone, Lawrence is the guy you'd want noticing."

Ruth lightly slapped her sister's hand. They both broke into schoolgirl giggles, but inside Ruth was flying. Yes. Yes she *did* deserve this.

Maybe she wouldn't have to spend her money in Europe after all.

Chapter Twelve

Lawrence stretched and touched his toes three times before making his bed. It was his routine since basic training. He pulled his robe around himself and padded to the kitchen to put on the kettle.

Steaming mug in hand, he walked to the windows overlooking the park. It wasn't a terrible view, but he was painfully aware of the three stories above his head. He wondered if his parents were also aware when they signed the lease that he wouldn't be on the top floor. They probably didn't even consider it. Charles, of course, got the penthouse in his building, but Lawrence? Lawrence should be grateful to have a nice view, right? To have anything at all, as far as his father was concerned.

Hell, he marched off to war just to get their approval. To finally show his father the kind of man he could be.

It wasn't much different than the boarding school his parents squirreled him away in when he turned fifteen, but the food was slightly better. Lawrence excelled at all the physical challenges his corporals threw at him. He was the fastest, strongest, and had the most endurance, but he couldn't fire a gun for shit.

Turned out while he was right-handed, his dominant eye was his left. To try to compensate, and not get honorably discharged, Lawrence started shooting with his off hand. His marksmanship improved, but not to the level of the other cadets. If it wasn't for his mile sprint times, Lawrence was pretty sure he could have been cut.

It was the one time where he felt like he'd earned his right to be there. No one cared what his last name was. It wasn't going to keep him from having to run one more lap, lift one more sodden bag above his head. He was successful because he worked at it, plain and simple.

And because of Marco.

****

They'd started basic the same day and were one-two in the rankings from that moment on. Marco pushed him to be better. Stayed with him on the range long after everyone else left to help him sight his targets. Touched his hands lightly to correct Lawrence's hold on his gun. Lawrence dragged Marco by the elbow, forcing him to keep pace.

Whatever they could do to spend more time together. To help each other. To make each other better.

When Lawrence's division got word they would be deployed to Italy, the fact that Marco was going to be there helped qualm his building fear.

His regiment, once appearing large to Lawrence, was a drop in the bucket when they arrived. Their five thousand paled in comparison to the million Italian fighters.

They headed to Vittorio Veneto to hold the river. Word came that the Italian army had the upper hand, pushing the Austrian-Hungarian army to the brink of surrender. Lawrence was about to breathe a sigh of relief when a small group of soldiers—possibly retreating?—barreled toward them. Lawrence lifted his rifle and without thinking, held it with his right hand on the trigger. It wasn't until he shot over the right shoulder of a man coming toward him that he realized his mistake. He tried to correct, but adjusted too much and hit the man's left arm.

"Shit!" Lawrence shouted. "Marco, I need your help!"

He looked back to where his friend stood moments before, but there was only empty space. Lawrence shifted the rifle to his other hand and took aim again, hitting the barreling man between the eyes. He moved to pick off the man running behind him, but someone else's bullet got there first. As quick as it started, the fighting was over.

About a half-dozen men lay dead on the muddy ground and another ten held their arms above their heads in surrender. A few of the American soldiers rounded them up and started stripping them of their weapons.

Lawrence's heart raced. To be so near death, so near the end, and to have a bullet save him. To have his own wits and abilities spare his life. The adrenaline was greater than even that of jumping out of an airplane for the first time. He turned to share his excitement with Marco, but found him on the ground, eyes wide and unblinking.

The sounds around Lawrence disappeared. He sank to his knees and cradled Marco's bloodied arm. Without thinking, he picked his friend up and threw him on to his back, then ran back to base camp where he knew the medics were. Shouts behind him broke through the whooshing sound in his head, but he ignored them. It was probably a superior yelling at him to stop. To not leave his command post.

They could kick him out if they wanted to. He needed to save Marco.

Three people in white outfits rushed to meet him as he arrived, probably because of his mad calling as soon as he saw the camp. Lawrence knew the truth as soon as they placed Marco on a stretcher, but he appreciated them putting on a show for him, working over his body for several minutes before sadly shaking their heads. A nurse came up to him and pulled at his sleeve. Her words weren't clear and it took him a few moments to realize it was because she didn't speak English.

He followed wordlessly. It wasn't until she lay him down on another stretcher that he felt the sharp pain in his side.

The pieces came to him slowly. One of the surrendering men decided he didn't want to give up his weapon. A struggle ensued. The man's gun fired, hitting Lawrence in the side just as he picked up Marco. The yells weren't for him being insubordinate, it was calls for him to wait for a medic for help. That Marco was beyond help. Yells to the man for shooting his gun. More gunshots as the man was killed.

It wasn't until Lawrence was on a plane home that he found out that the war was over. Almost forty thousand men died during the battle of Vittorio Veneto, but Lawrence really only cared about one of them.

The Purple Heart he got for trying to save Marco sat in Lawrence's desk drawer. His parents were so proud, their little war hero. They paraded him around town when he arrived home. If it weren't for the deep depression he fell into when he got back stateside, he would have reveled in it. Finally, finally the approval of his parents. They were proud of him. But it didn't last. Almost everyone had someone coming back from war. Soon the praise faded away.

He'd done it for them. Enlisted for them. Met and lost Marco because of them.

He bounced around a few cities, Baltimore, Philadelphia, Miami, and Chicago. Gambling, stealing, gambling some more. He began to realize the wealthy, like his parents, were all the same. They had more than they needed, but never wanted to share. He relieved them of their burden.

But the parties and double life felt empty. If there was no one around to impress, what was the point? After a few years, he took up his parents' offer to house him back in New York. They owed him that much for all they put him through.

They had acted like they were the ones saving him when in reality, it was the least they could do to get him a place with a decent view.

****

The apartment suddenly felt claustrophobic. Lawrence dressed and braced himself against the cold January air. He would pay a quick visit. It would feel so nice to warm up. It was the second day of the year; surely that side of town wouldn't be under surveillance anymore. Surely people would be getting back on with their lives. The cops were too busy with other matters to care about simple vices.

He entered the bathhouse after a quick glance up and down the street.

After ascending the stairs, he checked in at the front desk, making sure to scribble an eligible name in the ledger before handing over his dollar. A towel was handed to him, but he waved off the key.

He knocked on the door he knew Paul would be in. Paul, who helped him forget about Marco.

The door opened and he was dragged in with a long kiss.

Chapter Thirteen

Ruth was in such a panic as the end of the day neared, her coworker Trixie pulled her aside.

"Spill," Trixie demanded.

Ruth looked around before lowering her voice. "It's so silly, but I have a date tonight and I've got nothing to wear. And even though we are in the middle of one of the largest department stores in the city, I can't afford a single damn thing, even with working here for practically ten years." Her face flushed with embarrassment. "I am so sorry," she rushed to say. "That was too much sharing."

Trixie, who was, Ruth estimated, five years younger than her, waved her off. "No worries at all," she said. "Sounds like you are in a real jam. I don't live too far from here and have plenty of dresses. What time is your date and where?"

"We have seven o'clock theater tickets, then I think we're going to dinner after, but I don't know where." The panic rose again.

They'd been on three dates so far, which was exactly how many dresses Ruth owned, including the green one Lawrence had bought for her. That in it of itself was embarrassing, but she knew she couldn't recycle the green dress again. This late into January it was out of season. Plus, it would be a red flag to Lawrence what a lack of wardrobe she had.

Shot

Trixie lightly touched her shoulder. "I get off at five. You here until five-thirty?" Ruth nodded. "I'll give you my address. It's not far from here. Why don't you come to my place to get ready? I have one or two things that will work."

Ruth took a breath and let her shoulders relax and the tension left them. "Oh, Trixie." She was shocked to feel prickles of tears sting the back of her eyes.

"We have to get back to work now." Trixie eyed their boss across the floor. "I'll write down my address before I leave. Don't worry," she said, touching Ruth's shoulder again. "And next weekend we'll go out shopping. There are plenty of places to buy dresses that aren't here."

Ruth smiled and nodded her head.

Two hours later, Ruth stood in Trixie's cramped seventh floor walk-up as the former mild acquaintance-turned-savior zipped her into a long black dress. The fabric was a bit stiff from being laundered a few times, but the color was still rich and dark. It was made of a silk blend, not quite as nice as her green dress, but the lace details on the back and sleeves gave it an air of expensiveness the dress didn't actually possess.

Ruth and Trixie were about the same size, the latter a few inches taller, but Ruth had dashed home to fetch her heels and beaded purse before rushing back to Trixie's. There wasn't much time for her hair and makeup, but thirty minutes later Ruth was walking down the stairs looking better than she would have expected.

After the millionth thank-you to Trixie, Ruth was on her way to the theater district. It was cold, but the air was still, so she needn't waste money on a cab as her hair was likely to stay set in the up-do Trixie helped her with.

It was still a longer walk than she expected, and she found herself slightly out of breath when she spotted Lawrence in front of the ticket counter, looking as dashing and put together as always.

While typically she would have found it unfair that a man only needed to own one good suit and could wear it at will, where a woman needed to have clothes to fit a variety of occasions, she understood that Lawrence didn't just own one suit. The one he wore was cut slightly different than the ones he wore out to dinner with her. The fabric a little heavier, slightly more luxurious. Ruth hoped he couldn't notice that her dress was from last season and clearly had some use to it. His beaming smile as she approached betrayed nothing.

"You look wonderful!" he exclaimed, chucking his cigarette to the ground, then quickly embraced her.

When she pulled back and got an up-close look at him, she noticed a cut above his right eye, along with some bruising and swelling. She immediately reached out her hand to touch it, but he grabbed her wrist lightly.

"It's nothing, really," he said. "But a bit sore all the same."

"What did you do?" she asked, trying not to sound like her mother.

"Oh, there's a good story about that," he said.

At that moment, the ushers opened the door and people began to file in. An older man bumped into Ruth so forcefully, she almost fell, grabbing on to Lawrence to steady herself.

"You owe my date an apology," Lawrence said. He dropped her arm and grasped the man roughly at the elbow.

The man's face turned as pale as his shirt. They blocked the doorway, causing a bottleneck outside as voices shouted at them. Ruth burned in embarrassment.

"Lawrence, I'm fine, it's okay," she said, trying to pull his hand free.

"This gentleman owes you an apology," Lawrence said.

"There's a lot of pushing," the man said. "Everyone is just trying to get in."

Lawrence's fingers dug further into the man's arm, the latter yelping in pain. His date also tried without success to pry the two men apart.

"Fine. Ma'am, I'm sorry for running into you," the man finally said, a pinched expression to his face.

Lawrence immediately let go and placed his hand on the middle of Ruth's back, directing her toward the main lobby.

Ruth wasn't sure how to feel. She'd never had a man defend her honor before. That's what happened, right? The man *did* almost knock her down. He should have said sorry. It just felt an odd demand to make him.

They stopped along a wall, far enough away from the crowd to not risk being swept into it. Ruth looked away from the masses as Lawrence handed her a ticket printed on fine, thick paper.

"Lawrence, what happened to your eye?" she asked again.

"Let's just say defending someone's honor sometimes is messy work. Come on, we are going to miss the show."

He smiled, showing all his perfect teeth. She smiled back. Maybe this was just another aspect of his world she would never fully understand.

She wanted to ask him more questions, but also didn't want to miss the show. She'd only ever been to plays put on by local schools or churches where, more often than not, she knew most of the cast and crew.

She recognized some of the names in her playbill, but only from seeing them in marquee lights. It was a different experience to have no real connection to the actors.

The theater was magnificent. Plush red carpet lined the floors, stairs, and part of the walls. Gold chandeliers dripping with jewels hung like hornets' nests above. She fought the urge to duck as they walked under them.

Gold was everywhere. The railings, door handles, even the plaques on the chairs that told them what seats they were in. It was a lavishness she'd never seen before even during the short time she'd spent gallivanting through Lawrence's world. Even more of a wonder, no one seemed as enthralled as she.

"You may want to shut your mouth or you could spit on the floor," he teased.

She was too overwhelmed to be embarrassed. "This place is amazing."

"You don't have to whisper. We're not in a library and the show hasn't started yet."

"I think the lights in the entryway cost more than my house."

Lawrence laughed. "I wouldn't be surprised, frankly, if they cost more than mine as well."

"Do you come here often?"

He shook his head. "Not as much anymore. Used to

a lot as kids. My parents have had tickets for years, but they don't really go."

"So they have tickets, but choose not to attend?" The wastefulness amazed her.

"They usually give them up to me or my brother or friends who are in town. We've had this box for years. They don't want to lose it. If there is one thing my parents care about more than anything else in the world, it's their image."

"Oh, don't be flippant."

"I'm not," he said.

She narrowed her eyes, trying to read his expression. His features were smooth without the slightest indication of jest. She reached for his hand.

"Well, that is a great loss to them," she said, locking gazes with him. "They clearly don't know what they are doing if you aren't the best thing in their life, because…" She hoped she wasn't stepping over some social etiquette line, but deciding she didn't care. It needed to be said and he needed to hear it.

"Because you are wonderful, and anyone is bonkers who doesn't see that."

He kissed her right there, in front of anyone who wanted to see.

The show was almost as magical as the kiss. Ruth fought the urge to lean forward in her seat to get a little closer to the action. She laughed when the dog ran out with the woman's undergarments, gasped when the two men swung swords at one another, and wept as the young couple had to part ways because their worlds were too different and they simply couldn't be together.

She couldn't help but think of herself and Lawrence. She wasn't naïve enough to think she grew up on the wrong side of the tracks or anything. But her station and his were miles apart.

When the curtains closed after the second standing ovation, Lawrence finally pulled her from the enchantment.

"That was amazing," she rushed to say before he could get a word in.

"I am pleased that you thought so. I…"

"What?"

"I don't want to offend you."

"After I spoke so freely, without prompt, about your family. I can only owe you the returned favor."

She meant the comment in jest, but her heart raced to hear what he would say. Did he have the same thoughts as her after the play? That they were as different and doomed as the characters on the stage?

"You are just so refreshing," he said. "Like a breath of clean air when I've been inhaling smoke my whole life."

Ruth laughed to hide her nerves. "I'm afraid I don't really know what you mean."

"I've been going to the theater my whole life. It became a chore of sorts, as terrible as I know that sounds. Sure, the audience laughed and clapped at the appropriate times, but we were there more to be seen by each other than to actually enjoy an evening. At least that's what it had always felt like to me."

"How terribly sad," she said without thinking.

He smiled. "See that? Right there? That's what I mean. It *is* sad. And I didn't realize that until I watched you engrossed in the play. You were visibly moved. You laughed because you thought it was funny. You cried because you thought it was sad."

"It *was* sad," she said, feeling like she needed to defend herself.

"It was, but only if you're actually paying attention. I love that about you. That you pay attention." He kissed her again. "Come on, let's get some dinner."

Chapter Fourteen

Detective Kelly walked up the five steps to enter the brownstone townhouse and already met ten people who weren't supposed to be there. She pushed her way through men with bulky cameras as they jostled one another to get inside. Others shoved their way out, hopeful smiles on their faces to be the first with the scoop, and thus, be paid. They gave her dirty looks even though she was in uniform. It didn't matter. No one really saw her for what she was.

She elbowed her way inside, looked around to see if there was any actual authority on the scene, and found an officer standing in the hallway to the kitchen.

"You just letting anyone in here?" Kelly barked at the man.

"Who the hell are you?" the man challenged.

"The detective on this case," she said. Her back and feet ached and all she wanted to do was take a nap and maybe puke her guts up. She didn't have time for this shit or pretenses. "Get these goons outta here," Kelly ordered.

The officer narrowed his eyes at her, but since she outranked him, he was forced to order the reporters and photographers to leave. He told them they could stay outside and he'd send the lead detective out to come speak with them in a bit. Kelly glared at him for setting her up, but wasn't particularly surprised. A short stint in the pickpocket squad before becoming a prison matron gave her a lot of experience with male officers, most of which was negative. The kid had to follow her orders, but he would still try to put her in her place as much as he could.

She entered the kitchen and found two more uniformed officers, plus three detectives, standing around a body covered in blood.

"Oh, look who it is," one of the men said "Looks like Mom's arrived to tell us all how we're fucking up."

She ignored them and went to one of the few men in the department who gave her the time of day, "Hi, Carlson."

"Hey, Kelly," Carlson said quietly.

"What happened?"

"Guy's dead," one of the uniforms said.

Kelly wasn't sure if it was supposed to be a joke, but no one laughed.

"Stabbed, then shot," Carlson said. "Wife came home and found him."

"Where's she now?"

Carlson pointed toward the front door. "Side room, still needs a statement taken, figure you're probably the best to do it?"

"All right, just give me a minute," Kelly said. She moved closer to the body.

The prone man looked to be in his late fifties to early sixties, with white hair and no beard. His suit looked well-tailored. Maybe a banker. Kelly guessed the shirt he was wearing was supposed to be white, though it was so stained in red, it was difficult to tell. Kelly didn't need the coroner for cause of death.

She counted seven deep slits in the man's shirt, as

well as a round hole above his left eyebrow. The brutality of it took her aback a minute. It wasn't often they found victims practically hacked to death.

"Did you find a knife?" Kelly asked.

Carlson shook his head.

"No, but one's missing from the block." The other detective—Kelly thought his name was Green—gestured behind them.

"Check the sink and cabinets to be sure, but that may be our murder weapon."

The men didn't move and Carlson repeated the request.

She looked around again. "Not much looks out of the ordinary. Clock still on the wall, watch still on his wrist. Was anything stolen?"

"His wallet, and the wife says a bank deposit from a bag," Carlson said.

Kelly walked back through the hallway and picked up a burlap-colored bag with "G. Astor" written in black marker across the top, sitting on the console table..

"This bag?" she asked, holding it up.

"You must be the second coming of Sherlock!" Carlson said.

She rolled her eyes at him and he gave a friendly laugh.

Lord, it was refreshing to have a man not treat her like an imbecile because she had tits. Hell, if someone like him ran the department, she bet a lot more would get done because he'd put the best people on the case no matter what their makeup was.

"All right," he relented. "Not the actual bag, the money inside it."

Kelly nodded. "So, the guy broke in, robbed and murdered the homeowner for the cash only, leaving expensive items behind?"

"Appears that way, what do you think, Aubergene?" Carlson said, addressing the man Kelly thought was named Green.

"Well, I was the first one here, and according to the wife, the door was unlocked, but doesn't seem kicked in."

"Did you check the rest of the house?" Carlson asked.

"I did, sir," the kid guarding the kitchen said. "Everything else is locked up."

"Back doors? Basement?" Kelly asked.

The kid nodded, but addressed Carlson. "All locked, sir."

"Good work," Carlson said.

"So maybe our guy followed Mr. Astor in then. Saw him with the envelope perhaps? Possibly someone who lost money in the crash and is taking it out on a wealthy man?"

Some shrugs and nods met her words. No one was ever interested in her theories.

"The coroner's office?"

"Someone should be here to pick up the body soon," Aubergene said.

"In that case, why don't you introduce me to the wife? I'll get a statement from her and meet you all back at the station."

Kelly found the shaken wife with bits of dried blood on her hands. She wanted to bite the heads off the guys who didn't insist the woman clean up.

She looked up at Kelly after she introduced herself.

"You're a detective?"

The men and their disbelief she could handle, expected almost. But the women saddened her when they give her bewildered looks. This was 1930 for Christ's sake. How long would society keep up the pretense that certain professions were only for men?

"I am," Kelly said. "And I am so terribly sorry to hear about your husband. May I sit?"

The woman nodded.

"Can you walk me through the events of this afternoon?" Kelly asked.

Mrs. Astor had lunch plans with her husband, but he'd forgotten the deposit slip at home and sent word that he would get it, then drop the envelope off at the bank before meeting her. She expected him to be a bit late, but when almost an hour passed, she became concerned their signals had been crossed and maybe he'd canceled on her. When she opened the door and saw the envelope sitting on the table, she became alarmed. He'd had a heart attack two years prior and she worried maybe he'd gotten sick and couldn't call for help.

It was her screaming that alerted the neighbors, who phoned for the police.

"What does your husband do?" Kelly asked, careful to not use the past tense.

No need to remind her of the situation in the next room.

"He owns a shop. He sells very nice coats and jackets." She sat up a bit straighter, as if challenging Kelly to refute her.

"Is there anyone who may want to cause him harm? Maybe a partner who lost some money and blames him? I know a lot of people lost money in October."

She shook her head. "No. No, just him. And sometimes I help when they are busy during the holidays or wedding season. Everyone loves him. Loved him…"

"Do you have a place to go?" Kelly asked.

"My sister's. She lives upstate."

"Make sure you give their contact information to the officers here in case we need to get in touch with you." She stood and shook the woman's hand. "Mrs. Astor, I am so sorry for your loss."

Her grip on Kelly's hand tightened. "I am trusting you. Will you find the man who did this?"

"Yes." Kelly promised, just as she had done a dozen times before.

And like every other time, she hoped it wasn't a lie.

Chapter Fifteen

Lawrence couldn't believe how sloppy it went, and a day later, he still cursed himself. Gregory was an old man. He'd been in poor health the last three years. Anytime his parents spoke of the Astors, his mother always remarked about how sad it was that Peggy was spry, fit for her age, while Gregory hadn't been right since his heart attack almost two winters prior.

Lawrence knew they owned a successful shop and, as any shop owner did, would be depositing his slips and cash on Friday. The idea popped into his head when Ruth said she had switched shifts with someone at work and would have Saturday off instead of Thursday, so if he wouldn't mind, could they do something Friday night instead?

His parents willingly gave him the tickets without even a question as to why, which was for the best. He wasn't quite prepared to bring Ruth to them. He needed to lay a little more groundwork first. Make sure she wouldn't run for the hills after meeting them.

He cursed when he saw it was for the earlier show, so he'd have to take her out to dinner after. If it was the later, he could make some excuse that he'd have to meet her there. No such luck.

The string of nice dining places became increasingly difficult to fund. So a chance mention of the Astors when Lawrence went to pick up the tickets proved the perfect opportunity to pad his bankroll.

Lawrence got to the shop right before noon, expecting to have to wait him out until the end of the workday, but was surprised when Gregory shuffled out of the store, bank bag in hand. What luck!

But as quick as his elation came, it whipped away. How would Lawrence rob him in the street? He doubted he'd be able to lure him down an alley. His panic subsided when Gregory turned, not toward the shopping and dining district on 5th Avenue, but down 57th Street into a residential area.

Lawrence strolled a few paces back, paused to take in the Heckscher Building. An ugly thing in a style Lawrence knew was needed to get passed the zoning board, but in his opinion made it look like a cake. After putting a little space between him and Gregory, he followed the man.

Save for two woman pushing babies in matching buggies, the street was empty. Lawrence pulled his scarf up, covering most of his face and didn't make eye contact as he passed the pair. He doubted they'd notice though since they seemed engrossed in conversation with each other.

He matched Gregory's footsteps up the stairs to the brownstone and pushed in through the front door behind the old man. Gregory and the bank bag went flying, spilling cash all over the marble floor of the foyer. The foolish man scrambled after the money, but Lawrence held him down with a foot in the middle of his back. Thinking fast, Lawrence wrapped Gregory's scarf around his nose and mouth. He didn't need Gregory calling out his name or anything for nosey neighbors to hear as Lawrence kicked the door shut behind him.

The brief unbalance enabled Gregory to stumble to his feet, and made his way to the kitchen. Lawrence followed through the narrow hall, a few steps behind, unhurried, unworried. All he needed was one shot.

When he came around the corner, Gregory punched him right above his eye. Sparks flashed across Lawrence's vision. The shock of this frail man fighting back gave him the momentary edge. Gregory slashed a knife at the air. Lawrence wrestled it from him, but not before the man pulled Lawrence's own scarf down.

His eyes turned wide in fear. "Lawrence?"

Instead of trying to pull the knife away, he pushed it back, plunging the tip into the old man's chest. Gregory gasped and let go of the hilt. Lawrence cut him a few more times, but somehow the man was still standing, still trying to fight him, some sort of animalistic need for survival pushing through the pain.

Lawrence grabbed a kitchen towel, wrapped it around his gun, and shot Gregory in the head. The fabric helped muffle the sound of the shot, but the body crashing to the floor still made a racket.

He paused for a few moments, but didn't hear any commotion in the adjoining units. Maybe the two young mothers lived on either side. A lucky break.

The towel smoldered and Lawrence ran it under a cold tap. The last thing he needed was someone smelling fire.

He went back into the hall and gathered all the money. At first, he stuffed it back into the envelope, but thought the better of it and left that on the entry table. He was about to leave when he realized the man may have more money on him. Lawrence was rewarded with another sixty-seven dollars in his wallet. He stuffed the money and towel into his coat pocket, and went back out into the cold.

He kept his pace steady and even as he strolled toward the river. Men returning from their lunch breaks filled the streets and Lawrence shuffled in behind them, trying to blend in. He peeled away on a side street and took the towel out of his pocket, then stuffed it into a dumpster before making his way back to the street.

He walked a few blocks before it became clear he needed to get cleaned up. As the sidewalks became more crowded, the stares toward him increased. He dabbed at his eye a few times, drops of blood clinging to his fingertips. He was close enough for Charles's place, so rang for him.

When his brother opened the door, his face registered more exasperation than concern.

"What happened this time?"

"You wouldn't believe it if I told you," Lawrence said, pushing past him.

"I bet. Use the hall bath please, don't muck up my master one."

Lawrence gave him the thumbs up sign before going into the small half-bath off the dining room. His eye looked worse that he'd imagined. The brow was already twice its normal size and had a mix of crusted and fresh blood smeared over it. No wonder people gave him looks.

Charles appeared over his shoulder, holding out a towel with ice. "Here, this will help keep the swelling down."

"Thanks, old chap."

The scratchy fabric of the towel irritated the

sensitive skin, but the ice felt good against the cut.

"You going to tell me the truth of what happened?" Charles asked.

"Two men were trying to rob this poor mother pushing a stroller."

"Uh huh," Charles said, inspecting his fingernails. "And what, you swooped in to save the day?"

"Hardly," Lawrence said with a laugh. "I got my ass kicked." As if to drive home the point, he pointed at his eye.

"So they got her bag?"

Lawrence shook his head. "No, the commotion drew enough attention and they decided to scram. She was very thankful, offered me ten bucks for my trouble."

"I'm sure she did."

"Well, of course I didn't take it," Lawrence said. "But it was a kind gesture. Normally when people show appreciation for each other, they make some sort of offer. That's usually how it works."

"I'll keep that in mind," Charles said.

"Thanks for the ice."

Lawrence squeezed past his brother and headed back toward the front door.

"Oh, don't get sore," Charles said.

"No, no I'm not, really," Lawrence said, looking at his brother with his one good eye. "I have a date tonight. Gotta try to make this mug presentable."

Charles raised his left eyebrow. "Is this the same girl from the party?"

Lawrence nodded. "Ruth. Got tickets to the show tonight. Can you believe she'd never been to a Broadway play before?"

"You gonna let me meet her?"

"Maybe one of these days."

Lawrence tipped the towel-wrapped ice to his forehead in a mock salute before leaving. As he meandered back to his place, he realized he was close to a gambling house and considered going inside, his pockets deliciously filled with money. With great restraint, he passed them by and headed home.

He needed to stay focused on his plan. It came to him the past night as he walked home alone, past the speakeasies and clandestine watering holes. How much money flowed through this city for one vice: alcohol.

And with Ruth's help, he'd grab a piece of it for himself.

Chapter Sixteen

Ruth pulled down on the brown dress, not liking how it rode up now that they sat at the table.

"You look wonderful," Lawrence said.

Ruth froze. She didn't realize he was watching her.

"Is that a new dress?"

She nodded, grateful for Trixie showing her the discount stores around town. One sold used dresses and while Ruth initially balked at the idea, Trixie showed her how most of the garments still had their tags on them. Those that didn't were from such nice brands, Ruth stopped caring what previous lives they'd lived. Trixie said after the New Year lots of the cash-strapped wealthy were selling off their nice clothes in droves for extra money. She paid almost a full week's salary, but her closet was now filled with eight new options.

He said something else to her and Ruth shook her head to say she didn't understand. The dress, about a half size too small, felt like it was riding up again. She fought the urge to keep tugging at it, not wanting to draw more attention.

"Ruth, you look fine."

Her face burned. "I'm sorry, what were you saying?"

"The investment."

Ruth had no idea what he was talking about "Investment?"

A flash of anger passed over his features, but he smoothed it away. "Yes," he said slowly. "I mentioned it to you at dinner after the play."

A kernel of memory burrowed its way out of her head. "I'm sorry," she repeated. "I was so excited about the show, I must not have been paying attention. Please, tell me again." She leaned forward and placed her hands on the table to really show she was listening.

His expression softened as he took a deep breath.

"I want to open a pharmacy and I'm looking for investors," he said.

"I think that's wonderful," Ruth said. "I didn't know you were a pharmacist."

In that moment Ruth realized with embarrassment that for all their laughter and discussions, they rarely spoke about him. She had no real idea what he did or how he made his money.

"No, I'm not a pharmacist, I'd have to find one, but that's not the point, the license allows you to sell alcohol."

"I don't think I follow…"

"See, you can get a prescription for alcohol for things like anxiety."

She'd never heard of such a thing. "Who told you this?"

"My doctor, who prescribed it to me."

"For anxiety?"

The pieces weren't quite fitting together.

"Yes, from the war."

"You fought in the war?" Her mind was overwhelmed with new information, trying to hang on to one piece before the next got chucked at her.

He waved her off. "I don't want to talk about that, I

think you are missing the point. I can open a pharmacy. I found a location already and am going by later to take a look at it. There isn't another for one square mile and it's in a populous section of town. I think in a year's time I can quadruple an initial investment. Let's say a couple hundred dollars."

"Wow," she said. "That sounds impressive, I'm really happy for you."

"So, does that mean you are interested?" He leaned forward expectantly.

"Of course, I am interested, I am proud of you for thinking of such a thing," she said, wanting to be supportive, but also having trouble following his train of thought.

"So you'll invest?"

Ruth almost dropped the glass she held. "Me?"

"Well, of course. I want you to be a part of it. I want you to share in this wealth."

She was flabbergasted. "Lawrence..."

"Ruth, I know you want to move out of your parent's, and I want that for you as well."

"Not like this."

She wanted to move out, but only to move on. To move to something else, something with him.

"Can't you ask your parents for the money?" she asked gently. "Or have they been affected by the crash..."

"No, of course not," he snapped. "I don't need their money. Plus, it's not about the money." He took a breath and lowered his voice. "I care about you Ruth, and I think you care about me."

"I do."

He took her hand. "This is something we can build

together. We can build all sorts of things together."

Her heart soared. Was he alluding to what she thought?

"How much are you thinking?" she asked, against her better judgment.

She already felt in so deep with him. Spent so much money already to play along with this make-pretend life. She'd feel a fool to walk away from it all now.

"Five hundred dollars." He rushed to add, "But I'll guarantee your investment. If in a year, you want to take your money back, I'll give you every penny, plus interest."

"I don't know…"

"You don't trust me?"

That stung and tears welled in her eyes. "Of course, I trust you. And I want your dreams to succeed, but Lawrence, you have to understand, that is a lot of money for a person like me. I have saved my entire life for that amount."

"And you don't think investing in our future is a good purpose for all that hard work?"

Her mouth went dry, sticking her tongue to the roof of it. She wanted this. Hell, everyone in her life wanted this for her. She could hear her mother murmuring in her ear to do whatever the rich man asked. But then, if he was rich, why did he need her money? It was all so confusing. What if it really was for her? She heard about business ventures all the time. People going into partnerships and coming out rich on the other end. Maybe this was how it worked?

"I can't say yes to you, not yet," she said after he started to pull away from her. "But I promise to think

81

about it, *really* think about it."

He nodded and smiled at her. She hoped, prayed with every bit of her being, that the right answer would come to her.

And that it wouldn't result in the end of their relationship.

Chapter Seventeen

Kelly knew she was obsessed. Her fellow detectives, already adept at avoiding her, refused to make eye contact for fear that she may corner them. They didn't care about her theory. Frankly, they didn't care all that much that three wealthy people were killed.

Finally, someone from the other side, they joked. Maybe they'd get more funding. Maybe if enough outcrying happened, they could get raises. Once the rich were affected, that's when change started to happen.

When a file got slapped on her desk, she jumped up. "Another one?" she asked, grabbing her coat.

"Murder? Yeah, that's sorta your job," her supervisor, Lieutenant Porter, said. "But if you're losing the drive for it, I can transfer you— "

"No." Kelly worked to keep her face neutral. "Where's this one at?"

"Don't get your knickers in a twist there, Kelly. Just a run of the mill prostitute this time. Sorry to disappoint."

Her fist clenched with the throw-away line. She hated, *hated,* working murders of the call girls around town. All killing was sad, sure, but the way the men in the department spoke of these cases made her blood *whoosh* in her ears in anger. They literally could not give a shit if they tried. They'd make lewd comments over the body, commenting on the victim's figure or clothing. Half-ass worked the crime scene and save for asking a few of the other girls around town if they saw anything, didn't bother investigating.

But Kelly found herself having trouble focusing when she arrived on the scene. She told the photographer where to shoot, bagged and tagged the evidence that would surely be put in a box to rot. The woman, remarkably, had an ID on her. Must have been a new girl; they almost never carried cards on them so they could give false names when picked up. She lost count of how many Betty Boops walked through the station in a year.

She passed the ID to one of the uniformed officers and told him to notify her family.

"Might want to look through the missing persons files. Sometimes we can cross one off that list."

The man nodded and walked away.

Twenty minutes later, Kelly released the body and wandered back to the precinct, lost in thought. She wanted this death to matter, matter to her and everyone else in this shit-hole city, but her mind wandered to the other cases and the puzzle pieces she couldn't quite fit together. Even this one she found herself trying to connect.

The girl was found without any cash on her, but no gunshot wounds. Looked like she had been choked. Kelly knew in her gut it wasn't the same guy, but there was a pull to make it work anyway.

When she got back to her desk, the mail clerk stopped her cart in front of Kelly. She rarely ever got anything, so she looked up in anticipation.

"From Chicago," the young woman said with an impressed tone to her words. "You heading to college?"

Kelly shook her head. "No, why?"

The woman shrugged and handed it over. "Thought maybe one of us was gonna get out. Northwestern University return address."

Kelly ripped the envelope open. She didn't anticipate such a quick response.

A letterhead with *The American Journal of Police Sciences* was at the top of the paper, followed by neatly typed lines.

Detective Kelly,

As a recent New York transplant, I am pleased with your interest in our upcoming journal. Publication is slated for late 1931/32 as articles are acquired and copyedited. Unfortunately, at this time, the journal is not meant to be an avenue of connecting unsolved cases together, though that is an interesting path that may be followed in the future.

At present, its main goal is to connect the laboratory side of investigation with the policing side, so that both can work together toward a common goal: the correct prosecution of guilty parties.

However, as a member of the Bureau of Forensic Ballistics, it is our goal to connect the otherwise unconnectable. I encourage you to consider us in analyzing your projectile evidence. It is possible we can not only link your homicide cases together, but point you in a particular direction for a possible murder weapon.

Your interest in this budding field is both humbling and validating and I look forward to conversing with you in the future.

Sincerely,

Lt. Col. Calvin H. Goddard

Kelly read the letter three times before putting it in her drawer. When she saw the notice about the journal, her first thought was the East-to-West Murders, as the press dubbed them. Maybe she could pull in the minds from across the county to help her solve them. Especially since it was clear there wasn't a lot of brain power in her own department and she only had a couple more months to hope to crack the cases.

She hadn't thought she could use the bullet evidence itself to do that, but now that hope lit a new fire. She went to the evidence vault and sorted through the two boxes until she came back with the three manila envelopes, one from each of the bodies. Dark brown stains littered the outsides, confirming their contents, and Kelly held them gingerly by the corners. She placed them in a new envelope and scrawled Goddard a quick letter of thanks before tracking the mail room girl down.

"Can you make sure this gets in the post today?" she asked.

"Don't worry, Detective, your secret about going to school is safe with me. I'm rooting for you." She winked.

Chapter Eighteen

When the man unlocked the glass door and pushed it open for Lawrence, he gave a small flourish as if he were a circus magician. See what box of treasures I have opened for you?

Lawrence stepped through and was less than overwhelmed.

The floors and walls were both a sickly yellow color, which may have once been white. By the smell, Lawrence thought the discoloration probably a combination of tobacco and water, as evident by the newly patched ceiling.

"Leak?" Lawrence asked, pointing up.

The man nodded enthusiastically. "Oh yes, sir, yes, but fixed, sir. No issues. We had rain the other day, and no issucs."

The room was large, with some shelving units pressed up against a wall. There was a back room that would be a good place to hold supplies and items that the pharmacist would dispense. Lawrence envisioned a short half wall as a barrier between the stock and the customers. There was an additional small room that could serve as his office, as well as a counter up front with a cash register. It looked in good shape, except for a desperate need for some oil.

"The space will need to be painted," Lawrence said.

For the rent this man was charging, it was akin to highway robbery. The least the gentleman could do was throw on a fresh coat.

The man nodded. "Yes, sir. We have blue or white."

Lawrence looked around. "White."

Make it look more official. Clean. Trusting.

"And you said there are no pharmacies on this block? No buildings going up for lease that I have to worry about undercutting my business?"

The man vigorously shook his head. "Oh, no, sir. This is it. The only property. A real find, a real steal, you are lucky you found it when you did. It won't last long."

Lawrence's lips tightened into a line. He knew for a fact this place had been empty for eight months. Knew that while this may be prime real estate, the inside of the building was less than desirable. Money would need to go into it. Money that no landlord wanted to pony up and no business wanted to incur on their own. Lawrence knew he had the upper hand.

"There is a lot of work that needs to be done—"

"Cosmetic."

"Cosmetic still takes money. I will take the space."

"A good decision sir, a good decision. It won't last long."

Lawrence saw the man's pinched lips and furrowed brow relax in relief. Evidently glad to have the place take money in again.

"But," Lawrence said, sensing the opportune time to give his conditions, "in exchange for getting this place up to snuff and the lost revenue since I can't open right away, I will sign a year lease, but make payment for nine months."

The man's eyes widened. "Sir?"

"Three months free of rent," Lawrence said. He brought out his checkbook and moved to the dusty counter by the register. He began writing in the payment line.

"Sir, sir, wait." The man held up his hands.

Lawrence hovered his pen, then recapped it for effect.

"You know as well as I do how much work this place needs, which is why it's been vacant for months," Lawrence murmured, so the man had to lean toward him to hear. "I am offering you more than anyone else has or will."

"Two months," the man said.

Lawrence straightened and moved to put his checkbook back in his pocket. The man rushed to block the door.

"All right, all right," he said. "Three months. But I will need the nine months paid in full. *Today*." He puffed up to his full height, as if he was suddenly calling the shots.

They agreed and the man crossed out a few lines on the lease before Lawrence signed it and handed over the check.

"I expect the painting to be done by the end of the week," Lawrence called out as he left the building.

His heart pounded. The check he wrote was for almost every penny he had to his name. He *had* to convince Ruth to loan him the money. Or he'd have to…

He shook his head. The press had gotten wind of the murders, and while the cops weren't willing to link them officially, the reporters had no problem wildly speculating who was killing the city's rich. They acted like dozens had been murdered. Lawrence knew if he did another, especially now, there would be so much scrutiny he'd risk being caught.

He needed a game. A few bucks and a chance. He was sure, *sure*, he could double his money. His palms itched. He *needed* to play.

His watch told him it was out of the question, and his light billfold reiterated the fact. He didn't have enough time before his meeting.

In a stroke of luck, a family friend's daughter had just graduated from medical school. Lawrence heard his parents lamenting over it the other night at dinner.

"Well, what did she expect," his father said. "Women aren't meant to be doctors. She knew that before she went to school. Her parents told her, encouraged her, to find another path. Maybe *marry* a doctor, but don't become one. And here she is, bills for school and living back with her parents because no one will hire her. I mean, would you trust a woman to treat you?" his father asked Charles.

"Of course not," Charles said.

"I don't see the fuss," his mother said. "If she can pass the tests, why shouldn't she be able to work?"

"Your mother, the abolitionist," his father said to laughter from his brother.

An idea was planted in Lawrence's head. He knew he couldn't afford to pay the salary of a pharmacist, especially not right away. He was trying to figure out how to employ someone he couldn't adequately compensate until the business got off the ground. This could be the perfect solution. So he had arranged to meet her for coffee.

Emma Anderson was beautiful, at least, once you got past the expression on her face, as if she'd just smelled the air by the stockyards.

Lawrence put out his hand and was surprised when she grasped the whole thing in a manly shake, not the delicate three fingers he was used to from women. Her whole persona was gruff. She moved without an ounce of grace or self-consciousness.

He liked her right away.

"I hear you just graduated," he said when they sat down with their steaming mugs of coffee.

"With honors," she said flatly.

"Impressive."

She huffed a laugh. "Well, you are the only one who thinks so."

"I doubt that is true."

"I graduated the top of my class. High marks and recommendations from all my professors. And I am unemployed. It's true."

"That's actually what I wanted to talk to you about. I am opening a pharmacy."

"Good for you," she said.

"I want to employ you."

"I am a doctor."

"And…" he said, baiting her, enjoying watching her anger rise.

"I didn't work for eight years of my life to stock bandages and make change for ornery customers."

"No. You didn't."

She narrowed her eyes at him, sizing him up. "Explain."

"I want you to work as a doctor in my pharmacy.

See patients and prescribe them medication that we will then fill."

"Is that legal?"

"I have the license. The visits will be run of the mill, just simple exams, no procedures. You will give them a prescription. They don't *have* to fill it with us; heck, they are more than welcome to traipse across town. But if they want, we can certainly provide any recommended medications you suggest."

She nodded slowly. "I've never heard of such an operation."

"I don't think it's the first time you've been at the forefront of something."

The visible shift in her persona showed him he hit the right tone at the right moment. She struck him as someone who fought tooth and nail for everything she had. And would work twice as hard to prove herself. And more importantly, would take half the pay.

She agreed, balking at her wage, but relenting once he said he would offer her profit sharing.

"Five percent of all sales," he said.

Initially he wasn't prepared to give her any more, but when she hesitated, he panicked. Plus, this would incentivize her to sell more. A win-win.

They parted ways and agreed to meet at the store in a week's time. It was coming together. Lawrence would prove to everyone that he could be successful.

And he wouldn't need a dime of his parents' money to do it. He just had to reel in Ruth a little more. He knew she was close. Close to signing her whole life over to him.

She just needed a little push.

Chapter Nineteen

Ruth paced in front of her building as she waited for Lawrence. She checked her watch for the fifth time in as many minutes.

She swung her arms back and forth in an effort to bring warmth to them under her thin dress coat. She should have opted for the heavy brown one, but against her better judgment, she listened to her mother and picked the silky one that matched the black and white dress she wore. The hat pinned to the top of her head did little to warm it, and because she didn't have gloves in the same red color, her mother said she had to go without.

Customs be damned. She tucked her hands under her arms.

Lawrence pulled up a moment later and leapt out of the car to open her door.

"You're late," she said as she warmed her fingers in front of the heat vents.

He slid into the seat and pulled away, the car behind them honking at him blocking the street. He made a rude gesture out the window.

"Hit every red light on my way over here. Sorry, did you have to wait long?"

"A few minutes. And it's awful cold out there."

Her mood didn't improve as they drove on. She found herself yelling at the other drivers for going too slow, braking too soon, or just existing on the roads.

"Ruth," Lawrence said, after a particularly strongly worded outburst. "What is going on with you tonight? Did I do something wrong?"

His voice was so sweet, so filled with caring, she lost her composure. The tears she'd been fighting a battle over all day burst from her eyes. Lawrence pulled into an empty spot and put the car in park.

"Hey, talk to me," he said, rubbing his hands between his. They were large and warm, and the gesture made her cry harder. "Ruth, you're frightening me." He let go and put his arms around her, pulling her across to the space between their two seats.

"It's fine," she managed after what felt like too long of a time to be blubbering to a man you were trying to impress.

"Well, it's obviously not. Tell me what's going on."

"I have worked at my job for ten years. I have spent long hours, weekends, huge amounts of my life there."

"I can tell that you work very hard and care about what you do."

She nodded. "I do care. And a few months ago, I received word that one of the managers was leaving. I mentioned to my boss how interested I was in the promotion. It even allows travel as the managers get a say in some of the items stocked on the floors. They go to Paris once a year. *Paris*." She said the word as if it was a secret place, one filled with magic. From the stories she heard, it was.

"And, did the woman not leave?" he asked.

"Worse. She left and they gave the promotion to

someone else. Trixie. A friend, actually, which makes it even worse, but I was barking mad. All those years. All that time I put in, to be passed over by a girl five years younger than me, who's only worked there for less than two. I marched into Mr. Gulliver's office and demanded to know why I wasn't picked."

"I bet that shocked him," Lawrence said, his eyes wide.

"He looked about ready to call security on me," she said, thinking back to the panicked look on the man's face, having a raving woman stomp around his office. "But he did admit that it was a calculated move."

"How so?"

"My age. He said since Trixie is younger, there is less of a risk of her leaving them soon for *domestic life*. The nerve."

"You should quit!"

"Lawrence, you know I need this job. My family… I need this job."

He shook his head. "No, you need *a* job."

"No one is going to hire a woman my age. Especially with so many people losing their jobs. He's right. I am too much of a risk. I'm piss and vinegar and there's no teeth behind it. He said what he did because he knew I couldn't do anything about it."

"Prove him wrong. Hear me out," he said as she opened her mouth to protest. "A family friend who owns a clothing store just passed away. His wife is running the shop in his absence, but I know for a fact that's not what she wants to be doing. I can put in a good word for you, I'm sure I can get you a management position there."

"Really?"

Her mind swirled. Just imagining what it would be like to walk into Mr. Gulliver's office and putting in her notice gave her a small thrill.

"Ruth, I would do anything for you. You know how much I care about you, right?"

She wiped away her tears, his kindness causing more to spring up. "Thank you."

"And don't worry." He leaned over and kissed her before merging back into traffic. "I'll take you to Paris one day. I'm sure we'll have more fun than any stuffy fashion show."

She couldn't help smiling as she looked out the window. What did she do to deserve such luck? To deserve such a man? She was thirty, well past the social prime that should have allowed her to land such a catch. She said a silent prayer to whatever saint resided over such matters.

They drove down the street in silence, Ruth lost in thoughts and dreams for the future.

Chapter Twenty

Ruth's happiness at his offer made Lawrence feel like his plan could work. He'd get her in deeper and deeper. A good paying job would also give her extra cash to invest in him. She'd be so grateful to him for getting her out of that crappy job, she'd do anything to repay him. It was all working out better than he'd imagined.

He phoned Mrs. Astor at the store and asked if he could make an appointment to speak with her in person. She sounded surprised and pleased to have heard from him and enthusiastically agreed.

"It will be nice seeing a familiar face that Gregory was so fond of," she said.

"Yes, of course," Lawrence said.

While Lawrence had seen the couple at his parents' parties over the years, he only recalled exchanging words with the man on that fateful day. And his wife, of course, knew nothing of that encounter. She must have been mistaken, but if it helped Ruth, he wasn't about to correct her.

She gave him the address of their brownstone. Thirty minutes later, a woman, looking frailer and older than he remembered, greeted him at the door. She embraced him in a bony hug and led him to a sitting room off the entryway. Lawrence took a glance down the hall and into the kitchen. It looked white and pristine. As if nothing terrible had happened there.

Lawrence wondered for a moment how he would be remembered, or if history would swallow him up just the same.

"I was so terribly sorry to hear about your loss, Mrs. Astor," Lawrence said.

"Elise, please, call me Elise."

"Elise," he echoed.

"To what do I owe the pleasure, Lawrence?"

"I understand from my parents that you are running the store. My mother is very worried about you, about the toll of this stress."

His mother cared for no one. If Elise lost the store, it would be good fodder for gossip. Sympathy wasn't her strong suit.

"It is very tiring," she said.

Lawrence couldn't remember seeing Elise and Gregory at the New Year's party, but previously he'd remarked to his brother how much younger the wife looked, twenty years or so, though he was pretty sure it was less than ten. But now she looked about a hundred. He was intrigued that a single event, like a loss of a loved one, could do that to a person.

He wondered if he looked different after Marco, or if he was able to hide behind his injuries.

"I hope I can be so bold as to offer what I pray is a bit of a reprieve, at least until you get yourself back on your feet and figure out what you would like to do."

She sat up, a faint smile tugging at her lips. "You are going to help out at the store."

"No..." he stammered, not expecting this. "No, but I know a very special woman who would be perfect for the role. She has almost ten years of retail experience at a large department store, but is looking for an opportunity at a smaller operation."

The smile broadened. "Mr. Henry, who exactly *is* this woman?"

He lowered his gaze in mock embarrassment. "To be frank, she is the woman I plan to marry."

It was the first time he said it out loud, but it was true. He knew how earnest Ruth was each time they met. Laughing at his smallest jokes. Complimenting him whenever she got the chance. Agreeing to any date he proposed. And to get her on his side, to fully commit, he knew this was the move he'd have to make.

Elise's face lit up, shaving a few of the stacked years off her features. "Lawrence, that's wonderful! I am so very happy for you both. Are you parents dreadfully excited?"

He nodded. "Oh, yes. Everyone is. That's why I'm hoping to help her out as well. She is looking for something new."

"A department store is very exciting, I'm not sure she will find our work as interesting," Elise said.

"Oh, no she will. She is unhappy with the store, feel like it's so large she doesn't get to know her clients well. She's looking for a more intimate experience. When I heard of your…predicament," he lowered his voice. "I thought she could be of great help to you."

Elise nodded. "I am not sure how long I will keep the shop, frankly. I'd hate for her to leave her position and then be without a job in a year or two."

"If I may speak truthfully again," Lawrence said. "We are hoping in a year or two she can transition to a more domestic lifestyle."

Elise broke out into a huge smile. "Oh, Lawrence,

you would make such a wonderful father. That is spectacular news."

Again, she spoke as if she knew him. But he played along and thanked her.

"She was planning on leaving anyway, actually," Lawrence added, to really seal the deal.

"Oh, whatever for?"

"I am opening my own pharmacy."

"A pharmacy!"

"She was going to work for me, but I think this is more important."

"I can't take her away from you."

"No, I think she will be happier with you anyway. She didn't really want to work for me." He laughed. "We need some time apart, I suppose!"

Elise laughed and wiped at her eyes. "Gregory and I liked our alone time as well. Fridays though, we always lunched together on Fridays…"

Lawrence grabbed her hands. "It will be doing me a favor. She will be happy to be making a difference."

"You're certain you can spare her?" she asked.

"For you, for Gregory, of course."

"It's settled then." She patted his hands.

Moments later, Lawrence made up an excuse for having to leave.

"Expecting a shipment, you know how it is," he said, waving her off at the door.

"I do know. And Lawrence, thank you again."

"You are very welcome Mrs. Astor. You take care of my girl now."

He passed the same two women pushing strollers again, but made no attempt to hide his face this time.

He couldn't wait to see Ruth's expression when he

told her about the new job he lined up for her. She'd be indebted to him for helping her.

And he couldn't think of a better position to have someone in.

Chapter Twenty-One

Ruth sat on her bed, drumming up the motivation to get up for dinner when her mother entered her room.

"This came for you," she said, handing her a cream-colored sealed card with Ruth's name scrawled in Lawrence's handwriting.

She sat straight up. "Is he here?" she asked, scrambling to get out from under the covers.

"A man dropped it off. Don't hurt yourself," she said as Ruth's foot caught on a pair of pajama pants on the floor, and she tumbled into her dresser.

"He wasn't here?"

"No, don't worry. Your mother did not meet the man you've been spending so much time with. That you're so smitten with. You know, in my day, the man had to come around and ask permission of the parents to even call on their daughter."

Ruth groaned. She'd been hearing this complaint since the night of her and Lawrence's first date.

"Mother, it has only been a few weeks. I am sure when he feels more comfortable and the timing is right, he will come meet you."

What was left out was the fact that she never invited him. She knew her life was simple and quaint, and on some level, she knew Lawrence was aware of this too. But she also didn't want to drive the fact home and scare him off.

Her mother huffed and left the room. Ruth ripped the note open.

My darling Ruth—

Her heart fluttered. She paused and clutched the letter to her chest.

I have the most wonderful news. I spoke to Mrs. Astor, the woman who lost her husband, and she is most eager to have you come help in her shop. She would like you to start right away, but understands that you are currently employed. When you have parted ways with that wretched Mr. Gulliver, please call on her to inform her of your start date (sooner than later, I'd suggest.)

I look forward to hearing about your first day when we go out to dinner this Friday for Valentine's Day. Wear something red. I will pick you up at 8:30.

Fondly,

Your Lawrence

Her Lawrence.

She read that last line over and over until it was so burned in her memory, she could see the outline of his words when she closed her eyes.

Then the reality set in.

She had a new job. Which meant she had to quit her old job. A moment she fantasized about with increasing ferocity over the last few months now churned her stomach. Sure, she'd been stomping mad in the car with Lawrence, but was she really going to leave? She'd never quit a job before. But how could she tell Lawrence she took it back? That she was too afraid to leave and would just settle for her comfortable life.

She had a feeling Lawrence wouldn't be very happy with her. Mr. Gulliver wasn't going to be very happy with her either, but only one of the two men she planned on ever seeing again.

A new job. She wasn't even really sure what it was for. Lawrence had said it was a custom tailor shop, but what did that really entail? She wasn't a seamstress and wasn't familiar with men's clothing. What if she did a terrible job and got fired? Then she would have no job.

She considered writing Lawrence back and thanking him profusely, but asking him to give her regrets to poor Mrs. Astor.

As she rummaged through a stack of papers to find her stationary, she dislodged her checkbook and it fell onto the floor. It opened to her balance sheet. $523.15.

Every cent she'd earned. All the hard work she'd done over the years, scrimping and saving and it amounted to this. She wondered what her commission would be at a higher end place. Maybe double what she made now? The prospect excited her. This could be a real opportunity for her. For them.

She pictured them shopping for their apartment. Maybe even a house outside of the city where he would take the train to work at the pharmacy and she'd stay home with the children. How could she back away now? Her mother would never forgive her if she mucked up a real opportunity at happiness this time.

She didn't have to give him the check right away. She wasn't a complete fool. Knew he could take the money and run. Without a ring promising him to her, he was under no obligation to stick around.

But she could write it. See how it felt. Carry it around a bit, try it on for size like that green dress. See if it fit.

She took out her pen and scrawled his name. Then

wrote: *to the sum of five-hundred dollars* on the middle line of the check.

She could always tear it up, right?

Chapter Twenty-Two

Detective Kelly walked straight by the place, before doubling back. She didn't remember a pharmacy being on this side of town, but sure enough, there it was. Signs on the window announced its grand opening.

She was just coming back from investigating a double homicide. Two gentlemen murdered on their way home from a lunch club. The pink and white balloons drew her attention. She stepped inside and was hit with the smell of fresh paint and flowers. Red blooms lined the walls, along with teddy bears announcing all degrees of like and love.

"Can I help you?"

She turned and was surprised to see a woman in a white pharmacist's coat step out from between two aisles.

She cursed herself inwardly, knowing how she hated that people didn't think she could be a cop because she was a woman, so why the hell couldn't this lady be a pharmacist?

"I just saw the grand opening sign and was pulled in by all the balloons I guess," Kelly said.

The woman looked her up and down and smiled. "First time?" she whispered.

Kelly was confused by the question. "Didn't you just open?"

The woman laughed and it was deeper than Kelly

expected. "Come with me, officer."

"Detective," Kelly corrected but felt embarrassed the moment she did it. Why did she feel like she needed to get into a pissing match with this woman?

Kelly followed her toward the back counter where the woman rifled around for a moment before presenting Kelly with a brown paper bag.

"What's this?"

"Fresh ginger drops. Should really help with the nausea."

Kelly's blood froze. "Nausea?" How did this woman know? There was no way she was showing yet, the few pounds she never lost from her last pregnancy gave her a bit of padding and the heavy winter coat over her skirt suit hid her midsection even more.

The woman waved her hand. "The glow. Don't worry, doubt any man would notice, if that's what you're worried about. But these really should help. If they don't, come back to see me and I can maybe give you something else."

A noise to her right made her look over, but Kelly couldn't see anything.

"Yes," she said, as if answering someone else's questions. "What's your name?"

"Detective Kelly. Johanna Kelly. Why?"

The woman pulled out a pad, scribbled something down, and gave her a ripped-out page.

"What's this?"

"Whiskey," the woman said with a hitch in her voice. "It can also help settle your stomach down, and maybe your husband's as well." She laughed without much force behind it.

Kelly sighed. "You realize I am a member of law

enforcement?" Weary anger rose in her voice.

"I-I..." she stuttered.

At that moment, a man, presumably the one coaching her from the next aisle, appeared. He was dressed in a dark suit that fit him so well, Kelly guessed it was custom. Probably cost a month's rent. It never ceased to amaze her the number of items rich people found to spend money on.

"Can I help you, officer?" the dapper man asked, extending his hand.

"Detective," she corrected again. "Detective Johanna Kelly. This woman here just offered me a piece of paper to acquire whiskey."

"Oh, yes, this is Doctor Anderson. And Ms. Johanna—"

"Detective Kelly."

"Of course, Detective, I assure you we have all our licenses. I can show you if you'd like."

I bet you do.

"Doctor, you said?" Kelly asked, addressing the woman.

"Yes, ma'am. Doctor Emma Anderson. And really, in combination with the ginger, the whiskey may really do the trick."

"And what did you say your name was?" Kelly said addressing the man.

He didn't look like any pharmacy owner Kelly had ever seen. There was an air about him Kelly instantly didn't trust.

"My manners, I am Lawrence Henry."

"Henry," Kelly said, eschewing Lawrence's outstretched hand.

"Yes, ma'am. And Dr. Anderson, can you believe

it! Look at us here, an epicenter of progressive woman if I ever saw one!" He clapped his hands and displayed an ear-to-ear smile.

"Are you related to Charles Henry?" Kelly asked, ignoring the diversion.

"Which one?" Lawrence said. When Kelly didn't respond, he rushed to add. "Both, actually. My father and brother are both Charles."

"Do you know the Chanlers or the Astors?"

"Both, actually. Tragic."

"And I assume you were at your parents' party?"

"Yes, but I didn't see either couple there."

Kelly perked up. "Either?"

"Well, they both would have been there, wouldn't they have? They were friends of my parents."

"Do you recall seeing anyone who *wasn't* supposed to be there?" Kelly asked, hoping not to betray her excitement at this connection. She also fought the urge to reach into the bag for a piece of the supposedly magical ginger.

Lawrence shook his head. "I didn't know most people who were there. I can't keep track of all their friends, my brother's friends, hell, even all my own friends. Sorry I can't be of more help."

She held up the bag and gestured to Doctor Anderson. "What do I owe you for this?"

"On the house," Lawrence said. "Oh, here." He grabbed a heart-shaped box of candy and pressed it into Kelly's hands. "You and your husband have a wonderful Valentine's Day. Congrats and I hope you feel better soon, but if not." He tapped on the prescription slip. "Feel free to come back and see us and we can fill that for you."

Kelly nodded and strode out, her arms filled, her mind and stomach churning.

Chapter Twenty-Three

Ruth walked into work that Monday and informed Mr. Gulliver that, while she appreciated all the years, she felt that the acknowledgement of her value had waned. It was time to move on. She offered to finish out her shift, but he said that wasn't necessary. He didn't even stand or shake her hand. She'd wanted to leave, and nothing he said would change that, but it still hurt he didn't try.

She held her head high and went to say goodbye to Anna. The two hadn't talked much since Anna moved upstairs and she was shocked to learn that first, Ruth and Lawrence were in a relationship, and second, she'd put her notice in, effective immediately.

"How has your whole life changed in the six weeks since we left that party?" Anna asked.

"Your guess is as good as mine."

"Well, if anyone deserves it, it's you. Don't be a stranger," she said, leaning over to kiss her cheek. "I want an invite to that wedding."

"I'll deliver it myself," Ruth said. She embraced her old friend and left.

Walking through the hall with the few items from her locker, she ran into Trixie, who had the decency to lower her gaze. They hadn't spoken since the promotion, and Trixie knew what being passed over meant to her.

Ruth strode by her, but thought better of it and turned back.

"You take care, Trixie," she said. "Thanks for everything, really."

The girl looked up and smiled. "You too, Ruth. I know you're going to do big, great things."

Ruth nodded and walked out of the store, closing a chapter of her life in a burst of cold, New York air.

****

She started at Mrs. Astor's shop the next day, in a management position.

Any fear she had in direct selling men's clothes vanished and was replaced by being in way over her head. She'd never had to run schedules before, make sure correct stocks were on the floor, or appease disgruntled customers. The learning curve was steep, but by Friday, she started to get the hang of it.

Mrs. Astor still came to the shop every day to help out and show her the ropes, but she told Ruth in no uncertain terms that it was an arrangement that would be short-lived.

"This was my husband's business," she said after they'd closed on Ruth's second day.

"I understand," Ruth said, but she wasn't really sure what she was commenting on.

"He worked his entire life to build this. I am not about to run it day-to-day, but I'm not also letting someone burn it to the ground."

"I am taking this very seriously," Ruth said.

"I know you are, dear." Her voice softened. "Lawrence does think very fondly of you."

"And I of him, but I'm not here for Lawrence, I'm here for you."

Mrs. Astor smiled.

Ruth thought that would buy her some time, allow a bit more hand-holding, but that afternoon before she left to deposit the bank envelope, Mrs. Astor announced that she would be staying on only through the end of the following week.

"Next week?" Ruth asked, a lump in her throat.

"I am going up to my sister's for the rest of the month. I'm sure you'll get the hang of it, but just ask me anything you are still having trouble with before I leave."

Ruth nodded, but the building fear made it difficult to breathe. How would she manage without her? The other shop girls and one man obviously resented her coming in. They could see from a mile away that Ruth didn't really know what she was doing and questioned her on how she landed the position they'd all felt deserving of. They spoke of Mr. Astor often and how wonderful he was, obviously trying to rub in her inadequacies.

It was just like Trixie. Coming in and taking what Ruth thought was hers. Ruth regretted the way she cut Trixie out of her life, not even considering the other girl's feelings. She made a mental note to ask for input when she could and be as good a leader as possible. By the end of the week, even though she'd only been there four days, her head swam with new information and the daunting task of only having a few more days until she was left on her own.

Ruth's feet ached by the time she got home. The subway was packed and she didn't get her normal twenty minutes of sitting down that she'd grown accustomed to. She sat on her bed and counted to ten, knowing she needed to start getting ready now if she had any hope of being halfway decent by the time Lawrence picked her up at eight-thirty. The new job was amazing, exciting, and exhausting.

Her mother's knock at her door startled her so much, she realized with horror she'd fallen asleep sitting up.

"Do you need any help getting ready?" her mother called through the door.

"No, I'm fine, thanks. Be out in a few minutes."

Her mother had insisted after Lawrence's card to walk Ruth to his car so she could officially meet him. Then her father chimed in that he'd be coming as well. Not to be left out, Sally also said she'd delay going out so she could meet him too. Ruth groaned, but knew telling them no would just make it worse and relented.

She checked her watch and realized in a panic her family may be meeting him on their own, if she couldn't get herself together in time. Luckily, she'd had the forethought to hang her dress and shoes out the night before, so she just had to slip her current outfit off and change it out. As requested, she wore a garnet red, ankle-length dress, flattering, but weather inappropriate. She pinned her hair up and put matching lipstick on before dashing out to grab her coat.

Sitting in the kitchen, her family looked expectantly at her, already clad in their finest coats. It was a small gesture, and Ruth knew that they also wanted to look their best to meet Lawrence. She appreciated their effort.

Sally was wearing one of Ruth's black dresses for her night out with her fiancé and Ruth tried not to notice how much better her sister filled out the hand-me-down garment. She defaulted to jealous thoughts so much over the years, she inwardly chided herself for doing it now.

You have a wonderful man, just be happy that your sister has also found someone and is going to marry him.

She knew this, but sometimes it was easier said than done.

"You look lovely, darling," her mother said. "Do you think tonight will be the night?"

"Mother," Ruth said, rolling her eyes.

"What? It is a romantic night. You aren't getting any younger."

"Mom," Sally said, "let's not make Ruth more nervous than she probably already is."

Ruth smiled at her younger sister, silently mouthing, *Thank you.*

"I just want to meet this Lawrence we've all heard so much about."

Ruth sighed. They hadn't heard much of anything about Lawrence because she wasn't one to gossip about such matters. If Sally heard anything about Lawrence, it was because she'd asked around town, which Ruth was pretty sure she had.

Ruth tried not to feel like a fool when Lawrence's car pulled up. He looked shocked for only a moment before enthusiastically reaching his hand out to her father and then kissing the hands of both her mother and sister. All three of them appeared to swoon as Lawrence shone his attention on them. Ruth beamed with pride as her nerves faded away. She needn't have been worried.

In that moment, in stunning clarity, she realized

she loved this man. And desperately, more fervently than she'd ever wanted anything, hoped he loved her back. She knew he was flawed. Hell, she was flawed, too. No one made it to thirty without a prospect and didn't have some issues. Her mother was quick to point this out multiple times to her when Ruth rejected any suitors.

"It's not like you're perfect," her mother would say. "You're thirty."

It felt like a curse.

But she wasn't perfect. She also didn't fool herself into thinking Lawrence was either, as he held her mother's hand and gaze, so handsome, so polite.

But he was pretty damn good.

Chapter Twenty-Four

Lawrence eased the car up to the valet station as Ruth chattered next to him. She said over and over how pleased she was with her family meeting him. Of how impressed they clearly were. Of how wonderful he was.

He nodded, talking when she left a pause open for him to do so. Tried to hide his annoyance of being blindsided by the introductions. It wasn't part of the plan. She wasn't calling the shots in this, he was. His fingers twitched at the loss of control as he gripped the wheel.

It wasn't that he assumed he'd never meet her parents. Of course not. He knew it was the proper thing to introduce himself, especially when he had to declare his intentions, but he wanted it to be on *his* terms. He didn't like his hand played for him.

He tried to clear his mind. He needed to focus on his task tonight. He needed Ruth to believe in him, in *them.* He'd purposely picked a restaurant that ran a Valentine's special. For one, it was mercifully cheaper, but with the pink and red decorations covering each wall, he knew it was the kind of tacky that would have a simple woman like Ruth wide-eyed and amazed.

When dinner was over, he pushed a long rectangular velvet box toward her. Her face fell in an emotion he couldn't quite read.

"Is everything okay?" he asked.

She hesitated, fingers poised over the box.

He could tell instantly he played his hand wrong. His heart and mind raced from the stress at potentially screwing this up. Maybe having to start all over,

"Ruth," he said, words falling out of his mouth the second he thought them, "I see my future with you, I've hesitated to be so bold to tell you that, but it's true."

Her shoulders relaxed and her face softened. "Oh, Lawrence, I do as well."

"I know there are ways this is supposed to go. I guess I *have* met your parents." He forced out a laugh which she returned. Yes, he was getting her back. "But I want to be able to offer you a real life. A real chance of happiness. I don't want to rush that. This pharmacy…"

"This is a real life," she said.

He shook his head. "I want you to be able to have whatever you wish. I want to be able to take care of you and your family, don't you want that?"

"Of course, I do. Yes."

"I am building something that will do that. I am building something for us, something we can share."

Ruth closed her eyes and Lawrence worried he'd played it too strongly. Did he swing the other way and now risked scaring her off? He'd pegged her as a girl desperate to please her family, and he knew marrying a rich man ticked those boxes.

When she opened her eyes, she reached into her bag.

"*This* is for you," she said, "but not because it's Valentine's Day. It's just because I think we believe in the same things. And I believe in you."

He took the envelope but gestured for her to go

first. When she tilted the lid open, the effect he was going for worked. Her eyes widened. The emerald and diamond necklace sparkled in the middle of the box.

"This is too much," she whispered.

"It is exactly enough," he said.

"You need this money for your business, I can't accept this."

"Well, don't think too highly of me," he laughed. "It is a family jewel. My great aunt passed it down from her side of the family."

He took the necklace from the box and clasped around her neck. He stood back to take in the view. Just as he knew they would since it was the same color combination Mrs. Chanler wore, the jewels perfectly complemented the dress. She looked stunning.

Ruth touched the necklace with her fingertips. "It's so heavy."

He laughed. "There are quite a lot of diamonds."

She took a deep breath and flashed him a huge smile. "Thank you."

He moved to open the letter, but she reached out a hand to stop him.

"Now I feel silly. Please, don't open it now. Tomorrow. Another time, it's not appropriate for now," she said, her voice squeaking.

"Nonsense, now I need to know what it is." He opened the card, wondering what could possibly be contained to make her squirm so.

He unfolded the check. Five hundred dollars.

"Ruth…" He pretended surprise when all he wanted to do was jump in the air. Shut his eyes and throw his fists up in victory.

"I know, it is such a paltry amount. After this…"

119

She touched her neck again. "But it's all I had. Well, save for a few dollars."

He took her hand, wanting her to believe his sincerity. "Ruth, this is amazing. Thank you. Thank you for trusting me, for believing in me. I am so lucky to have found you."

Tears welled in her eyes and she leaned forward to kiss him.

After a decadent dessert and short walk, he dropped her back off at her place with apologies for having to end the night so early.

"I have a meeting in the morning with some suppliers," he said.

She yawned, as she had been doing the entire drive. "I have work tomorrow. I really do love this job, but it is very tiring."

"You'll get the hang of it in no time, I'm sure." He kissed her three times before opening her door. "Happy Valentine's Day, Ruth."

"Happy Valentine's Day, Lawrence."

As he drove toward the dock, Ruth's check felt like both a lead weight and a feather in his pocket. He kept touching the fabric to feel its outline on his chest. He expected her to give him the money, sure, but also anticipated he'd need to trade her a diamond ring for it. He probably still did, especially if he wanted to milk any more cash out of her, but the necklace probably bought him a bit of time.

And all that nice stuff he said about helping her family. Flying by the seat of his pants. He was impressed with himself for thinking of that.

When he pulled up to the dock, a man in a dark trench coat met him before he was even fully out of the car.

"You're late," the man barked.

"Let me tell you a story," Lawrence said,

But the man held up his hand. "It's cold. I don't have time and I don't care about no stories. You got the money?"

Lawrence nodded and handed over the envelope with cash inside. He practically had to dig through his couch cushions to come up with the full amount. The two men leaving the club had a paltry sum between the two of them when Lawrence relieved them of their money. Almost made the whole ordeal not worth it.

The man quickly thumbed through the bills in the envelope and nodded. "Stuff's round back. Pull up and I'll help you load it."

Once they'd put the three cases in Lawrence's car, the man turned to walk away.

"Hey, wait. I need to talk to you about the next shipment. I'm going to need double what you gave me this time."

The man shook his head. "Double, nah, I can't do that. Can barely give you what I'm giving you now."

"I'll pay. Business is going well, I need more supply. If I run out, people will find someplace else to get it. I can't let that happen. You understand."

He shook his head again. "If Lucky gets wind that I'm selling you *any*, I reckon he'll have a thing or two to say to me. And Lucky don't really like talkin', if you catch my drift."

"Why don't you worry about getting me more whiskey, and I'll worry about Lucky," Lawrence said.

"We all need to worry about Lucky," the man said. "Whether we know it or not."

Lawrence shrugged. He'd seen worse in life and survived.

A mobster certainly didn't scare him.

Chapter Twenty-Five

The glow Detective Kelly took to work the next morning faded once she walked through the door and saw a group of detectives standing together.

The night had been pretty perfect. She'd taken the chocolates home to her children, who rewarded her with a series of kisses and the ginger had finally given her some relief. The kids were freshly showered when she got home and she sat in the big chair in the living room and read them stories as she breathed in their clean, strawberry scent.

They ate heart-shaped cookies the children baked that day for dessert and she tucked everyone into bed after telling them one more tale of the princess falling in love with her handsome prince.

"I want to marry a prince one day, Mommy," Mollie, her youngest, declared.

"Well then, you will, *a stór,*" she over-exaggerated an Irish accent while saying the term of endearment just like Mollie liked.

"I'm going to be a prince one day," Alvie echoed.

"Then you surely will."

She kissed both of them and went to sit with her husband by the dying fire.

"The chocolates were good," Patrick said. "You should bring them home more often."

"Well, usually I'm just trying to get straight

home," she said. "It was a fluke I caught a case near a new pharmacy. You know how it is."

The sentence hung in the air. They didn't often talk about life *before*. When he was working the long hours and she worked part-time at the jail. When she was at work and got the call he'd been shot. How she rushed to the hospital in a panic after sending a message to the woman upstairs who watched her children while both parents were working.

Seeing him hooked up to all those machines, the hallway lines with head-hung officers, was an image she pushed away any time it entered her mind. The terror that she'd lose him. The knowledge that she wouldn't but he'd never walk again. He had some feeling and movement, but not enough to be able to get up. Certainly not to work again.

"Come here," he said, gaze searching her face.

She perched on him in the wheelchair and he wrapped his arms around her.

"How much longer do you think you'll be able to work?" he asked.

She let out a long-held sigh. "Three months, maybe? Luckily I have a bit of room to grow in my uniform and can wear a winter coat to hide it, but that will only last so long. I fear I'm going to outgrow my girdle before then though. I could kick myself for not hanging on to my old one after Mollie."

"We can buy another."

She smiled at him. "Seems like an extravagance for such a temporary need."

He kissed her on the forehead. "Do you think they'll let you go back? Or give you a desk job?"

"I doubt it. Gosh, I don't want to leave it."

"Are you upset?"

"About the baby? No. It was unexpected, but no, a blessing. Always a blessing. It's just…" She didn't often like to talk to him about her work, more to spare him the reminder that she was doing what he couldn't. And that he did what she couldn't because she was away.

She never asked him how he felt about being the caregiver to their children. In some ways it didn't matter, not like they could change anything about it, so better not to have the added guilt of leaving her babies if her husband also resented the work.

But she did often wonder. When she walked out the door, how did her home make it through the rest of the day or evening? Were there hugs and love or clock watching? As the kids got older they would give her snippets of their day. Talked about how they went to the park across the street where Daddy could see them from the window. How on nicer days he'd join them, the blessing in all this being they had a first-floor apartment so he never needed to go upstairs.

She couldn't help but wonder if they missed her when she was gone, like she missed them. How a part of her brain was occupied at all times by their absence. How even when she was deep in a case, there was a small string pulling her home.

This baby would be a blessing in some ways. They'd had some savings and her working these last few years increased the amount of pension she'd get when she left. They'd be able to get by. Maybe it was the universe telling her to slow down and be there for her kids.

But then she thought about those dead men and

women who littered her streets. The officers too dim-witted or uninterested to care enough. Of the ones who brushed off a dead prostitute just as easy as a dead socialite.

Where was the justice for them? How could she leave them behind?

The same string that pulled her home tugged her back out there.

It seemed she was never where her body told her to reside.

"Hey, where did you go?" he asked, pulling her back.

She shook her head. "I am right here. Let's go to bed."

****

In the morning, she slipped out before any of them woke to make it to the office in time. It was a simple life, work and home. It created a structure she liked and on most days, she was fulfilled and happy.

But lately, the work had been harder and harder to forget. The cases traveling home with her until she became distant at dinner. Patrick or the kids would repeat questions to her several times before she realized someone spoke to her and she had to answer.

So, when she arrived and saw so much commotion so early in the morning, she knew something terrible had happened.

"You hear?" Carlson asked, handing Kelly a cup of coffee. She smiled and thanked him, ignoring the looks from those around who probably expected Kelly to hand out the coffees and not the other way around.

"Probably not," Kelly said.

"Buncha pharmacies got hit last night," he said.

The image of Lawrence and the chocolates popped into her head.

She was about to ask Carlson which ones, when their lieutenant came out barking orders.

"All right listen up. Kelly, good, glad you could finally make it."

She looked at the clock. It was five minutes *before* her shift was supposed to start. God, he was such an asshole. Would never speak to the male detectives the way he spoke to her. She dug her nails into her palms to calm herself.

He pointed at her. "You and Carlson will take Kappie's on Twelfth. JoJo and Abrams, you take Martin's on Tenth."

He rattled off more, but Carlson was already tugging on Kelly to get going. She didn't recognize the last two names, but knew they weren't Lawrence's.

"Kappie's?" Kelly asked.

"Of course he's gotta give us the one with the stiff," Carlson said, taking the keys from Kelly's hand. "Think that's your bad luck rubbing off on me."

It was a sort of joke she never found funny, how she always got the worst cases. The most gruesome. She was sure it was in an effort to make her quit, but the bosses swore cases were handed out in order. Just a simple round robin, nothing more to be read into about it.

But she knew. She wasn't an idiot. Luckily Carlson didn't seem to mind too much. She didn't have to worry about him later putting dog shit in her locker or stealing her panties to hang from the bulletin board in the hall while she showered. Some of the other guys, they had no qualms about airing their grievances in such ways.

"So, what exactly happened?" she asked, taking two steps for every one he did.

"Told ya, pharmacies got hit."

"Give me the long story."

Carlson sighed. "All four cleared out of cash and booze. Two set on fire. Well, actually all four set on fire, but two burned down. At Martin's some passersby were able to douse water on it. Kappie's is close enough to the fire station. They got there pretty quick. Good, too, because it would have been hell trying to ID a crispy body."

"Someone dead inside?"

"Yup, our unlucky break. Well, I guess the guys too. Other buildings weren't occupied, but for some reason this guy was in there when the place was broken into. Word is a backdoor lock was broken. Guy must have stumbled on the robbers because they found the body in the storage area, stabbed a few times."

"And only money and alcohol were taken?" Kelly asked. "No narcotics?"

He raised an eyebrow at her, like he was surprised she could ask an intelligent question. He was nice, but he wasn't immune to prejudices.

"Doesn't appear so," he said. "Well, to tell you the truth, apparently the booze wasn't even taken, but smashed."

"Who would smash alcohol and not take it?"

"You can't think of a single person? Someone who isn't too happy about these places competing with his business?"

"You think Lucky is behind this?"

"I'd bet my shitty apartment on it."

When they pulled up, they'd missed the coroner by

a few minutes, but enough blood puddled on the floor. It was pretty clear where the body had been. The officers said the photographer had taken pictures of the scene and they handed Carlson a bag with the man's personal effects, reaching over Kelly to do so.

The place reeked of alcohol and burnt wood and plastic. The walls were licked in black streaks and some of the shelves were melted and misshapen. Kelly walked to the front and saw the open cash register. She went into the side office and found a wall safe with some scratches on it, but it appeared intact.

Someone called out from the front of the store. Kelly and Carlson reached it at the same time. An older man stood with keys shaking in his hand, the clinking of the keys hurting Kelly's teeth.

"Can we help you?" Carlson asked.

"This, this is my place. I got a call that something happened."

"We are sorry sir to have to tell you this, but one of your employees was killed here last night and it appears that a portion of your store was set on fire. The fire department was able to put it out, but there is some damage back there," Carlson said.

"And your register was cleared out," Kelly added. "But looks like your safe is untouched."

The man looked Kelly up and down. She was obviously with the department, her blue skirt, jacket, and matching hat with emblem couldn't be missed, but he still narrowed his eyes and turned to Carlson.

"Billy is dead?" the man asked, bewilderment in his tone.

"His name was Billy?" Carlson asked, flipping open a notebook and jotting the name down.

"Does he normally work late?" Kelly asked.

Again, the man looked at Carlson. "Only when he closes. Only when I ask him to close. I had plans with my wife last night. I was supposed to, it should have been me…" The man's words fell off as he started to cry.

Kelly grabbed a chair from the office and placed it in the entryway and gently moved the man to sit in it. Apparently emotional support was okay for her to give because he accepted it without comment.

"Were there problems with any customers lately? Someone who may want to cause Billy harm?" Carlson asked.

The man shook his head.

"No one you can think of?" Carlson asked.

The man furrowed his brow in concentration then looked up abruptly. "Come to think of it, two nights back when I was leaving here, two men approached me in the alley. They offered me protection and a supply discount. I said I already had a supplier. They said they'd like to take over, but I've been using Pete for thirty years, I told them. I wasn't interested in switching."

"And they didn't give you any trouble? Try to shake you up?" Carlson asked.

"No. Just asked if I was sure and left me alone when I said no."

"Would you be able to describe them? If we took you down to the station, think you can provide enough information to get a sketch?" Carlson asked.

"I can try, but it was dark, and I was in a rush."

"We understand," Kelly said. "But all the same, it may help." She put a tentative hand on the man's shoulder and was pleased he didn't shrug it off. Small victories.

"Anything. Anything to catch the monsters who did this to Billy. It should have been me. It should have been me."

The man mumbled it over and over to himself. Carlson motioned for one of the unis to take him down to the station.

"All right, think that's our cue to leave as well," Carlson said. "And if I hear one damn thing about you trying to link this to the East-to-West shit, so help me God, Kelly, the coroner will have to come back for you."

Chapter Twenty-Six

Emma was so close to the door when Lawrence opened it, he almost hit her in the face. She didn't react, moving right back into the space when it shut behind him.

"Did you hear?" she asked, her eyes wide.

Lawrence moved past her, brushing her shoulder with his. He walked to the back to take his coat off, her at his heels like a hungry alley cat.

"Hear what? That detective didn't try to cause any trouble, did she?"

She shook her head. "Kappie's, Martin's, Calder's, and Roland's got robbed last night."

Lawrence's gaze flew up to her face. "What?"

"And one of their stock boys, Bobby or Buster or something, was killed. Lawrence, *they killed him.*"

He pulled her over by the arm so they could sit side-by-side on the small leather couch. Lawrence's mind whirled.

"Who Emma, who killed him? Who broke into these places? Does the police know?"

She shrugged. "I don't know, I didn't hear. I just heard they stole the money, set them on fire. *Fire*, Lawrence! And smashed their alcohol."

"Wait, what? They destroyed the alcohol? Anything else? Did they take any meds?" His voice rose. Could it be? Would that scoundrel have ratted him out?

She shook her head. "No, or at least, that's what the rumor is," she said, her voice less sure.

Just then a firm knock on the door made them jump.

"I forgot to leave the door unlocked," Lawrence said, removing her gripped hand from his knee. "Probably just a customer angry at finding it not open. Are you going to be okay? Why don't you lock the back door? That way there is only one way in and out. I'll stay all day. You won't be alone," he said. He planned on meeting Ruth for lunch, but now wasn't so sure.

As soon as he turned the lock on the front door, it burst open. Three men exploded through and tackled him. Another man's shoes clicked on the floor and the lock moved back into place.

"You the only one here?" one of the men asked before punching him in the stomach.

"Yes!" Lawrence gasped. "I'm the only one here." He hoped Emma heard and had the wherewithal to either leave or hide.

Two of the men held him by the arms and dragged him to the back office. Lawrence looked around wildly, but saw no sign of Emma. He was thrown in a chair, and when he tried to get up, the third man—the one who punched him before—socked him hard in the face. Stars burst across his vision and he temporarily lost hearing in his right ear. It came back in painful shockwaves. A ringing echo followed it.

"Do you know who I am?"

"Mmmm," Lawrence managed through gritted teeth.

"Look at me, son." The man pressed a gloved finger under his chin and lifted his head.

Lawrence's eyes came into focus, merging the two men into one. He was shorter than the three goons surrounding him. Lawrence estimated he'd probably come up to his shoulders. That is, if he was ever able to stand again. The man wore a fine blue and pin-striped suit with a matching hat. A taupe scarf resting over his lapels, one of which housed a single red rose. His hair and eyes were almost the same shade of black.

"Do you know who I am?" the man asked again, the smell of cigar smoke fresh on his breath.

Lawrence tried to nod, but found his chin held too tightly for movement. "Yes, Mr. Luciano, sir."

"Good." Lucky Luciano let go of his chin. "That will save us some time. Now, Mr. Henry, my partners here tell me they came to you with a business proposition that you were uninterested in."

"Well, s-sir..."

Lucky put his hand up. "No need. No need for lies or apologies. I am going to make this very clear to you. We are now your supplier for spirits. You will get your deliveries by the docks behind the third warehouse on the left. I believe you know where that is."

Lawrence nodded. He knew exactly where it was. That little rat.

"Good. You will pay us ten dollars a gallon. Plus, an additional twenty-five-dollar protection tax."

Lawrence's mind whirled. He typically paid six a gallon, which he turned around and sold for three dollars a pint. This gave him a decent profit, which this man was about to take a huge chunk out of.

"Mr. Luciano, I am a new business. I can't afford

that much money."

Someone's hand pressed his neck, then lifted him out of the chair and cut off his breathing. He scrambled for purchase on the floor, but found nothing to grab on to on the slick surface.

"Tito, that's enough," Lucky said evenly and the hand disappeared.

Lawrence coughed, sputtered, and rubbed the sore place. Involuntary tears welled in his eyes. It had been years since he'd been in a real fight. Even the war felt more like an ambush, not a planned attack like this. The feeling of helplessness both angered and terrified him.

Flashes of his youth, locked closet doors. His father beating him with whatever object was close by. Of boys in boarding school questioning his sexuality as they kicked him. But then he grew up. He'd gained control. Hell, even the tussle with Mr. Astor still was on Lawrence's terms. Even when the old man fought back, Lawrence knew he wasn't in any real danger.

Not like this.

He just hoped Emma got away. Would hate if something happened to her. Maybe she'd already escaped out the back door. Alerted the police. They could be on their way right at this very moment.

"From what I hear, there was a series of unfortunate events with some of your competitors last evening," Lucky said. "I have a feeling that your business may just pick up."

"Yes, sir, yes it may, sir." He worked hard to keep his voice steady. To not let the anger slip out. Words were his only weapon usable at this moment.

"You should feel grateful that I have come today and am offering you such a good deal. The protection alone will be worth one hundred dollars a week. You are in a dangerous profession, it appears, Mr. Lawrence."

"Thank you, sir. Thank you for looking out for me." Lawrence hated groveling to the man, but he knew enough to play along. He'd get revenge somehow, but he needed to live first.

"You're welcome Mr. Henry. I think we have can have a successful partnership together. Don't you?"

"Yes, yes, Mr. Luciano. Thank you."

"Boys," Lucky said and turned to leave. "Oh, and Mr. Henry."

"Yes, sir?"

"I don't think this is something you need to worry about mentioning to the authorities, do you?"

Lawrence shook his head. "No, sir. No, of course not."

"Good, because I'd hate for something to happen to your lovely Dr. Anderson or Miss Smith. Good day, Mr. Lawrence."

He waited until he heard the front door open and close again before slumping from the chair on to the floor. How in the world could he come up with kind of money Lucky wanted? Ruth's check sat in his wallet, suddenly meager, mocking him. Only moments before and he was on top of the world, his plan of striking out on his own right around the corner. Who the hell was Lucky Luciano to try to take that from him?

Emma rushed around the corner with a small first aid kit and began cleaning him up. He was glad not only to see she was okay, but that she hadn't left to alert the authorities. While he was already working on plans to double cross Lucky, he was also smart enough to know to listen to the man.

"What are we going to do?" Her hands trembled as she pressed gauze to his eye.

He grabbed her fingers and looked straight into her eyes. "Emma, you can *never* mention this to anyone, do you understand?"

"But the police—"

"No." His words came out more forceful than he'd anticipated, and she jumped. "No one. They will kill us. We are going to act as if this never happened. I will meet them once a week where they say and pay them whatever they want, and we will be safe. As far as you are concerned, you have no idea where we get our supply from. I am in charge of restocking and purchasing. You've never heard of Lucky Luciano. If anyone asks, no one strange has come around the store. You know all your customers and you trust them. You heard what happened, so we will keep the back door locked and make sure there are always two people here. I will hire a shop boy to help out. We never speak of this again, do you understand?"

She nodded.

"I need you to tell me that you understand," he said, his voice firm and urgent.

She leaned back from him, some fear in her eyes. "I understand."

"We have work to do. Let's clean all this up and get to it."

He took the gauze from her and stood, wobbled a little, but regained his footing. He put the chair back in its place and began restocking the shelves. He kept catching Emma looking over at him, but she had the decency to lower her gaze without further comment.

Now he just needed to figure out how to make it all work. The money from Ruth wouldn't be enough, and while the store was doing okay, it also wouldn't float the operation how Lawrence needed it to. Maybe ask Charles? Or talk to his parents about investing?

Or there was always that place down the street. The rumors they ran a table all day and night.

And even as he willed himself to ignore it, he knew he'd give in to the delicious urge.

Chapter Twenty-Seven

Rebecca popped her head into the office, interrupting Elise telling Ruth how to add new client names to the circular books so ads could be sent to their homes for all major sales. "Pardon me, Mrs. Astor, but there's a gentleman here to see Miss Smith."

"Someone to see me?" Ruth asked.

"A Mr. Henry," Rebecca said, a foxy smile on her face.

Elise clapped her hands. "Oh, Lawrence. What a pleasure. I would like to see him as well, to thank him for recommending you."

Ruth looked back at Rebecca, whose eyes shone with pure delight. Which meant something had to be wrong because Rebecca openly disliked Ruth. Elise gasped softly. Ruth maneuvered around her to see what the problem was.

Her hand flew to her mouth. Lawrence's right eye was swollen and sported a bandage above it. His lip was cut and his hunched manner indicated to her his jacket was hiding other injuries.

"My dear Lawrence," Elise exclaimed. "Whatever happened to you?"

"Oh, it's nothing really." He flashed a smile that cracked the cut and blood droplets built at the corner of his lips. "I was hanging some signs up at the store and fell off the ladder."

"You do too much," Elise said.

"Ruth, can I speak with you please? Mrs. Astor, I am terribly sorry to interrupt your day, but this will only take a moment."

"Take all the time you need, dear," she said.

Ruth motioned for him to follow her into the back. She was pleased to see Rebecca's smug smile had turned into a disappointed scowl. Serves you right.

Ruth embraced Lawrence when she'd gotten him safely behind the office door. He stiffened and pulled back.

"Okay, what really happened?" she demanded.

"Do I have a story for you," he said.

The line, endearing at first, wore on Ruth. She just wanted the truth.

"I don't want a story, Lawrence. I want to know what is going on. I heard Kappie's got broken into. That a man died. Is that what this is about?" She gestured to his face.

"I'm fine, really," he said. "Just a little mishap at the store. Nothing I can't fix or handle."

"I am an investor, unless you forgot," she said. "Unless you want me to pull my funding, I need the truth from you."

"It's too dangerous."

"Lawrence." She looked him in his good eye. "Look at you. I'm scared. For you. For me. For my family, which you said you'd protect."

He opened his mouth to speak, but she held up her hand.

"I need you to give it to me straight. I need to know what I'm also involved in." She crossed her arms and her heart pounded in her chest.

His eye narrowed. "This doesn't involve you, Ruth. I'm handling it."

"Oh, it sure looks like you are."

He took a step toward her, invading her personal space a little too much.

"Lawrence, what are you doing? Are you going to fight *me*?"

He shook his head and staggered back. "It's been a long day."

"Tell me."

"You can't breathe a word of this to anyone. I mean that, Ruth. Any single person or you risk both our lives."

Lawrence looked at her full in the face. She tried to stare back without wincing at his rapidly swelling eye.

She mimed locking her lips and throwing away the key, trying to break some of the tension between them. "I promise."

"I'm under the thumb."

"Of who?"

"Doesn't really matter. But yes, they killed a boy last night, robbed and set three other places on fire. I don't really have any options than to do what they tell me to."

"What are we going to do?"

He smiled and leaned forward to kiss her. He smelled of rubbing alcohol and iodine.

"I need more money."

"Your parents—"

"For the last time, I don't need a handout from my parents."

"Lawrence, it's not a handout, I am sure—"

"I don't need anything from them."

Anger darkened his features and she took a step back, scared and unsure of what to do. Not liking these mood swings and hoping their commotion wouldn't make someone from the store check on her, embarrassing her further.

"Well, I don't have any more. I gave it all to you." Her mind spun. "I can probably sell some things." Flashes of green sped through her mind. "The necklace and the dress."

"Out of the question," he said, what little color he had draining from his face.

"Lawrence, please. I am sure both will fetch a pretty penny. I love them, but I love you more." The words were out of her mouth before she could stop them.

"You love me?"

She took a deep breath. "I do."

"I love you, too."

A small voice in the back of her head screamed in excitement. Another part wanted to pull the words back. To shelve this moment for something better. A story she could actually tell someone. Not this one. She couldn't say that the first time they said they loved each other was in the back of a dingy storeroom, while he was bloody and they were figuring out how not to get killed by people who wanted money. No, that wouldn't do.

"Ruth," he said, pulling her back to the present. "You must promise me you won't sell that necklace."

His words were cold and stern. She nodded.

"I need you to say the words to me."

"I promise that I won't sell the necklace," she said.

"Don't worry, I will figure this out. I need to go."

"Wait, just wait a second. Okay, look, we can figure it out. It won't be much, but I am making more here. I suppose I can invest that back into the store," she said.

Uneasiness nestled in her stomach as she said the words. As she dug herself deeper.

Lawrence nodded, but she wasn't sure if he entirely heard. He stared out the small, dingy window onto the street. Part of her hoped he hadn't. If she thought too much about the few dollars left in her bank account, she'd lose her appetite and need to sit down. She prayed she hadn't misjudged Lawrence and his abilities. Hoped that one day soon they would be married and she wouldn't have to worry about money anymore.

"Let's plan on a party at my place this weekend. Invite all your friends. We can let our circles meet..." He was lost in thought for a moment. "Yes, yes, a party."

"Do you really think that is the best idea right now? Shouldn't we be saving? Not draw attention to you?" Ruth hated to question him, but it seemed necessary.

"No, it will be perfect. I need to go."

She walked him to the front of the store. He was halfway out the door before he turned back and kissed her again. "I really do love you."

And he was gone.

Emotions swirled in Ruth in his wake. As crazy as it sounded, she hoped they'd turned a new leaf over in their relationship. He'd shared something with her she knew he didn't want to. He'd seemed angry about it at first, but she'd gotten through to him. He'd trusted her.

Now they could figure their future out, together.

Chapter Twenty-Eight

Fear had a strange effect on Lawrence. He felt reckless and bold. He went to the bank and cashed all but one hundred dollars of Ruth's check. It had been weeks since he'd seen Paul and his insides itched with anticipation. He didn't even look up and down the street before climbing up his steps to his apartment.

Paul was all over Lawrence before the door even shut behind him.

Clothes were tugged off, lips kissed too hard, bruises ignored. Paul didn't even ask Lawrence what happened to him or if he was all right. The need to just be together was too strong. Afterward, on the mattress which sat directly on the floor, Paul traced the bruises on Lawrence's chest.

"Are you going to tell me how that happened?" Paul asked.

Lawrence shook his head.

"Your girlfriend?"

Lawrence laughed. They didn't talk about Ruth, but Paul wasn't a dumb man.

"This have anything to do with those robberies last night?"

"Doesn't matter," Lawrence said.

Really, it didn't. There was nothing he could do about it. Lawrence knew enough about Paul to realize he didn't have any money. There was no point in asking.

"Do you know of any good games going on right now? I need one that is a little higher end than normal."

One of Paul's many jobs was dealing cards at the underground casinos scattered through the city. He knew what was going on at any given moment.

"Yeah, sure, right above Everyard's, actually. We can stop in first…" Paul trailed kisses on Lawrence's chest.

Lawrence sat up. He didn't have enough time for another romp. "Not today, I need to make that game. You can come to that, though."

"Naw, bosses don't really like us showing our faces when we're not working. And they especially don't like us taking money from guys we try to get coming back the next night. It never ends well. They think we're working in cahoots with the dealers, things turn ugly. You're on your own."

He gave Lawrence directions for how to get in the back entrance and walked him out.

"Look," Paul said, holding on to the half-closed door. "I know you have a whole other life out there, but don't forget me for this long next time, got it?"

"Got it," Lawrence said.

Lawrence walked to Everyard Baths, but instead of entering through the front door, he followed Paul's directions and went around back, knocking three times on the delivery door. A rectangular piece of metal slid aside, revealing a set of eyes.

"Help you?" a gravelly voice boomed.

"Here to see a man about a dog," Lawrence said.

The metal slid back and the sound of turning bolts and locks radiated behind the door. The man let

Lawrence in and told him to go up the stairs and to the room on the right. Lawrence turned back in time to see the man go down a narrow hall and wondered if someone saw him coming and had sent the man to let him it. He waited for several more minutes, but no one came back to man the relocked door.

The room Lawrence found was dark and filled with a choking amount of smoke, weakening the overhead lights even more. Men on stools surrounded three green felt topped tables, with a dealer sitting at the head passing out cards. Chips in an array of colors littered the centers and were stacked around the outside.

A woman with a tray met him at the door and gestured him toward the small bar.

"Getcha a drink?" She snapped a piece of pink chewing gum the same color as her dress.

"Is there a table limit?" Lawrence asked.

She shook her head.

"I need four hundred."

He noted that her eyes didn't widen at the sum. Paul was right about this place. She pointed to the man standing behind the bar. He placed stacks in a cardboard holder and passed them over once Lawrence counted out the money.

"Good luck," the man said, without any real warmth behind it.

Lawrence lost track of time as hand after hand was dealt. The only marker that he'd been there for a while was when he lit his last cigarette. At one point the other tables were consolidated and two new players sat on either side of him as men left with empty hands and the dealers parted ways.

Lawrence's stacks grew. He estimated he was at a

thousand dollars. He knew he should leave. This would be enough to get them through until he could figure something else to do. He was about to stand when the marker stating he was required to put the minimum bid passed to him along with a pair of cards. And not just any card. Aces.

He could have folded. Could have walked away, out a few bucks from the blind, and cashed out. He should have just walked away. Instead, he pushed his entire stack into the middle.

An ace and two kings were turned. A full house. Lawrence could have kissed the dealer and his good luck. He was about to rake the money back toward him, when the man on his right said. "Now wait a minute. Let's see this play out."

He'd been the only one to call Lawrence's bid, and while he still had a good-sized stack of chips in front of him, Lawrence knew the man was about to lose quite a bit of money. Lawrence nodded his apology and motioned for the dealer to turn the last two cards.

A two and a seven. Lawrence beamed as he flipped his cards.

'Full house," he announced, though it was probably unnecessary.

The two other men around the table nodded their appreciation. One whistled at the other man's bad luck. Lawrence moved to drag the stack toward him when the man reached out his hand again and flipped over his cards. Two kings. He had four of a kind.

He'd won.

Lawrence lost the ability to breathe. This could not be happening. It was impossible. He stood to get a better look at the cards.

"No, no, you must have cheated," Lawrence said.

The other men lamented at his bad luck. The dealer helped push the chips to his right. He'd lost it all.

The gun was out before he knew he'd drawn it.

"Hey, easy now," the dealer said with his hands up.

The bartender stormed out from behind the bar with his own gun out and Lawrence shot him without hesitation. He knew once the sound of gunshots rang through, he'd only have so much time to get out. The clock was ticking. He hoped the man hadn't returned to the door downstairs.

He pulled the trigger four more times, dropping the men around the table. The guy to his right fell forward, hands still clutching the pile of chips. The woman with the drink tray didn't scream, but she dropped to the floor and covered her head. He stood over her.

She looked up at him. "I swear, mister, I swear I won't tell nobody I was here. I won't breathe a word to nobody."

Lawrence nodded and shot her between the eyes.

He stepped behind the bar and shoved the cash into his coat pockets. His heart raced. He stuffed the gun in his suit jacket, still warm and smoking. He thanked his lucky stars there were only six people left as that was how many shots he had. He cursed himself for not thinking to bring ammo, but lucked out yet again when the bartender's revolver was fully loaded. He placed his hot gun in the man's hands. Tucked the cool one in his suit.

He took the stairs two at time and paused a moment before unlocking the still mercifully unmanned door. He straightened his tie and hat then pushed through into the cold. No shouts behind him. No one was coming.

He expected bright sunlight, but the world had darkened in the time he'd been upstairs. He stumbled along and it wasn't until he stepped under a streetlight that he realized how much blood he had on him. His coat was covered. He took it off and tried stuffing it under his arm, but thought that would create more suspicion. Voices rose from down the alleyway toward the street. It was evident they were getting closer.

Lawrence walked a few paces back from where he came, and stopped by an old metal trash can. He forced the rusty lid up and stuffed the coat inside.

He straightened his hat once again to compose himself and stepped into the street, just as a group passed him, too busy laughing to notice the panting man who rushed away.

Chapter Twenty-Nine

Detective Kelly lay in bed hoping the phone would stop before the seventh ring. Four. Five. She got up and moved down the darkened hall. Six. Hand hovering over the receiver. Seven. Stop.

She groaned and picked it up.

"Mrs. Kelly, it is very late in the night to be receiving phone calls."

"Yes, Mrs. O'Malley."

"You need to tell the phone company that you need a new ring number."

"I know Mrs. O'Malley."

"You need to be first so it only rings one time," the old woman said for the millionth time.

"I will ask. Please, go back to bed."

Kelly waited a few minutes, but grew impatient when she didn't hear the click of her hanging up. It was too late. She didn't have time for this.

"This is Kelly," she said.

She supposed her landlady would just have to listen to her call. The woman was already horrified that Kelly worked and her husband took care of their children. Now this was would be one more thing to add to the list: how her job kept them all up at night. How it was dangerous and terrible work for a woman to do. She'd heard it a million times from a million people. She would ignore Mrs. O'Malley like she did everyone else.

"Gonna need you to come down," Carlson said.

"How bad?"

"Six."

"Jesus, Mary, and Joseph," Kelly said.

It got the desired effect, the click of Mrs. O'Malley hanging up. She'd have to pay for that, too.

"Where at?"

Carlson sighed. "You're not gonna like it."

"I never like it, but it's late. Stop messing around. Where at?"

"Everyard."

"Jesus," she said again. She'd owe about a thousand Hail Marys by the end of this phone conversation.

Kelly avoided that part of town as much as possible. While the other girls in the department didn't seem to mind going undercover at the gay bars or abortion clinics, that wasn't work Kelly was interested in. She wanted *real* criminals, not people just trying to live their lives the best they could. She'd quit before turning on her fellow humans like that.

"Come around back," Carlson said. "There's a big metal door. Apparently, they were running an illegal gambling house out of the place as well."

"Why doesn't that surprise me? Be there as soon as I can."

"Sooner," he said and hung up.

She kissed her husband and slipped out the door, thinking for the umpteenth time how she wished she could just wear slacks instead of a skirt. Her legs burned in the cold of the midnight air. Her stockings still damp from washing the day before and her girdle dug uncomfortably into her stomach. She pulled her thin coat as tightly as she could around her body, careful to keep her hands in her pockets around her midsection to hide the bulge growing there.

Light was just coming up the horizon when she stumbled down the narrow alley and was met by several officers standing outside of the door Carlson described.

"Ma'am," one of them said as he stepped forward.

Her annoyance peaked. She was in a freaking uniform. Was wearing her agency issued hat. What did they think? She woke in the middle of the night, beat up some matron, and stole her uniform just to get to a shit part of town and see something gruesome?

"They up there?" Kelly asked the one standing by the door, ignoring the one trying to block her.

"You can't come up here," the officer in front of her said.

She wasn't familiar with the beat cops in this area and they clearly weren't familiar with her.

Screw it.

"I don't have time for this," she said in her most biting tone. "I'm Detective Johanna Kelly with the four-five and unless you *boys* would like to go up those stairs and deal with whatever shit-show is going on, I'd suggest you let me pass."

They all froze, puffs of hot air emanating from their mouths the only movement. After what felt like a million heartbeats, the one at the door nodded and held it open for her.

"Thank you, sir," she said as she brushed past the other two.

She climbed the long staircase which smelled of booze, smoke, and sin, in that order. She turned on the landing. Carlson stood in the middle of a dimly lit room littered with bodies.

"A total goat rope," Carlson said.

"I can see that."

"Looks like a poker game gone bad. Money's gone. If I were a betting man, I'd say whoever was in this seat"—he pointed to the overturned chair—"shot this guy for taking his money." He pointed to the man slumped over with arms on the table, piles of chips in the middle of them. "At some point, the gun came out from this guy and then the shooter probably realized he needed to off the rest of the crew, including the bar girl, so he could steal the money and get away."

Kelly bent over the large man with the revolver on his chest. She picked it up and opened the cylinder. All six chambers were fired. She showed it to Carlson, who shrugged.

"Ran out, switched it with the bar guy in case he came under more fire trying to leave?" he said.

"Sounds about as good a guess as I could come up with. And no guy at the door downstairs?"

A part of her reveled in this exchange. To have a sort-of partner in this. Someone to bounce ideas off of and work a case side by side. She'd never had that before. It was a nice change.

Carlson shook his head. "Owner is claiming he didn't even know this game was going on. Said they don't use that door for anything but deliveries and he never goes up here. Used to be offices but he switched his to the basement."

"Yeah, I'm sure. And the peep hole is just a coincidence."

"Well, I'm sure he'll be cooperative. We rounded

up everyone here and brought 'em to the station. Been a while since this place was raided. Need to make sure these buggers know we don't tolerate this behavior in our city."

Kelly was one person and knew she couldn't correct a whole city, but it bothered her she couldn't even speak up to this one person. She felt a little less like herself in moments like this, when she had to balance her own survival over what she knew was right and just. So she let the comment go.

The brutality was out of the ordinary. The girl, still on her knees, was slumped back against the bar. There was a hole in the middle of her forehead. No witnesses. This was more than a reaction to losing a poker hand. This guy had some experience.

"Any thoughts on who did this?" Kelly asked.

"Nah, probably some rival bathhouse or gaming house. We'll threaten to charge anyone we brought in if they don't speak, but I have a feeling no one saw nothin', even if they did."

"You think inside job?"

"You know of people that come to this area unless they're looking for what this area offers?" Carlson asked.

They whirled around at a noise in the corner of the room.

"You didn't check 'em all?" Kelly yelled.

Carlson looked stricken. "The boys said they did."

They hovered over a man with frothy blood gurgling out of his mouth.

"What did you see?" Kelly asked.

She fought the urge to shake the man by the shoulder. Carlson shouted down below for someone to call a doctor.

"A man… Blond hair… Nice…suit."

Each word was a struggle. The man's lungs wheezed with an evident hole somewhere in them. Kelly leaned her head down and pressed her ear against his lips, ignoring the warm blood splattering against it.

"What else? Did you know him, recognize him, did anyone say his name?"

"He had two aces… thought for sure…he'd won."

"Two what, what was his name?" Kelly asked, trying to keep the dying man on point.

"Four kings. Tough luck. Beat by four…"

Blood covered the man's chin and his eyes were wide open. Kelly felt for a pulse, but none resided.

"Tough break," Carlson said, placing his hand on Kelly's shoulder. "Come on, let's get you cleaned up. Who knows what shit is in that blood."

Kelly didn't have the strength to turn this into a teaching moment about tolerance. It was a losing battle anyway and she was just so damn tired of it all. The hamster wheel she was stuck on and no one gave a shit about how her legs pumped in frantic motion, but she didn't go anywhere. More murders. More cases she couldn't clear. More hatred in the world than she could ever hope to extinguish.

But she saw that poor girl's face in her mind's eye. Wondered like no one else at the department would about her life. What caused a pretty thing like her to get swept into a place like this? How she was expendable to everyone. Everyone but Kelly.

But the weariness was in her bones. All she could do was step over the girl and follow Carlson out.

Chapter Thirty

Ruth had a mouthful of pins, trying to talk around them. She'd helped the seamstresses pin dresses all the time when she worked at her old store, but wasn't familiar with the process with men's clothes. The seamstress barked orders at her as they scrambled to fit the jacket on an older man who was impatient with the whole process, even though he decided to come in the day before he needed the alterations completed. On a Sunday.

"Miss Smith," the seamstress said, her eyes narrowed.

"Farey," Ruth said through the pins. "Sowry," she tried again with more success.

She placed the pins where the seamstress pointed, then discreetly moved back.

She couldn't stop thinking about Lawrence and the shock of the day before. Nightmares littered her dreams that night. In one, Lawrence was shot in front of her when he refused to give her the handfuls of emeralds in his pockets. Ruth screamed at him to turn them over. But he said no, that was how he would pay for their future. In another, a man berated her to pay him more money, but she said she didn't have any. She turned out her pockets, but the man didn't believe her. How can you say you love me if you won't give him your money? Lawrence asked right before the man shot him in the head.

She woke with her sheets wrapped around her like serpents. She didn't try to go to sleep after that. She decided she'd go to the pharmacy after work today to visit Lawrence. She needed to see him and make sure he was all right.

"Ruth."

She lunged forward to pin the indicated spot and tried to weave the needle too quickly, stabbing the man in the leg.

"You daft woman!" the man shouted.

The pins fell out of her mouth. She apologized over and over as she scrambled to pick them up.

"Can I be of any help?" Rebecca asked.

Ruth groaned. Plus, rightly so, there was no way the man would let her near him again. She nodded and slipped away.

This would be the first day Mrs. Astor wasn't stopping by the store. She had told her she needed to spend the time at church praying for her husband's memory and her own future. There wasn't any way Ruth could argue with that.

Her life had been so simple less than two months ago. She was in too deep, drowning in the change and stress of it all. She wondered if Mr. Gulliver would give her job back. He'd probably love to have her crawl in and beg. She was certain he'd cut her pay. Up her hours. Probably put her in intimates or housewares. Her days of beautiful dresses would be over in every sense of the word.

She could ask for her money back. Tell Lawrence that, while she loved him, this was not the life for her. She'd always imagined the rich lived an easy life, but she could see it was anything but. The endless struggle to acquire more when they already had so much seemed so ridiculous to her. Why couldn't he just be happy in his nice apartment and whatever life his parents wanted for him? But then she pictured his face and her resolve melted.

She knew she couldn't walk away.

Chapter Thirty-One

Lawrence took large, steadying breaths. He'd left the jacket.

The jacket with all the money in it.

He was in such a harried rush, the weight of the revolver in his suit made him forget he'd stuffed the cash in his outer pockets. When he saw all the blood on the coat, he knew he had to get rid of it lest someone see him and turn him in. He did it without thinking. By the time he realized and doubled back to get it, cops swarmed the alley. He cursed under his breath.

He spent the rest of the early morning pacing his apartment, trying to calculate how long it would take to clear the bodies from the scene. Did the cops do that? No, must be some medical place, or the coroner. Would the cops be the ones cleaning the place?

His mind spun wilder and wilder. What if someone emptied the trash? Or a transient went through it looking for food scraps?

By the time the sunrise gave way to day, he couldn't take it anymore. He grabbed an old coat someone left after a party and one of his larger hats, hoping he could conceal his identity. In retrospect, shooting all those people probably wasn't the best idea, but if he could recover that money in the jacket—easily a thousand dollars—it would all be worth it.

He walked by the alley twice, noting the trash can

still had a lid on it, before he moved down it in measured, strolling steps. He didn't want to draw attention to himself by running, but it was all he felt like doing. When he opened the lid, the coat was where he left it.

"Thank heavens."

The jacket was frozen from the dried blood. It took some effort to maneuver it out and unfold it without clanging around the can too much. The cash was still there. He inhaled a long, steadying breath of crisp air. It would be okay. The cash was still there.

Minutes later, his suit pockets weighed down with the money, he replaced the lid and strolled back into the street. The day was just starting and groggy working-class men filed in around him. A few casual polite nods in his direction, but no one really paid him any mind.

"Mr. Henry?" a hesitant voice said behind him two blocks past the bathhouse.

Lawrence froze, reflexively tightening his arms against his sides where he could feel the wads of bills.

He turned, but didn't immediately see a familiar face. Then he spotted her, the red hair tucked haphazardly under her cap and her uniform making her stand out amongst the rest of the crowd.

"Mrs. Johanna," Lawrence said, keeping his voice bright, as if she was the only person Lawrence wished he'd run into.

When the truth was anything but.

The detective took several long strides to catch up. "It's Detective Kelly. What brings you to this part of town?"

Lawrence caught a bit of annoyance in her tone at not being addressed correctly, but she tried to keep her tone light. Two people playing the same game. There was very little this area of town for a man of Lawrence's status.

"Supplies," he said after a two-beat pause.

The detective wrinkled her nose for a moment. "Supplies?"

"Yes," Lawrence said, feeling emboldened. "I'm not sure if you've heard, but I've recently entered in what has turned out to be a dangerous business venture."

"Yes, but I assure you, we are doing everything we can to track down and arrest whoever killed that poor boy and set those fires," Kelly said.

"Well, in the meantime, my clients are scared to come in and my suppliers are scared to sell to me, lest they be associated and targeted next. Desperate times," Lawrence said, opening his arms to indicate it was the police's fault he had to come to an area like this.

Kelly narrowed her eyes. "Like I said, we are doing everything we can."

"As am I, *Detective* Kelly."

"You may not be aware, but this area of town has a reputation. One your social status may not want to be a part of. Unless…do you frequent these businesses?"

Lawrence boiled with rage. How dare she try to turn this back on him.

"I don't like your tone or accusation."

"Forgive me, that was not my intent," Kelly said, holding her hands up. "We had a few murders here last night. Nothing to worry about, but if you have come here for supplies in the past, maybe you've seen something? A gang hanging around, anything out of the ordinary?"

Lawrence shook his head. "No, detective. If I come here, it is to do my business and then leave. I try to spend as little time as possible. And hopefully, if you are correct and are close to catching the monsters who are terrorizing us, then I can spend no more time here."

Kelly nodded. "I understand. Thank you for your time. And please thank your Dr. Anderson for the advice. The ginger did the trick."

Lawrence touched the brim of his hat and walked away, relieved he was in the clear, and vowing never to put himself in a similar position again.

On his way back to his apartment, he stopped by two other gambling houses. Doubled security at both. Clearly, word had already traveled about the Everyard shootings. Lawrence assured the men he was only there to pay off his debts.

He felt free. His gambling days were over, he promised himself. This feeling was too wonderful to risk giving up. He didn't owe anyone anything, still had enough cash to float the business for a few weeks until he could figure out how to get Lucky off his back. It would be all right.

He passed the store once before turning back to walk by the window again. He hesitated for only a moment before walking in. He wasn't quite sure what he was looking for, but the salesman was very helpful.

He was getting himself some insurance. He wouldn't do it now, but it would be nice to have it already, to not scramble when he needed it.

Forty-five minutes later, Lawrence left with a diamond ring in his pocket.

Chapter Thirty-Two

Kelly hesitated, her hand on the knob for a moment before going inside. It was a strange ritual. Her husband used to walk through the front door and *then* take off his coat and hat, removing all traces of the outside. She needed to do it before.

Everything she wore looked clean, sure, but it helped her mentally peel off the layers of the last few hours. Scrub the image of that poor girl on her knees surrounded by a pool of blood, the stench of sweat and bodily functions that burrowed in her nose and pores.

Patrick never commented, but he had to notice. He knew what it was like. You didn't spend that much time with death and not get a little on you. Have bits permeate and follow you home. But he never asked her details about any of her cases. Probably didn't want the reminder of what he'd lost and all this wife had to deal with because of it. The horrors remained unspoken between them.

When she opened the door, the first thing she saw was her husband sitting in his chair by the windowsill, blowing cigarette smoke outside. The window was cracked a half inch, fighting the push and pull of cold air coming in and his breath pushing out. The temperature in the apartment suggested this wasn't his first one.

"Hey," she said, startling him and throwing his

hand to his waist, an automatic reaction for a weapon which no longer resided there.

"Lord, I didn't hear you come in. Kids, Mommy's home!"

She was momentarily assaulted by small hands and arms, feet standing on hers to get just a little closer. It was the best part of her day. She gave them all hugs and kisses and told them to go play.

"It's almost seven," Alvie, her youngest, said.

"I won't miss it. Why don't you turn the radio on now and let it warm up so it's ready? Then go play for a few minutes so I can talk to Daddy."

The two kids dashed off, sounds of pushing as they fought over who got to touch the radio.

"You'd think the world would end if they missed an episode," Patrick said, exhaustion lacing his words.

"Hey, I want to know what happens, too. Everyone at the station mentions it at least once a day, I've gotta at least try to keep up with the conversation of what Amos and Andy did last night."

She tried to kiss him, but he turned his head, giving her his cheek.

It felt like a punch to her gut.

"How are we doing to start all over again?" he asked her. "And what are you going to do about work when you don't have a station to go to and gossip and get your fill of people?"

"First off, there's practically no one who talks to me anyway. *You* are my people. You and the kids are the only ones I want to talk to and see."

"What do you think they will do?"

She sighed and shrugged, sitting on his lap and taking the cigarette from his fingers for a long drag.

"Maybe they won't notice."

He laughed and took the cigarette back. "They are detectives."

"Most of them aren't any good."

He looked at her straight in the eyes. "Jo, really, how will we do this?"

"I don't rightly know, but somehow we will. This baby will come, and I'm sure they'll muscle me out but maybe I can go back. We can see if one of the girls in the building can help out during the day while I'm gone. We'll get some of that evaporated milk, so that'll be easy to feed the baby when I'm away. I'll probably get reassigned, but I can keep working. I only need a few more years anyway until I can retire."

She leaned down to kiss him and he let her this time.

"It'll all work out. I don't know how, but this baby is a blessing. God wouldn't give us a blessing like that and not also the means to take care of it."

Tears poured down her face and she was so shocked at their sudden appearance, it took her a moment to brush them away.

"I didn't mean to upset you," Patrick said.

"No, no, I think it's just the hormones. Gosh, this one's been rough on me. Probably a boy, if I had to guess," she said, rubbing her hand on her burgeoning belly.

"You think?"

"For all the trouble it's causing me, yeah." She laughed.

"Just a few more months," he said.

The truth made her palms itch.

She did believe this baby was a blessing. Believed

all her children were and she loved her life, but the closer her due date came, the more her concern intensified. What if she couldn't solve these cases? What if a killer was left on the loose and that was on her? More blood would be shed and that would be her fault. She'd be ushering one life in, but dooming others.

She just hoped God knew what he was doing.

Chapter Thirty-Three

"Why am I the one answering the door?" Lawrence hollered over his shoulder. His frustration peaked as he stepped aside to let Ruth in. "Can *anyone* be bothered to take this lady's coat?"

A man in a tuxedo rushed forward, tucking a silver tray under his arm as he took Ruth's jacket from off her shoulders.

"You know that's not necessary," Ruth said. "Is there anything I can help with?"

"Find me a new staff at short notice?"

Lawrence meant the comment to be a joke, but Ruth wrinkled her brow. He waved his hand and leaned down to kiss her cheek.

"Never mind, just last-minute jitters. Welcome, please come in."

Ruth's eyes widened at the movement all around her. Lawrence tried to take it in from her point of view. About a dozen men in fine black tuxes raced around, filling glasses of Champagne, plating food, and generally busying themselves to be ready for when guests arrived in about twenty minutes. Lawrence was used to this sort of beehive activity moments before a party began. Clearly, Ruth was not.

"I wanted everything to be perfect for you," he whispered in her ear.

A visible shiver ran over her as his hot breath hit

her.

"This is the first time you'll be meeting many people from my circle. I just wanted it to be special."

"Lawrence, how much is this costing?"

"My parents paid for it. They were sorry they couldn't come and wanted to show how excited they were as well."

It was a half-truth. They were paying for it, and they weren't coming, but only because they had no idea it was happening. He'd invited his brother who was unable to come, but Charles knew better than to mention anything to them about it. Both he and Charles hosted parties and called on the backup staff their father always had on retainer. If he ever noticed when the monthly bills came in, he never mentioned it. It wasn't really stealing if no one cared, right?

Wasn't stealing if they owed it to him.

"Well, I am sorry I won't be seeing them, but that's awful sweet of them." She pulled her gold cigarette case out of her bag and held it up to him. "Is there someplace I can go smoke? Sorry, but I need something to calm my nerves."

"Sure, follow me."

He escorted her through the living room where a man in tails played softly on the baby grand piano. The wall of windows gave way to a door at the far end and onto a small balcony. The staff had removed the furniture earlier in the day, save for a few spindly tables, to make it appear larger than it was. Candles flickered in the cold air, giving off a romantic effect.

"This place." Ruth breathed out along with cigarette smoke.

Lawrence took one from her case and lit it from

hers.

"The view could be better, but it will suffice for now. I came back with such short notice, it was a bit of a scramble to find a place," Lawrence said, keeping his voice light and casual.

No hint to the disrespect he actually felt at the second-rate apartment.

"I think it's lovely." She stood at the edge of the railing and gazed toward the sky.

Of course she thought it was lovely. Everything was so special and magical to her. He probably could have lived in a tenth floor walk-up and she'd think it was the Taj Mahal. If she only knew the struggles and rat race all the rich people went through to maintain what they had. The stress of needing to stay on top. How quickly it could all slip away. How fast someone could take it from you. Then she'd be less wide-eyed about the whole thing.

But he needed her just the way she was. Needed someone so enthralled by what was going on around her, she didn't notice what was happening right in front of her face.

"Let's get you inside and warmed up before guests arrive." He put his arm around her and guided her inside.

An hour into the party—and four glasses of Champagne—the stress Lawrence carried in his shoulders finally started to relax. He'd regaled the party with his feats of heroism as he saved a woman being harassed by a group of men, and got a nice shiner for his troubles. Ruth's sister Sally came with her fiancé. The two stood in a semicircle of Lawrence's prep-school friends. Ruth chatted with Albert, one of his friends from Chicago who also moved to the city, and Emma. Lawrence was floored she actually attended. When he'd offered yesterday while they were closing the pharmacy, her acceptance seemed more like a polite brush-off than actual consent. But here she was, drink in hand, acting like a typical girl at a party. It was a stark contrast to the normally tight-laced way she acted at the store. He liked it.

Albert excused himself from the conversation.

"I like her," he said, slapping Lawrence's chest.

"Emma or Ruth?"

Albert barked a laugh. "Both actually, but I was referring to Ruth."

"Yes, I like her too."

"She was telling me a bit about herself. Your parents will be red, old chap. The look on your father's face…"

He patted Lawrence's chest hard several times with his open palm. Lawrence wanted to slap it away, but kept a smile on his face.

"That'll be fun." Oh, it will be.

"But now that you mention it," Albert murmured, "Is Emma spoken for?"

Lawrence shook his head. "You have my blessing. Good luck."

Albert held his glass up in mock cheers and returned to the conversation. Now it was Ruth's turn to extract herself and come over. Her cheeks were flushed from the mix of breathless chatter and alcohol.

"I really like Dr. Anderson. Emma, I guess," she said.

"Yes, I am very lucky to have snagged her for the pharmacy. The customers also like her."

"I wasn't so sure about a woman doctor, but she's so personable."

Lawrence was just about to answer, when someone grasped his elbow.

Lawrence almost dropped his Champagne glass. Paul. Standing right in front of him in a suit that was probably a uniform from a gig he was either coming from or on his way to.

"Lawrence, are you going to introduce me to your friend?" Ruth held her hand out.

"Paul, ma'am. Nice to meet you," Paul said, dipping his head to kiss the top of Ruth's hand.

Lawrence swore her cheeks flushed a shade darker.

"Paul," Lawrence said, finally recovering his voice. "I thought you said you couldn't make it."

"My thing got pushed back. Turns out I had enough time to stop here first."

Paul smiled broadly at him. Lawrence wanted to strangle him. Wanted to take him into his bedroom, throttle him, and more. He was a breath away from ripping the man's clothes off right here in front of everyone.

"Splendid," Lawrence said. "Come with me, I'll get you a drink. Ruth, we'll be right back."

As soon as they entered the kitchen, Lawrence grabbed Paul's upper arm and dragged him into the pantry. His heart raced.

"What the hell are you doing here? What the hell are you thinking?"

Before Paul could answer, Lawrence's mouth crushed his. The combination of cigarettes and alcohol swirled into an intoxicating mixture. A voice in the back of Lawrence's mind screamed at him to stop. He couldn't get caught. Not with Ruth here. There were people right outside this door. Nothing was stopping someone from finding them. His desire doubled at the risk.

Paul's hand slid from his face, down his chest and to his belt. Reality snapped back into focus for Lawrence and he pushed the hand away.

Both men panted on opposite sides of the space, like boxers in a ring.

"You can't be here," Lawrence said.

"I think you like that I'm here. Want me to tell everyone to go home and you can have me right in this pantry?"

Lawrence let out a soft moan. "Yes. Yes, but no. Paul, this is too dangerous. We can't let people see us together. How did you even know—"

"I work with half the people you've employed for this party. Frankly, I'm a little sore you didn't hire me." Paul played with the buttons on Lawrence's suit jacket.

He slapped the hands away.

"You need to go. Say that you are needed elsewhere. You lost track of time, I don't care. You need to go."

Paul nodded. "Fine. I just needed to see her."

"What?"

Those in the kitchen averted their gazes as they left the pantry. Lawrence fixed his jacket and Paul smoothed his hair. Great, this was the last thing he needed, staff gossiping about his love life. He could never hire them again. Too risky. He'd have to come up with some story about how one stole something, make sure his father and brother cut ties as well.

"Ruth. I just needed to see her."

"Well, now you have," Lawrence said. "Now you can go."

Paul nodded. On his way out he gave his apologies to Ruth, saying he wished he could stay longer, but the nightlife called.

Lawrence walked him to the door, waving off the guy manning it.

"Don't ever do that again," Lawrence said. He wanted to bash Paul's head in for the risk he just took. The position he put Lawrence in. "I mean it."

"You'll have to punish me next time you see me." Paul winked and left.

"He seemed nice," Ruth said when he returned to her, fresh glasses of Champagne in his hands.

"Oh, Paul? Yeah, I guess. Don't know him too well, actually. He's the son of one of my father's business associates. Somehow heard about the party and stopped by. Sorry, he wasn't supposed to be here."

"Ah, well it was nice to meet him either way," Ruth said and clinked glasses with him.

He smiled and downed the drink in one gulp, heart and mind racing a mile a minute.

****

A few hours later and the party finally wound down. Emma was the last of the guests to leave, kissing both Ruth and Lawrence on the cheeks before departing.

"See you tomorrow, boss."

"Don't be late," he joked.

"Ditto."

"I need to be leaving as well," Ruth said.

She'd been quiet as the party wore on. She drank glass after glass of Champagne before Lawrence caught the eye of the servers and shook his head, an indication they could bottle up the rest and stop serving.

"Is everything all right? Did you have a nice time?" he asked.

"Simply lovely. This evening was more than I could have imagined. Sally and Walter had a wonderful time. Thank you for inviting them."

"I'm sorry Anna wasn't able to make it."

"I wasn't expecting her to."

"Still…"

He was honestly lost at what to say. He thought the party had been a success, but Ruth looked so forlorn. That's not what he needed. To keep up the façade he built for Ruth, he needed her to be having a good time, always. To be too scared of losing what all she had.

"I had fun, honest. Thank you again." She kissed him and left.

Lawrence told the staff to turn off the lights and blow out the candles before they left and he headed to bed. He noticed the small box on his dresser drawer.

He knew just what he had to do.

Chapter Thirty-Four

Ruth decided she would have to end it with Lawrence.

She fingered the emerald necklace in her drawer, sad that she was going to have to give it back. The last few weeks were, for the most part, a magical whirlwind, but it was a life for another person. The party solidified that, being surrounded by so many fancy people. She didn't belong.

There was a soft knock at her door and Sally peeked in.

"Come in," Ruth said. "It's going to be strange when you don't live here anymore."

"At the pace you are going, you may be outta here before me," her sister joked.

Ruth burst into tears.

"Ruthie!" her sister cried and rushed to her sister's side. "Whatever is the matter?"

Ruth sniffled and shook her head, composing herself. "Oh, Sal, I don't know. I think I'll have to leave him."

Sally pulled her toward the bed and they sat facing each other, holding hands.

"The party was so lovely and Lawrence clearly adores you. Did something happen after we left? Tell me!"

How to put it into words? Lawrence did seem to

adore her. He threw a lavish party for her, just so she could meet some people from his circle. Hell, he even invited her sisters. But how to put her finger on her apprehensions? How to say what she really felt?

He scared her.

"It *was* lovely. That's just it. He just…"

She overheard him telling story after story at the party. About his eye. An exaggerated tale on how the two of them met. Of how he stoically would remain open no matter what, to serve the great people of New York City who had few pharmacy options now.

But who didn't tell tall tales? Who didn't embellish from time to time at a party to seem more important? He couldn't exactly say the real reason he had a black eye. Why he needed the pharmacy to stay open. It wasn't the lies exactly, but how effortlessly he told them. Like he was so used to fabrications, he didn't even notice when they blurred with the truth.

"He what?" Sally asked.

"It's just that I'm not sure how our lives will mesh with each other," she said.

The easier answer, and also true.

"I mean, look at him, at his family."

Sally bristled. "What's wrong with our family?"

"You know what I mean. I have been working my fanny off for years, and almost three months into the year, and what do I have to show for it? Just a bunch of secondhand dresses."

"Well I think that's a little simplistic. Plus, all your hard work doesn't go away just because you find someone. You still have all of that."

Tears welled in Ruth's eyes. "It's all gone."

"What's all gone?"

"My money." Her voice was small with shame. She hadn't meant to tell a soul what she'd done. How stupid she'd been.

"Ruthie, I don't understand. You've been saving for years. What do you mean it's all gone?" She looked at Ruth's closet. "Did you spend it all on outfits?"

"No, nothing like that. And, I guess if you want to be technical, it's not that I lost it, not yet, but I invested it."

"In what?" Sally asked.

"Lawrence's pharmacy."

Sally sat back, her eyebrows raised in shock as her mouth momentarily hung open before she composed herself. "Why did he need you to invest?"

"He said it would be a good opportunity for me, for us."

"He's a wealthy man. I still don't understand why he needed your money."

"His family is wealthy."

"There's a difference?"

"He is very bent on making his own way, of not taking handouts." She felt suddenly defensive of him. Or maybe, of her choice to believe his rationale.

"Unless they come from his girlfriend?"

Ruth's face must have showed the hurt she felt because Sally rushed to add, "I'm sorry, that was low; he seems like a very nice man. But all right, so he borrowed money from you, or you invested it. I thought the pharmacy was doing well? I hear now he's the only one open for a few blocks because of the fires and break-ins. Is all this stuff with the banks affecting him?"

Ruth wanted desperately to tell Sally what

Lawrence confided in her. About how they weren't safe. That she could lose both him and her money if the same thugs came after him. But she couldn't. She promised and didn't want to endanger Sally with the truth.

"It is doing well, but it's not without risk. And I think he's okay. He hasn't mentioned being concerned about the banks or anything. I'm under the impression his family didn't have a lot of stocks, so I don't think they were hit as hard as some of their friends. I just think I'm in over my head, in all of it."

"Okay, I can see that. What about this, why don't you get Lawrence to put something in writing. Something official that will protect you then. I'm sure he has lawyers, or at the very least a family one you can insist he use. Have you formally listed as an investor, that way you won't have to worry since it will be protected. Or, if it's really that stressful, just ask for your money back. He is a rich man, whether he wants to count his parents or not. I know what you have saved is a lot for you, but it can't be that difficult for him to give it back to you. Maybe remove the business aspect then you can just focus back on being together."

Ruth smiled. She wanted to agree. To see it that simply, but the fact was Lawrence had come and asked her for *more* money. Ruth suspected if she asked for her money back, he would make up an excuse and put her off.

"I will do that," Ruth lied. "Thanks for the advice. And whoever moves out of here first, I think we can agree the other will be the worse off for it."

They hugged and Ruth started to get ready for dinner, and possibly the beginning of the end.

****

She wore black. It wasn't intentional. She didn't realize the omen until she was about to leave. But it was too late to change, and anyway, it was probably fitting.

Her stomach roiled with stress. She wasn't sure what the fallout would be for her demands. Would he break up with her on the spot? Accuse her of not trusting him?

And really, *did* she trust him?

He met her at the restaurant, but seemed distracted. He kept looking around like he was waiting for someone to come.

"Is everything all right?" she asked.

His bruised eye was turning a sickly green and she noticed glances from the other diners in their direction. Maybe she was seeing things, but it felt like everyone was paying attention to them. Did they know who he was? Were they wondering about her? Or just what happened to his face?

"Lawrence," Ruth said, drawing his attention back toward her. "Are you feeling okay? Did something else happen?"

He narrowed his eyes in confusion. "No, why?"

"You haven't said more than a dozen words to me and keep looking around."

"Oh, yes, sorry. No, nothing is wrong."

"I need to talk to you," she said, taking a sip of water to steady herself.

He held up a finger to her, looking around again. She fought the urge to throw her napkin at him.

"Can, can you hold that thought for a moment?" He turned back at her. "For just a moment, please?"

She opened her mouth to protest, but at that

moment a man playing a violin came over, while another brought them Champagne.

"Ruth," Lawrence said.

She was so distracted by the arrival of the two, she didn't realize Lawrence had moved next to her. But then he knelt next to her. No, he was on one knee.

She stopped breathing. Her mind whirled. No, this couldn't be happening! She covered her eyes with her hands, but he pulled them down. Tears welled in her eyes and spilled down her cheeks. He wiped them away. He looked at her with soft eyes filled with love. This man who loved her, who wanted to start a life with her. Who was risky and a mystery and so appealing to her for reasons she couldn't put into words. "Ruth, will you marry me?"

The violin played and the man with the Champagne held a knife close to the cork.

She took a deep breath and stared straight into Lawrence's eyes. She'd played by the rules her whole life. Did what others told her to. Stayed on the straight and narrow for this moment. Never in a million years could she have imagined that man would be someone who could give her a ticket out of her life in so many ways.

She had apprehensions, but who didn't? How many girlfriends whispered reservations to Ruth over the years? He lived a life she knew nothing of. But he'd done right by her so far. Opened up more opportunities in a few months than she had her entire life.

And here was one more, if she was willing to take it.

"Yes," she said. "Yes."

Chapter Thirty-Five

The woman who sat across from Detective Kelly picked at the chipped paint on her nails. Flakes fluttered to the ground. Her coat looked old and tattered. There was certainly not enough fabric to cover the rest of her exposed body. Legs in fishnet stockings. Skirt so short it only peeked through the opening to her jacket. The buttons missing so her clothes beneath were exposed.

Not for the first time Kelly thought of the fine line that separated the two of them. How one of them got to go to work in a uniform and be respectable and the other donned her own business attire and was the scorn of her community.

If her husband had worked any other job that put them out after an injury, would this have been her sitting on the other side of the table? Dignity traded for scraps to feed her children?

She knew she'd have done it. Done whatever was needed to make her family survive. It was one of the reasons why she never judged the street girls. Why she always brought them hot coffee if they worked a neighborhood where she needed eyes and ears. Why she never betrayed them to work the undercover ring at the abortion clinics. They were all just trying to get by. Kelly just happened to be the one with the badge.

This girl had been in a few times over the years and most of the department knew her. "Pearl", she liked to be called, but Kelly was pretty sure that was only her street name. Most of the girls had them. She'd devoured the danish Kelly gave her and downed the coffee like it was a shot of whiskey. Probably burned her throat in just the same way. But no matter, the girls knew what was going on in the city probably better than any cop.

Kelly didn't like having her sit here, wished they could get information another way. Save the trip of bringing her in past the ogling eyes of the so-called upstanding men in her department, but the girls didn't trust all the uniforms. The detectives tended to have better luck and her especially. Usually they had better things to do than round up the hookers and take them in for booking so they weren't much of a risk. The detectives gave them lunch, a warm drink, and appreciated them for their info, not their professional abilities.

"All right Pearl, you got your food and coffee. Now, what brings you in today with the express need to speak with me?" Kelly asked, trying not to be annoyed that despite the relationship they'd built over the years, she still refused to speak until those items had been served. As if Kelly wasn't as good as her word.

"So, I saw a gent by 28th Street."

"Just get on with it. What did you see?" Kelly rubbed her temple, frustrated at this exchange.

"Well, he had a nice coat on. Usually don't see people with coats like that on."

"You came in here to tell me that a person who normally doesn't frequent the area, was there? Come on Pearl, I should book you for wasting my time."

It was a bluff and they probably both knew it, but Kelly didn't have time for games today. Or the mental wherewithal. She began to stand up when Pearl put out her hand.

"No wait, it wasn't the coat I was so worried about, but what was *on* the coat." She leaned forward. "Blood."

Kelly sat back down. "Blood?"

"Yeah, I heard something went down the other night and thought it was odd that someone I don't think I've ever seen before is hanging around with a bloody coat. Seemed like an odd coincidence."

"Pearl, I need you to tell me exactly where you saw this guy and the last time. I need you to give me a detailed description." Kelly snapped open a notebook.

Five minutes later, with Carlson in tow, they rushed across town.

"Think it's the guy?" Carlson asked as he drove, the siren flashing.

They decided not to put the sound on. No need to draw too much attention to themselves least the man get spooked and run away.

"Seem suspicious enough," Kelly said.

She tried to keep her voice even, casual, but she found it difficult not to yell at Carlson to go faster. She desperately needed a break. Something to keep her going and tell her it was all worth it. The long hours, the crazy looks from her coworkers, the ticking clock before her dismissal. She needed this.

Carlson parked around the corner from Everyard and they walked toward the alley Pearl directed them to. There were a few people standing in front of burning trash cans, but they paid the two detectives no mind. It was clear the men had lived on the streets long enough to know you kept your head down and out of trouble.

At the back of the alley, standing in front of a fire all his own, stood the man Pearl described. He had a tan coat that, even at a distance, Kelly could tell was covered in red swaths of blood. Dirty blond hair covered his eyes. Hadn't the dying man said something about the killer being blond?

"Sir," Carlson called out when they were almost upon him. His hand hovered over his right side just in case he needed to draw his weapon.

Kelly wished, not for the first time, she carried more than the billy club, but Patrick didn't like her carrying a gun, so she opted out. Most of the women in the department didn't carry one, so no one pressed her about it.

The man looked up. His glassy expression turned wild in a heartbeat. He tried to turn and run, but either didn't realize or was too drunk to remember that he was at the back of the alley.

"Easy," Kelly said. The last thing they needed was for the man to try to fight his way out. "We just have a couple questions for you about your coat."

"I finds it," the man said. "I finds it, it's mine."

"You found it?"

"Fair and square, I tell ya. Fair and square."

Carlson lowered his hand. "Where?"

"Trash can, block over. Perfectly good coat. Don't know why someone would throw away a good coat. But I found it, I tell ya. Fair and square." The man paced back and forth.

"Did you see who put it in there?" Kelly asked.

"I don't gotta give it back," the man said, ignoring Kelly's question.

"You can keep it," Carlson said.

"Damn straight. Fair and square."

Kelly wanted Carlson to rough the guy up. Her patience waned. "Did you see the guy who put the coat in the trash can?"

The guy shook his head vigorously and stood stock-still, staring straight at Kelly. All his nervous ticks went away. "A woman cop?" the man said in a tone of wonder.

"What did you see?" Kelly asked, capitalizing on the moment of clarity from the man.

"Didn't see nothin'. Was lookin' for food. Opened the can, and saw this nice coat." He touched the coat, as if he needed reminding it was still on him. He was lost in thought for a moment, and when he glanced back up, the wild look in his eyes was back. He began pacing again.

"Come on," Carlson said, touching Kelly's arm. "Let's go."

"Wait a sec, sir, can I see that coat for a moment? I promise I'll give it right back," Kelly rushed to add as the man pulled the coat tighter around himself.

"Fair and square," the man repeated.

Kelly sighed and pulled out a dollar. She held it up to the man, who swiftly took the coat off, exchanging it for the cash.

Inside the right lapel, stitched in perfect cursive, read *Astor's* along with a series of numbers. She showed it to Carlson who pulled out a pen and paper to write it down, but Kelly stopped him.

"Give me your coat," she said.

Carlson took a step back. "You've lost your damn mind. Just pay the man a few more bucks." He rifled through his pocket and produced two more ones.

"We can't let him freeze to death."

"Is that the sob story I'm supposed to give my wife so she doesn't thrash my ass?"

Kelly stood her ground with her hand out. Carlson cursed and handed over the coat. It felt heavy and warm in Kelly's hands.

"You know I'm about the only friend you have on the force and you're dangerously close to losing me," he said.

"I know."

She addressed the man. "Thank you, sir, and here, take this."

She handed him Carlson's jacket. The guy didn't seem to even notice the switch, quickly putting the coat on and turning his back, muttering again to himself.

"Let's check Astor's out," Kelly said when they made it back to the squad car, the jacket carefully laid out in the back.

"Anything to get us out of this god-forsaken place. Plus, you owe me a new fucking coat."

Chapter Thirty-Six

She was getting married!

Ruth repeated the proclamation over and over in her head her entire shift. It still didn't feel real.

When she'd gotten home after their dinner, Sally met her at the door.

"How did it go?" Sally whispered so their parents wouldn't hear.

Ruth raised her hand in response. Sally didn't react right away, just grabbed her hand and inspected the perfectly clear, large diamond.

"How do you feel about this?" she asked.

"I'm getting married!" Ruth murmured as loud as she dared.

"So, did he agree to sign the papers?"

Ruth was a bit frustrated. Sally wasn't catching on fast enough to what was happening.

"Papers? No, we're going to be married. Everything will be *ours*."

Ruth's mother came around the corner. Ruth squealed and showed off the ring. Her mother cried and immediately went to call on the priest.

"He is Catholic, right?" Sally whispered.

"Yes, of course," Ruth said, but she realized with a sickening feeling she had no idea.

Ruth's father, hearing all the commotion, came out to see. He was initially offended that Lawrence didn't ask for his permission, but grudgingly admitted that he liked the boy and would support their union. Sally asked her a few more times how she was feeling and if she was really sure. Ruth finally had to scold her sister.

"Are you not happy for me?" Ruth asked, feeling hurt.

Sally shook her head and embraced her. "No, nothing like that. I am very happy for you, Ruthie. And you're right. Once you are married, everything is both of yours anyway. I guess it doesn't really matter in the meantime." She smiled broadly at Ruth. "I am happy for you, really."

****

The next morning at work when Mrs. Astor arrived, Ruth couldn't wait to show her the ring.

"Oh, my darling! I am so happy for you!" she exclaimed, embracing Ruth in a bone-crushing hug.

Rebecca merely smirked, but the others seemed genuinely happy for her. Maybe she was growing on them after all.

The morning was a blur for Ruth. Some of the customers noticed her new jewelry, which led to discussions on the lucky man and how he proposed. Ruth couldn't stop smiling. The more she looked at the ring, the more she told people about the engagement, the more excited she got. The more real it felt. Even grouchy Rebecca couldn't dampen her mood. When a man and woman in dress clothes and hats entered the store, Ruth greeted them brightly.

"How may I help you?" she asked.

"Need to speak with the manager," the man holding a bag said. His gaze darted around the store in a manner that made Ruth feel uneasy.

"I am the manager, Ruth Smith," she said, dropping her chipper façade. "Who is asking?"

The woman flashed a silver badge. "Detectives Kelly and Carlson." She gestured to herself, then her partner.

Ruth's breath caught in her throat for a moment. *Detectives?* She rolled her shoulders back and tried to put on professional air to make up for her casual introduction.

Detective Kelly looked at her with a squinting eye, like she was trying to place her.

"Do I know you?" Ruth asked, unsure of what the attention meant. She'd never met a female detective before and wondered if they all acted this way or if it was some ploy.

Detective Kelly smiled. "My apologies, no. You look so much like my little girl. It's like I got a window into the future. Is there someplace private we can speak?"

"Of course, in my office, please follow me." Ruth walked with what she hoped was authority. She probably should have admitted she was in training and gotten Mrs. Astor right away, but figured the woman would be in the office anyway.

"Mrs. Astor! I am glad to see you back in town and well." Detective Kelly's whole demeanor softened, and she took the woman's hands in both of hers.

"You two know each other?" Ruth asked.

"This detective helped my husband…"

Heat flushed through Ruth's chest and neck. Of course. She was so stupid to not put it together and her stomach fluttered with worry that she was about to be privy to some information about the crime.

"What can we help you two detectives with?" Mrs. Astor asked.

"We are hoping you can help us identify a coat," Carlson said.

He placed the bag on the table and Ruth automatically reached. Kelly stopped her.

"Please, ma'am. It is not clean."

"Oh, that's okay."

She stepped closer and noticed the tan coat had dark brown paint all over it. It took a moment for it to register. Blood. She recoiled.

"I can take it out," Carlson said.

He wrapped his hands in handkerchiefs and fumbled with the coat, before showing them the tag. "That is your label, correct?"

"Yes," Ruth and Mrs. Astor said in unison.

Detective Kelly exhaled a low breath.

"Wonderful," she said. "Can we please see your records of sales?"

Mrs. Astor shook her head. "That is our most popular coat. We only keep records for custom orders, and even then, we give the buyer the information receipt for their records. I am sorry, detectives."

"You don't keep receipts for sales?" Carlson asked incredulously.

Mrs. Astor shook her head again. "Never had a need to. We know all our customers here. They can trust us. They know they aren't going to pay for an item that won't last. It's about trust, detectives."

"Plus," Ruth said, feeling like she needed to answer for something that both happened long before her arrival and wasn't her decision. "Most of our customers pay in cash, which we require in full at the time of sale. We don't do payment plans here, so there is no need on our end to keep records of payment. The only way someone will leave with an item is if they fully pay for it."

The detectives nodded and she was pleased with her addition to the conversation, even if she could tell by their hunched shoulders they were disappointed.

The female detective surprised her by asking for a coat for her partner and Ruth wondered if maybe there was something going on between the two of them. They each had wedding bands and didn't appear to be too friendly toward each other, but Ruth showed them to their least expensive section. When they refused the coat for free, Mrs. Astor gave them a price Ruth knew was about half what they'd normally charge, but all seemed pleased with the exchange.

The man put the coat on right away and Ruth went to show the pair out when Detective Kelly turned back to her.

"Ruth, you said your name was?" she asked.

Ruth nodded.

"Ruth, can you do me a favor? For the next few weeks, can you start keeping a record of whomever buys this same coat? I have a feeling the owner may be looking to replace it."

"Oh." Ruth hesitated. "My apologies, detectives, I assumed that you were trying to identify a deceased individual."

Kelly shook his head. "No, we believe the owner of this coat has been involved in a homicide."

"Murder?" Ruth asked.

"Afraid so," Carlson said. "At least six individuals."

Ruth's hand flew to her chest. "Oh my!"

"We'd be much obliged to any help you can give, ma'am," Detective Kelly said, touching the brim of her hat.

They were about to leave when Lawrence strode in.

"Mr. Henry," Kelly said.

"Mrs. Johanna." He paused for a second. "My apologies. Detective Kelly, I mean."

"You two know each other?" Ruth asked. She felt like the only person in town who *didn't* know this woman.

"I've seen *you* a lot lately," Kelly said.

"It's a small town," Lawrence said, matching the underlying hostility.

"Not *that* small," Kelly said.

She tipped her hat again and the two detectives left, Ruth not exactly sure what had just transpired.

Chapter Thirty-Seven

"What was that about?" Lawrence asked, trying to sound uninterested, when in reality, his heart pounded at the sight of his bloodied coat in the detective's hands.

"Awful," Ruth said after a quick hug. "And did you know that woman was a detective? Can you imagine, a female detective? I never…"

"So, what did they want?" Lawrence asked sharply.

"Some people were killed and they think the man who owned that coat did it."

"Do they now? And what did they want with you?"

"Wanted to know if we could tell them who we sold the coat to."

This was an avenue Lawrence hadn't thought of when he disposed of it. "What did you tell them?" he asked, his heart rate increasing even more.

"No, we don't keep records. They seemed pretty upset about it, but I explained that our customers mostly pay in cash. There's no need."

Lawrence relaxed.

"But, they did ask me to keep a record of any future sales. Said they think the person may come back to replace the coat."

"That's interesting."

"That's what I thought!" she exclaimed. "Boy, I hope the person doesn't, though. But now I will look suspiciously at everyone who comes in to try that coat.

I wonder if you can figure out who a killer is just by looking at them."

"I imagine you can. Well, don't think too suspiciously of *me*," he said. "But I came in to get two new coats."

"Two?" She winked. "I think that makes you *doubly* suspicious. But don't worry, your secret is safe with me." She laughed and brought him to the dressing rooms.

An hour later, and his father's account further in the red, Lawrence left with two new coats, one dark brown and one navy blue. He'd wanted to replace the tan one, but there was too much risk now. Maybe in a few weeks when no one was paying attention anymore.

Mrs. Astor came over to congratulate him and Ruth. He finally had to extricate himself, saying that he was expected at his brother's. He gave Ruth a quick kiss and rushed off.

Charles greeted him as if he knew he was coming. "Brother!" he exclaimed, shaking hands and embracing Lawrence. "It has been too long; to what do I owe the pleasure?"

"I have some good news, and some better news."

"The better first, please."

"I am getting married."

His brother's jaw opened in satisfying shock for a moment before he was able to compose himself. "Married? To whom? Don't tell me it's that shop girl?"

"The one and the same."

Lawrence was pleased with Charles's reaction. His brother didn't have any current prospects, due, in part to his busy work schedule, but Lawrence was glad for once to have something his brother didn't. The fact that it would infuriate his parents made it that much better.

"Well, oh boy, Mother and Father will flip their lids," Charles said, pouring Lawrence two fingers of scotch and handing him the heavy glass.

They clinked and drank. The liquid filled Lawrence's belly with fire.

"What did you say her last name was again?"

"Smith. Miss Ruth Smith," Lawrence said.

"The Smiths… Are they from Philadelphia?"

Lawrence laughed. Of course Charles would try to place her family. To figure out her social standing. So like their father.

"No, she is from here, actually."

"What does her father do? Do I know them?"

"Probably not, not unless you frequent the tile kilns by the river."

Charles's eyes widened in shock. It was deeply satisfying to create such a reaction. Lawrence drew this out longer than he needed to, but was having too much fun to rush it.

"He's—he's a factory man? But I thought you met her at the New Year's party?"

"I did."

Charles finished his drink and poured another. "Forgive my directness, but how did a shop girl without family ties get an invite?"

Lawrence tightened his grip on the glass. He shouldn't have been surprised, but expected more of this class talk from his father, not brother. Charles knew Lawrence's afflictions and subsequent struggles. He should have just been happy for him, even if Lawrence wasn't telling the full truth.

"She was there with a friend, if you must know."

"I see, well, I am happy for you old chap."

"Thank you. And that's not all."

"Oh, am I to be treated to a famous story?" Charles asked, a half-smile on his face.

Lawrence let the jab go. He needed Charles on his side.

"I wanted to let you know how splendid the pharmacy is going."

It was a lie. The money from the poker game was almost gone. Between the ring, his gambling debts, the latest shipment of booze—and a couple poker hands—Lawrence was close to being right back in the same mess he'd just gotten out of.

"Equally wonderful news to hear," Charles said.

"So, the offer still stands."

"Offer?"

"Well, to invest, of course. It would be a great opportunity for you."

A twitch of a smile broke out on Charles' face. Lawrence flashed with anger.

"What kind of money trouble have you gotten yourself into this time?" Charles asked.

"No, no trouble. Nothing like that. I thought, as my brother, you'd want to be a part of my success."

"Lawrence, you know your successes are my successes. Your joy, my joy. But pharmacies really aren't something I invest in."

"Aren't you always speaking to me about diversifying?"

"Yes, I am, but I don't think this is the right investment for me. But I appreciate your offer, really I do."

"Sure," Lawrence said, turning to leave.

"Brother," Charles called as Lawrence walked out the door. "I really am happy for you."

****

Lawrence roamed the city, too amped up to go home, but with enough sense not to try to find a game. He kept his gaze down as he traveled to the garment district, knowing he couldn't put off the conversation any longer.

"You're engaged?" Paul asked as soon as the door opened.

"What? How did you hear that?" Lawrence said, not expecting word to have traveled so quickly. He was hoping to break the news to Paul himself.

"Everyone talks about everything in this town. Especially when a poor, lucky shop girl gets pulled out of the slums by a rich, handsome heir."

"She's not from the slums," Lawrence said. He regretted the words as soon as they were out of his mouth. "Baby, Paul, look, I'm sorry." He rushed to Paul's side.

"I knew it," Paul said, tears brimming in his eyes. "I knew that this wasn't going to last forever. But I was hoping it would last a little longer."

Lawrence stared at him, the cogs in his brain whirling. If he played his cards right, maybe he could get the money and even a shot at happiness with Paul. A new city. A new life.

"And it will," Lawrence said. "Just a little while longer. Can you wait for me for just a little while longer?"

"And then what?" Paul asked, his arms crossed.

"She'll no longer be between us. And we can be free."

Chapter Thirty-Eight

Detective Kelly brought three boxes into the small conference room, careful to keep them poised right at her belly. Even with all the sporadic vomiting that followed her into the second trimester, her weight was rapidly increasing. It was the only time she'd ever been glad no one tended to pay her much attention, otherwise they'd be sure to notice the bulge poking out under her uniform jacket.

She carried the last box and shut the door behind her. Best to do this in private. No reason to give the boys anything else to talk about.

She started with thirty-nine files. The first, which she moved to a pile on her right, included the Chandlers' murder. There was no need to review that one again. She knew which side it was on.

For the next three hours, she went through every open homicide case from the last two years. Thankfully no one knocked on the door or came looking for her. Must not be any gruesome deaths on the docket. A frantic fluttering filled her chest. A need for order and some semblance of getting a handle on what odds she was against. Her internal clock ticked right along with the one on the wall.

The pile on her left grew as she weeded out cases where there was a clear suspect, like a jilted boyfriend, or a murder-suicide. She also excluded any robberies where no jewelry or money was taken. Several cases concerned prostitutes, but they were straightforward. She hated herself for disregarding them. But there was no reason to believe they may be involved, no matter how much she longed to nail the guys. Any sexual-related crimes also went into the pile on the left. Everything else joined the Chanler file on the right.

Twelve in all.

Next, she tried to figure out how to connect them.

Of the twelve, nine of the victims had been shot. Four of them were prostitutes, but the circumstances around their death, like location and missing personal items, warranted their inclusion. The others were wealthier citizens. She made a note to retrieve any bullets and send them along to Goddard. She'd already packaged the revolver found at the bathhouse massacre. She didn't understand exactly how it worked, but knew experts were cropping up in court stating that they could unequivocally say if a particular firearm shot a particular bullet.

A lot of the cops on the force called it voodoo, or lazy policing. Why use science to catch someone when you could use your brain, like cops had been doing for decades? But Kelly knew she wasn't making much headway. She was desperate to try anything before the chances of ever solving these crimes left right along with her.

She was convinced two of the cases, the Chanlers and Astor murders, were connected. The other ten were nothing more than a gut feeling, but if linking could help give them leads, she'd give it a shot.

She gathered the projectiles from the other cases.

"What are you taking all these bullets for?" Rogers,

the evidence room officer asked after handing her another brown bag containing three of them.

How much to tell him? She hadn't had much interaction with Rogers and didn't know exactly where he stood on the whole "female cops" line, so she decided on half-truth.

"Series of cases I got saddled with." She rolled her eyes in mock annoyance.

"And these hunks of lead are supposed to…"

"Shit if I know," she said and his eyes widened at her language. "But I'm not going to get anywhere if I don't turn over every rock, right?"

He pursed his lips for a moment before nodding.

"You know," he said as she turned to leave. "My sister is a jail matron."

"That right?"

"Yup, always wanted to be a detective though."

"Then she should go for it."

He gave her a weak smile and she was reasonably confident he wouldn't mention to anyone what she'd taken. She took the items back to the procured room and placed them, along with the revolver, in a shipping box. The revolver made it difficult to carry it without all the contents slipping to one side. She looked around the office, but couldn't find enough scrap newspaper to fill it. When she got to the mailroom she asked the boy there.

"What for?" the boy asked, clutching the paper he was reading tighter in his hands.

"Day old is fine," Kelly said with a smile. "Boss will have my behind if something in here breaks. Just need to pack this tighter."

The boy rummaged under his desk and produced a

pile of crumpled pages. She stabilized the box and left it with the clerk, with strict orders to make sure it went into the mail that day for express delivery.

"Express? You know that's gonna be a pretty penny. Chief's not gonna like seeing that bill."

"You let me worry about the chief," Kelly said. "It has to get there as quickly as possible."

She left her hopes in a small cardboard box filled with lead and newspaper.

Chapter Thirty-Nine

Lawrence met Pops down by the warehouses, but he hadn't even gotten out of his car before the man was shaking his head.

"Nope, no way. You go back the way you came," Pops said.

"Pops," Lawrence started, but the man held up his hand.

"If anyone hears you came here, we're both dead men. Get outta here."

"I'll pay you more. Five dollars a crate more than what I used to pay you."

"Lawrence—"

"Ten dollars more. Please, do me this favor," he begged.

"My favor to you is not telling Lucky you approached me. Now, get out of here," Pops said.

Fuming, Lawrence got back in his car. Who was this two-bit guy to tell *him* no? To act like *he* had the power in the situation, in the city. Like Pops held the keys. Lawrence was done. Done owing people something. Groveling for what should easily be his. His parents should just hand money to him like they did his brother. But no. He had to work for it. Scrimp and scrounge and slither in the shadows to pick up the crumbs of others.

He should have it all. Rich parents. A decorated

military stint. He had the girl, plus a discreet guy on the side.

It could just be him and Paul. It would be a simpler life if he and Paul ran away together. Start a new life in one of the communities just for men he'd heard about. Then he could give it up. He wouldn't need to gamble, wouldn't need to hide. He could just *be*.

There was the matter of money. And Ruth. But maybe one could take care of the other.

He was lost in thought when a car swerved in front of him and he reeled toward the curb. He recovered, but overcorrected and the car skidded along the icy road. It hit a slick patch and spun in a circle, before coming to rest in the middle of the street. Lawrence breathed heavily as the vehicle settled and spewed steam. He hit the steering wheel, about to yell at the other driver when his door was wrenched open.

The man's fist hit him before he could put a hand up to protect himself.

He was dragged out of the car and thrown against the still smoking hood.

"Now wait a minute," Lawrence said before he was punched in the stomach. He slumped down, but the man pulled him up, holding him by the coat lapels.

"Mr. Henry," a familiar voice said.

Lawrence looked through watering eyes to see Lucky walking toward him.

"Mr. Luciano," Lawrence said. "There must be some misunderstanding. I paid you your money."

"Yes, you did," Lucky said. "Which I appreciate. What I don't appreciate though, is you trying to double cross me. No, I don't appreciate that at all."

"I'm not trying to double cross you." Lawrence

flinched as the man holding him shifted.

"Funny neighborhood to be in. What brings you to this side of town outside of a delivery night?"

Lawrence decided a half-truth was the best method. "I was breaking it off with my old supplier. That is all."

"Is it then?"

"Yes, Mr. Luciano."

Lucky moved closer to him. "Because I think I've given you a fair price for what I'm offering. I'd hate to hear that you think I was being unreasonable."

"Never, Mr. Luciano," Lawrence said, regaining some of his ability to stand on his own.

"Because if anything, Mr. Henry, you should be paying more. We've gotta start squirreling away some money for the day when all of this goes away," he said, opening his arms and gesturing around him.

"I-I don't understand," Lawrence said.

"This, my boy. What you and I are doing. These days of rum-running are coming to an end."

Lawrence shook his head, which was a mistake. The world spun.

"No, Mr. Luciano. Business is good. There's no reason to stop."

"You need to pay more attention, son. Hoover's on his way out. Man named Roosevelt's about to put us all out of a job," Lucky said.

"No one's ending Prohibition," Lawrence said, uncertainly.

Could Lucky be right?

"Mark my words, Mr. Henry. Pretty soon, all of this will be a distant memory. A chapter of history soon to be forgotten. But in the meantime," he said, moving even closer still.

The cigar smell wafted toward Lawrence.

"If I hear you speaking to any other suppliers, to end your contract or otherwise, I'll kill ya."

Lawrence nodded. "Yes, sir."

"Ha!" Lucky said, shaking his head. "Can you imagine, us having to get real jobs again? Progress," he lamented. "What's the fun in that?"

Chapter Forty

Ruth stood on the stoop in front of her parent's apartment, holding her new coat tightly around herself. Mrs. Astor insisted she get one.

"How can you recommend our products if you don't own one yourself? I insist, all the people working here have an Astor's coat," Mrs. Astor said.

Ruth agreed, and was glad she did. The deep burgundy coat lacked a fur collar, but was still warmer than any she'd ever owned before. With matching buttons and a fitted waist, it was also more fashionable than her old ones, too. It was true she had a better appreciation now and would likely make a better salesperson. She made a mental note to ensure any new employee that she hired got the same treatment.

Under the coat she wore the green dress from her and Lawrence's first date. She tried on every dress in her closet before settling on this one. It was the nicest she owned. The better to impress his parents with. Plus, the emerald necklace matched it perfectly.

When she suggested meeting his parents—after all, they *were* getting married and he'd met hers—he'd hesitated, but relented. He said he'd send a car for her.

"You won't be picking me up?" she asked, crestfallen.

The idea of arriving to his parents' house by herself didn't thrill her. She wanted to ride with him the whole way so she could ask questions. Make sure she wasn't going to embarrass herself, or him. She felt ill-prepared for such a meeting as the driver pulled up.

She'd been to the house before, but it felt different this time. Intimidating in a way that it wasn't on New Year's. When the driver opened her door, another man met her in the driveway to escort her in. She'd never been to a rich person's house before as a guest like this and wasn't sure exactly how it worked.

A man took her coat as soon as she entered and she waited a beat before realizing that she wasn't getting a ticket in exchange. Then a woman came and said she was going to escort Ruth to the library.

They walked through a section of the house that was off-limits during the party, and Ruth tried to look every which way to see it all. Paintings, coats of armor, and sculptures lined every surface. It was like living in a museum. Goosebumps formed on her arms and she wished she'd kept her coat.

She was shown through a mahogany paneled room with a roaring fire, the heat giving her instant relief. Two plush velvet couches faced each other. A woman sat in one while Lawrence, and presumably his father, stood by the mantle, brandy snifters in their hands. The three leaned in toward each other, and Ruth had the sneaking suspicion she'd walked in on a heated discussion.

"My darling," Lawrence said and rushed over to her.

He paused for a moment, staring at her as if her appearance wasn't immediately pleasing, but he quickly washed the hesitation from his face. He embraced her and gave her a quick peck on the cheek. His instant change in demeanor made her even more suspicious.

Were they arguing about her? Does he think she was silly to be wearing the dress yet again? Did it highlight how she lacked money for a bunch of fancy clothes?

"Mother, Father, I am pleased to introduce you to Miss Ruth Smith."

Ruth took a small curtsey, unsure of how she was supposed to acknowledge being introduced so formally. For the hundredth time she wished Lawrence had driven with her here so they could go over all the intricacies of the meeting.

"Miss Smith," his father said, and kissed her hand. "It is lovely to finally meet you."

Lawrence's mother stood and took both of Ruth's hands in her, squeezing them once. "Yes, my dear, lovely."

Ruth thought they seemed genuine and nice, but were they putting on airs? Della said the first time she met her husband's parents they were sugar-sweet to her. But now they gave Della a hard time about everything, especially when it came to the children. Della constantly complained about how her mother-in-law commented how she raised her kids to be more respectful. Ruth hoped it wouldn't be a similar situation with Lawrence's parents.

"It is so nice to meet you, Mr. and Mrs. Henry. Thank you for having me in your home," Ruth said.

His mother smiled. "You can call me Lucile. We were just speaking about the unpleasantries of those men who robbed the bread trucks. Charles, can you imagine such a thing?"

"Thugs, the lot of them," Lawrence's father said.

"Over a thousand men. And what did they think? They could just take all that food? It was meant for the hotel, you know. My friend Betty Gaines was supposed to have a luncheon there and they had to cancel. What a pity."

"People are starting to get desperate," Ruth said, because she was a loss at what to add to the conversation.

The talk of the men in the bread-line overtaking the truck meant for a fancy party had sped through the city. Funny how her parents only spoke of sympathy about those desperate enough to try such a foolish act. They'd be spending the night in the cells, stuffed like sardines. She wondered what, if anything, it meant that Lawrence's parents were more concerned with the party it affected.

"Well, no need to discuss such matters." Lucile leaned forward, eyes squinting. "Your necklace…"

Ruth reflexively pulled her hands back and touched the jewels.

"Yes," she said. "Isn't it wonderful? Lawrence said it was from—"

"I gave it to her," Lawrence said.

"We had a friend that had a very similar one," Lucile said. "Joy Chanler."

"Yes," his father chimed in. "Hopefully you have better luck than the last person wearing one like that." He laughed.

"Charles," Lucile said.

"I'm just teasing. We knew someone who had a similar necklace and she met an ill-fated end."

"Oh, that's terrible," Ruth exclaimed.

"Don't worry," Lawrence said as the butler called

them all to dinner. "I won't let anything bad happen to you."

He put an arm around her, and squeezed her shoulder, but his eyes held a hardness that didn't match his words. An all-too familiar hollowness formed in her stomach, and her skin crawled.

Ruth couldn't quite put her finger on why these waves of emotion hit her sometimes. It was like some internal alarm blared, but she couldn't decipher it. Lawrence didn't have a reason to double cross her. It was clear he didn't need her money at all, so then the only logical explanation for asking for it was to bring her into the business. To have them build something together for their future.

But the alarm still blared, and she was unable to silence it.

Chapter Forty-One

The evening was a disaster.

Lawrence wished Ruth never suggested it. And really, why did she? What did it matter if Ruth ever met his parents? What consequence was it to her? Lawrence figured when she really pushed the issue, he'd just suggest a courthouse wedding anyway. None of their family would even need to attend. He bet she wouldn't be happy about it, but he could tell in their previous conversations he had her. She was going to do whatever he told her.

He'd arrived at his parents an hour before he told Ruth to be there, wanting to make sure he had some time to speak with his parents first about a few matters. His mother was cross that he'd propose to a woman without letting them meet her.

"A woman, this Ruth character?" his father asked, a laugh in his tone.

Lawrence wanted to smash his glass on his father's head, but took a deep breath to settle himself.

"Why haven't we met her?" his mother asked, salvaging the conversation as always.

"She was at the party. I can't help it if you don't remember her."

Originally, he couldn't wait to present Ruth to them. To shock them with his pick in a mate. As the evening drew near, he found the whole ordeal tedious.

The marriage plot seemed such a small speed bump to his and Paul's future life; everything surrounding it now felt like a chore. He wished he could fast-forward the evening and just be done with it. He hoped that by placing the blame on them for not remembering, they'd feel bad enough to let the matter drop. It only worked marginally well.

"All the same," his mother said. "You should have brought her by sooner."

"Well, we aren't married yet, Mother."

"Tell us how this business is going," his father said, already ready to move on. "Your brother informed me you are doing quite well."

"Yes," Lawrence said, grateful for the shift in conversation to something he wanted to speak with them about. "That is partly why I came over early this evening, to discuss business with you."

"Oh, and here I was, thinking you were going to give us a speech on being on our best behavior and checking to make sure the house was in proper form," his mother said.

"Father, you know more than anyone how difficult it is to secure funding the first year of operation, especially with all the bank failures. They are…hesitant to make loans. Which, of course, is completely ridiculous giving my standing and business model."

"Ahh," his father said, as if he'd been waiting for this. "Let's have it then."

Lawrence tried not to let the offense show in his voice. "Business is doing well, especially after the terrible matter of the robberies and fires with the other pharmacies."

"Oh, yes. Mr. Roland told me, a terrible shame.

And that poor boy killed. Mr. Roland was very upset," his mother said, a hint of real concern in her voice. "Are you in any such danger, my boy?"

"No," Lawrence said, but softened his voice. Played up feigned fear to make her worry a bit. "Nothing like that, but it has made it more difficult to acquire provisions and funding."

"So, I'm guessing you are here to ask us for some money? All right, come out with it. How much do you want?" he asked.

Lawrence bristled. "I'm not here asking for you to give me money. I am here with a business proposition."

"And what makes you think I am in the market for new investments?" his father asked.

"You are always in the market for good investments, new or old. You yourself have told me that." Lawrence clenched and released his jaw several times, willing himself to keep his cool, knowing his father wouldn't react well to anger or raised voices.

Why were they making this so difficult for him? Lawrence bet if Charles walked in asking for just about anything his parents would fall all over themselves to give it to him. But the one time he asked for anything, they pushed back against him. It was simply unfair.

"Well, yes, but I don't see how I am going to make my money back, much less a good return on investment on this one. I am proud of you, dear boy. You have really made something of yourself. Going off to war, making a good time of that, coming back and bumping around the county a bit. But it looks like you have found your place once you returned home. Found someone to settle down with. All in all, well done, but I'm not looking for such an investment at this time.

Especially with all the instability going on now, as you mentioned."

Lawrence moved to the bar cart and poured himself three fingers of brandy. His father joined and got one of his own before they sat back down.

"Though if you just want the money, you know all you need to do is ask," his father said. "It is yours, young man. I know you aren't interested in it and feel it some sort of affront to take it, but it's yours. We're lucky as all get-up to still have money. All these fools losing the shirts off their backs from this crash, they're calling it."

"I don't need a handout," Lawrence said, his hackles raising along with his voice.

It was always presented as such charity when they offered money to him. It was out of pity. No matter what his father said, Lawrence knew he wasn't proud of him. Didn't believe in him. He'd done perfectly fine earning money his own way. He was done trying to get them to see his worth.

Just at this moment, there was a soft knock at the door and the butler showed Ruth through.

Wearing the necklace.

Lawrence almost dropped his glass.

It didn't appear his parents fully recognized the item. Thinking it was similar was fine, he supposed. No reason for any of them to suspect him. Really, what cause would they have had? Sure, they didn't think all that well of their first-born, but a killer? No, he didn't need to worry about accusations from them.

Ruth was her normal lovely self at dinner, even with the fib his mother told about the bread-line mob. He was pleased and a little surprised she so quickly gave a possible explanation for their heated discussion. But they were quickly back to their typical backhanded complimenting selves.

"You are so well-spoken for someone who grew up in Chelsea," his father commented.

"Aren't there a lot of Irish there?" his mother asked, an expression on her face reminiscent of smelling something unpleasant.

"Well, yes, my father is the manager of the Gas Works. He thinks it's good for the employees to see he lives in the same area they do. Helps build camaraderie."

"Ah, I see," his father said.

She brightened. "They just opened the most beautiful new apartment building in our neighborhood. It even has a pool! I am trying to convince him and my mother to move there." She laughed, but the others didn't join in.

"What a beautiful dress. I think I remember seeing it at the end of the Christmas season," his mother said.

Ruth graciously accepted her comment. Lawrence burned with embarrassment and hoped that Ruth didn't notice how rude his parents were. Maybe she was proud of her father's morals and maybe his mother recognizing the dress as a worthy one was good enough for her, even if that's not what was really meant.

Mercifully, the dessert plates were finally removed and nightcaps passed out. Lawrence gave the obligatory thanks to his parents for their hospitality, then he and Ruth walked toward the door.

"A lovely coat," his mother said after he helped Ruth put it on.

She beamed. "Thank you, it's from Astor's."

"Ah, yes, I'd recognize their work anywhere," his mother said.

Lawrence waited, but there was no addition, no cutting down to complete the sentence. Was this a true compliment? Lawrence heard so few in his life, it was hard to tell.

"You simply must come to our St. Patrick's Day party," his mother said.

"Oh yes," his father said. "We have a wonderful view of the parade and get the finest Irish whiskey money can buy." He winked.

"I would be honored and delighted.," Ruth bowed slightly.

Lawrence fought the urge to roll his eyes and instead offered to take her home. She checked her watch.

"Home already?" she asked.

"I'm afraid so. There is some work that I need to do tonight," he lied.

Her eyes widened. "You aren't going into the office alone, are you? I know you said not to worry about those thugs, but I can't help it."

"No, nothing like that, a few hours, but at home."

"I think it went well," she said after a few minutes pause.

"Swimmingly."

"Penny for your thoughts?" she asked.

Do you have a penny you could give me? he almost asked. "Oh, nothing. I am very pleased with how the evening went." He kissed her hand. "Though I expected nothing less. Of course, they would love you like I do, how could they not?"

She smiled back at him. They kissed one more time

and Lawrence led her up to her steps.

"Home?" the driver asked when Lawrence got back in the car.

"No, garment district, please."

"Right away, sir," the driver said.

The soft chemical smell from the clothing manufacturer Paul lived over wafted through the halls as Lawrence made his way upstairs. Paul opened it and the smell dissipated as soon as the door was shut.

"Saw you from the street," he said, taking Lawrence's coat and hanging it on the back of one of the mismatched chairs in the small kitchen. "Twice in one week! To what do I owe the pleasure of the increased visits? Can't get enough of me? Having second thoughts about that fiancée?" He laughed and leaned forward to kiss Lawrence, who pulled away.

"I need your advice. Or help. Or anything."

Lawrence was horrified to find tears prickling the edges of his eyes. Why was it that Paul did this to him? Removed his defenses so much, that all the floodgates were left wide open?

They moved to Paul's cramped living room and sat on a wildly uncomfortable couch. Lawrence realized he hadn't really been anywhere but Paul's bedroom. Looking around the space with a critical eye, for the first time he saw how drab and sad it was. None of the furniture matched. Most of it had either a broken leg or was scratched up, presumably by a cat, though Lawrence never saw a feline in the apartment. Most likely all the items had been picked from the streets or second-hand shops, having run their course in one home and then moving on to another.

In that instant, Lawrence's need to save Paul was

solidified. This was his true path. In saving himself, he could also give this man a better life. This poor man he loved who worked multiple shifts at multiple jobs and for what? To get the trash of other people filling his house?

If Paul was embarrassed by his place, he didn't show it, endearing him to Lawrence even more. Ruth fretted all the time about the differences in their social standings. Paul dared him to say anything about it.

Paul held one of Lawrence's hands in his, drawing small circles in his palm. "Tell me what's going on, honey."

Paul had never called him honey before. Never looked at him with such caring. It broke what little remained of Lawrence's resolve and he started to cry. It felt like a rusted cage opening. All noise and pain, but relief also. Lawrence couldn't remember the last time he cried. Maybe when he was a small boy.

Paul held and shushed him, rubbing his back until Lawrence calmed down enough and could speak.

"The business. I think I am in over my head," Lawrence said.

"All right. So sell it."

Lawrence laughed. "As if it could be that easy."

"And why can't it? After the robberies, I heard there isn't a competitor within blocks of you. Sell to one of them. It will take months for any insurance pay-outs. I bet at least Roland's will want to open a new shop sooner than later. One that's already set up and ready to go will be ideal."

It all sounded so simple and possible. Lawrence lowered his head.

"I am too far underwater."

"But I thought you were doing well?"

"I was, I *am*," he said. "But I had to take out loans to open it, and securing all my product has made me tap any investor I could find. I took a second loan out of the place already. There's no way I could pay the bank off. Plus, with all this financial hoopla going on all over the city, it's not like they let me catch a break. They are trying to make examples of people. There's no way they'd let some rich boy off when every beggar on the street is asking for pennies to my dollars."

"We will figure this out, don't worry. Why don't you get that fiancée of yours to help?"

Lawrence nodded, as if those resources weren't tapped out as well. He was in a confessional mood, but still wasn't ready to let someone into all his deep, dark secrets. He needed to save a few for himself.

He left a few minutes later, stressed and amped after the emotionally draining evening, passing on Paul's offer to stay over. He wanted to gamble. *Needed* to gamble. But he had no money.

He walked down the street looking for a cab, something, anything, to take him away from this place.

Away from this life.

Chapter Forty-Two

A telegram sat on Detective Kelly's desk when she arrived the next morning.

Please call me as soon as you get into the office.
—Lt. Col. Goddard

Kelly's heart jumped into the back of her throat as she asked the floor secretary to get him on the line.

A few minutes later a scratchy voice was patched through.

"Lieutenant Colonel? This is Detective Kelly with the forty-fifth precinct in New York City," Kelly said, her pen hovering over a legal pad, poised to jot down notes.

There was a long pause on the other end.

"Detective Kelly?"

Goddard's question made her realize she'd never used her first name on their correspondence. He most definitely had expected Kelly to be a man and if she was being honest, she'd been banking on that. A phone call was never expected. She should have foreseen this.

"Yes, Detective Johanna Kelly, sir."

"Right, okay. Well, Detective Kelly, thank you for calling me back. I will be releasing you a report as well, but I thought it best to speak on the phone about my results."

"You were able to get results?" She wanted to shout at the man to hurry up but figured she was already on thin ice for her deception.

"We always get results, one way or another," Goddard said.

"And which way in this case?"

"The revolver you sent us was positively identified as having fired a number of the submitted bullets."

Kelly let out a long breath. "Oh, thank God." She *knew* her hunches were correct.

"Yes," Goddard said.

Papers rustled before Goddard rattled off a series of case numbers, including the Chanler, Astor, and Everyard.

"No one believed me," Kelly said. She imagined Goddard didn't really care, but felt the urge to say it out loud anyway.

"That is what makes science so wonderful," Goddard said. "Coupled with good policing, we can do anything. Even the impossible. But I'm sure you're used to doing the impossible."

She smiled even though she knew he couldn't see her. "Yes, well, I do try." Kelly felt like she was speaking with a kindred spirit, all previous awkwardness erased.

"The other cases you submitted are not involved with this firearm, but for what it's worth, two of them were identified to each other, so if you find a suspect weapon, I would suggest sending that along. A Colt Police Positive."

Kelly sat back in her chair. "A cop gun?"

"Yes, and no. Once departments switched over, sometimes the old revolvers were sold at auction. I wouldn't worry you have a rogue officer on your hands."

"Anything else?" Kelly asked.

"Yes, actually. Something very interesting."

"Go on." Kelly wished the man would just tell everything he knew.

"This revolver you sent us, the one that was involved in those other cases, was also linked to two cases from here."

"I don't understand," Kelly said. "I thought you said you can tell guns apart." She felt the whole case unraveling.

"Oh, I can, we can. That's what I am saying. This weapon was also used in two homicides in Chicago, where wealthy people were robbed of their cash and jewelry. No other items of value were stolen, even though their homes contained several expensive items. The details of the cases sounded familiar, so I decided to look against our unsolved cases. I came up with six with similar M.O.s. Your gun matched two of them."

Kelly was speechless. "So what do I do now?"

"Well, I think it's a pretty solid lead. I know we each have big cities, but it narrows it down to look for someone who was in Chicago during the summer of 1928 and in your city now. It's still a big pool, but hopefully you may be able to fish something out of it."

"Lieutenant Colonel, I appreciate all your time and effort," Kelly said.

"My report will arrive to you later today," Goddard said. "And I hope you find your man," he added. "When you do, I would be more than happy to testify to my findings."

"Thank you."

Kelly hung up, her head spinning with information. She slapped her desk once, twice, three times and fought the urge to call out in vindication.

"Hate to interrupt this celebration," Carlson said. "But looks like the lieutenant is determined for us to be partners. Must have royally pissed him off about something. We caught another one."

Kelly sighed.

"I may have good news for you, guy's not dead, and apparently he's blubbering on. Come on, let's go."

They got to the scene just as the man was being placed in an ambulance. It was a stabbing, which disappointed Kelly momentarily before she admonished herself. The neighborhood was right though, the victim clearly wealthy, his suit ripped open while a man held blood-soaked cloths over his chest.

"I can't believe it," the man said. His skin was as pale as the falling snow.

"What?" Carlson asked.

"I can't believe he did it."

"Who?" Kelly implored.

She just needed a name. A break. Anything to go on.

"I can't believe he did it," the man repeated, before his head lolled to the side.

"We gotta go," the ambulance attendant said, before pushing Kelly and Carlson away so he could close the ambulance door.

"Send for us the moment he wakes up!" Kelly called, running up to give the driver her card.

"*If* he wakes up," the driver corrected, taking the card, then speeding off, the siren wailing as the rig raced down the street.

Chapter Forty-Three

"And then," Ruth said, gesturing wildly with her hands. "He said that *I* was the one who owed him. Can you imagine? A proper gentleman like that accusing *me*?"

Ruth was fired up all over again. Even Rebecca had taken Ruth's side, which made her feel vindicated, but no less annoyed at being treated terribly by a rich client. Mrs. Astor was no longer frequenting the store and Ruth felt a shift with the clientele, like they were seeing what they could get away with in her absence.

After the disgruntled man left, one of the sales associates said she'd heard he'd lost the majority of his fortune in the crash. They all speculated if the man was trying to get a free coat because he couldn't really afford one. A terrible shame, but no excuse for how he spoke to her.

"Ruth, I am sorry that you're having a rough day, but please, can we talk about this?" Lawrence asked.

They sat across from each other at the crowded deli down the street from Astor's. Her roast beef sandwich was uneaten in front of her, creating more palpable frustration from the other patrons as they wanted everyone to rush and move on so they could sit.

"I am talking about it," Ruth said, confused at Lawrence's response.

It was all she'd been talking about since he met her

in front of the store and walked her to lunch. She took a bite of the sandwich to calm her nerves and prevent herself from speaking.

"No." His voice rose.

Several people looked in their direction. He promptly lowered his voice. "I have put you in my will," he said.

The change in conversation gave her whiplash and she struggled to swallow the too-large mouthful of food. "Why?"

"I know we are getting married soon, but I wanted to make sure if something happened to me, you'd be safe in the meantime."

He squeezed her hand before putting the last bite of his sandwich in his mouth. She continued to hurriedly eat hers, not caring if she spoke with a full mouth.

"That is very kind of you," she said. "But I still don't understand."

"Ruth, I am asking you to make a similar gesture of security."

"Security?"

"If something happens to you," he said in a tone suggesting she was daft.

"Yes, I understand what you are saying," she said defensively. "I just don't understand why you are saying it. Lawrence, we've been through this, I don't have any money. I've given it all to you."

"Invested," he corrected for the millionth time.

She nodded. "Yes, invested. But there isn't any more. If something happens to me, then you won't have to pay me back. I am sure no court will require you to settle a debt to my parents."

"The court doesn't work that way, not when an

investment is involved."

Now she was confused. "I don't understand."

"I signed papers stating that a portion of the business is yours."

"You did?"

She was shocked. They'd never spoken of it.

"Of course I did. You trusted me and invested a large portion of money. It was the right thing to do."

She agreed, making a note to tell this to her still-skeptical sister.

"So, I still don't understand, if something were to happen to me, then what?" she asked.

"The investment is tied up. It has been spent. You know this."

"Yes," she said. "But again, what does that matter?"

His hands tightened on hers and the discomfort made sweat warm the back of her neck. Why didn't she understand what he was saying?

"It would leave me in a tight spot since I'd have to deal with lawyers and such to transfer your portion of the business over to me. But since I already have it in my will, if something happened to me, you'll be fine. Do you understand?"

"Yes," she said even though she didn't. But she didn't want him to get angry with her. Especially not here in a public place.

"A life insurance policy would also help," he said.

"Life insurance?"

"Sure." He said it so casually, as if everyone got one. As if it was no big deal.

"For what?"

"I think five thousand dollars would do it," he said.

Lawrence gathered his empty plate and her nearly full one and placed them on the counter. She thought about protesting, but her break was almost over and she'd lost her appetite anyway.

They left and Ruth had to jog to keep up with his sweeping steps. The air was bitterly cold outside and it stung her lungs after being in the warmth of the deli.

"Lawrence, Lawrence, wait," she called and reached out her hand to stop him.

Her head spun and she needed an explanation. Why did he need money from her? Assurances from her? It didn't make any sense. She knew he was too prideful to take money from his parents, but she always figured he would in a pinch.

"Look, nothing is going to happen to you," he said and continued. "But if something did, I would need some help, financially. If something happened to me, you'd be taken care of, I have seen to it. Nothing will happen to either of us. But that is what insurance is for, the 'what if's.' "

"Why would you need help?" she whispered, half-hoping he wouldn't hear her.

He finally stopped and faced her, the kindness in his features a jolt. "Ruth. I am not trying to patronize you, but there is an awful lot of business dealings you don't understand. When capital is tied up, it's not easy to get to that cash. Just because someone has money, doesn't mean they have access to it. And if for some reason someone *did* want to go after me, since your name is also on the paperwork, that means they could go after your family also, to collect. Think of this as a bridge, a helping hand in a time of need until affairs can be settled. It's all very common."

She nodded, fears of putting her family in danger running through her head because of this man. He handed her a card.

"Call on this number. He will draw up the papers and you can sign them," Lawrence demanded, as if the matter had been resolved.

"I'll think about it," Ruth said, not ready to give him the victory quite yet.

His expression made it clear that wasn't the response he was looking for, but he nodded and strode away, her again jogging to keep up.

Chapter Forty-Four

Detective Kelly waited for ten minutes before a nurse finally helped her. Even though her uniform was obvious, she still flashed her badge for what felt like the twentieth time since arriving, exasperation hunching her shoulders.

"How can I help you, officer?" the nurse asked. Her white uniform had a single spot of blood on it below her left shoulder and the stain momentarily took Kelly's attention as the nurse looked her up and down. "Is everything all right with the…" She gestured vaguely at Kelly's midsection.

She felt her cheeks warm and nodded.

"That's not what I'm here for. My name is Detective Kelly. I am here about a gentleman who was brought in last night, who was robbed and stabbed. I haven't heard any updates and was hoping maybe he was awake and I could speak with him."

The nurse walked behind a counter to a large ledger. She flipped through two pages, and ran her fingers along a list of names. She looked up and bit her lower lip.

"Detective, I am so sorry no one contacted you. That gentleman passed away early this morning. Name of Walsh."

Kelly thanked the nurse who then held out a bag.

"Will you be doing the next-of-kin notification?

Here are his things. You may take them with you if you are."

"Yes, yes of course I will," Kelly said.

It wasn't typically something she did, but it got her access to the man's belongings, so it seemed worth it.

She walked the few blocks back to the precinct and went into the empty conference room that had become her ad hoc office for the East-to-West murders. The bag held Walsh's wallet with operator's license, a few scraps of paper, but no money of course. The man's clothing was also inside, the fine suit stained with blood. Kelly put the bag on the floor and it clinked softly on the linoleum. She picked the bag up and turned it upside down on the table. A small navy object fell out and rolled toward the table's edge. Kelly grabbed it before it fell.

It was a single button, an 'A' in fancy script on it. Kelly inspected Walsh's suit jacket and overcoat, but didn't see any missing buttons on it

Carlson entered and shook his head.

"You've lost your mind," he said.

"Maybe," Kelly admitted.

"Come on, better clear out of here before Lieutenant Porter sees this mess. He'll blow his top, especially with you. You know they'll fire you."

"Just turn the light off. No one comes in here. I took this place over a week ago and nobody noticed."

"Definitely don't tell anyone else that. But this is really dangerous for you, you know that, right? You won't get the same kind of leeway the rest of us might."

"I'm not interested in leeway at this point," Kelly said truthfully. Her days were numbered anyway, but it was clear in the way Carlson treated her he was none the wiser on that fact.

"You can't do any good from outside it."

Carlson turned to leave, but Kelly stopped him.

"Hey, you recognize this?" Kelly held out the button.

Carlson took it and turned it over in his hand. "Sure, isn't that the emblem of the Astor place we went to the other day?"

Recognition snapped in Kelly's brain, followed immediately by frustration.

"It keeps coming up," Kelly said. "What do you think the connection is?"

"Dunno," Carlson said. "Maybe someone at the store is killing clients? Upset at the rich coming in, maybe not being so nice? Did the other murders also have an Astor connection?"

"Don't think so. Doesn't seem too good for business though, to kill off your clientele."

Carlson shrugged. "Just a thought. Of course, unless it's just a rich person killing other rich people. Maybe settling a score or moving competition out of the way."

"How so?" This second theory intrigued her.

"All that old money just passes from one hand to another, hard to make any new fortunes, unless you take them out. That's how the mob does it. Could be some anti-Robin Hood is stealing from the rich to get richer."

The two walked out. Kelly closed the door behind her. She'd sweet talk one of the uniformed officers to inform the man's family of his ill-fated end.

The floor secretary handed her a telegram. She nodded her thanks.

"What is it?" Carlson said.

Kelly couldn't believe it.

"A message from that scientist in Chicago I was telling you about. Turns out," Kelly paused to read the note one more time, to make sure she got it right, "Same guy that's been killing here is linked to four homicides in Baltimore, as well as the two in Chicago."

Carlson stopped. "Wait, are you telling me that we have a mass murderer here on our hands?"

"Looks like it."

"Well I'll be damned." Carlson clapped Kelly on the shoulder. "Maybe you aren't so crazy after all."

Chapter Forty-Five

Lawrence's hands shook as he pushed all his chips into the middle of the table. His chest rose and fell as he breathed in and out slowly through his nose, a faint whistling sound emanating from his nostrils. The man sitting across from him narrowed his eyes. Half his chip pile was already in, but he apparently hadn't anticipated Lawrence re-raising him by going all-in.

"Fine," the man said in a huff. "I think you're a bullshitter. I'll call that bet."

The man had a few more chips than Lawrence, so he still had a small stack of about a dozen after pushing the majority of his pile toward the center. It was just the two of them as the dealer turned the river card. Lawrence flipped his cards over, his heart pounding in his chest as he prayed to his absent God that his cards, three kings and two sevens, were enough.

"Damn it!" the man yelled, standing so quickly he almost flipped the table.

The chips and drinks rattled before settling again.

A large gentleman moved from a dark corner of the room to stand by the man, ensuring the peace. The player put his hands up indicating he wouldn't cause any troubles.

Lawrence dragged the pile of clay chips toward him and began stacking it in the wooden trays to cash out.

"Oh no you don't," the man yelled. "You gotta give me a chance to win my money back." His face reddened and his cheeks puffed out.

"Sorry, boys," Lawrence said. "I've got someplace to be. Good game." He touched his forehead in salute and backed away from the table.

"Bullshit!" the man called out to him. "You yella-belly coward. That's no way to play a game. Be a man. Give me a chance to win my chips back."

"Wish I had the time," Lawrence said, trying to keep his voice light, though with the way the room was looking at him, he could tell the others agreed that he should give the man a chance.

Little did the man know, Lawrence desperately wanted to stay. Wanted to ride the chips until he took everyone's money, but he got what he'd come for and he wasn't going to make Mr. Luciano wait for it.

The scantily-clad woman who'd turned his cash into chips two hours before, reversed the process. He tipped her five dollars for the trouble.

"Thank you, sir," she said, tucking the money between her ample breasts. Lawrence tipped his hat to her and left.

He'd turned Walsh's hundred-and-fifty dollars into four-hundred-and-twenty-five dollars in the span of two hours. He'd debated on even gambling in the first place, wondering if he should risk being a little short with Lucky, but the urge was too strong.

He noted that there was more security than normal at the gambling house, probably in response to the Everyard murders all the players were talking about. Lawrence nodded along with them, commenting at the appropriate times what a travesty it was, the merits of losing gracefully, and how no self-respecting man should be in that part of town anyway.

When he got to the gambling house, he considered only cashing in for fifty chips. He could double that up and leave with enough to pay Lucky in full. Next week's payment, plus the bit he owed him from the previous week, could be settled at a later time. But the woman saw his billfold and began counting out the chips accordingly. He didn't want to embarrass them both by asking her to put some back.

He'd bet on himself and won.

Lawrence got to the warehouse a few minutes early, but Lucky and his men were already there. He got the cash ready, sticking the spare bills in his glove compartment in case they decided to shake him down and up the price once they realized he had more money on him.

"Mr. Luciano!" Lawrence called when he got out of the car, as if he was over the moon to see the man.

Lucky nodded to him. "Aren't we in a good mood, Mr. Henry?"

"It is a beautiful evening," Lawrence said, which was actually true.

It was unseasonably warm, the temperature almost hitting fifty degrees that day. The city swarmed with people coming out of the winter hibernation, excited to walk the city unencumbered by heavy coats, boots, and hats. Lucky snapped his fingers and three men, all ones Lawrence didn't recognize, started to move wooden crates into the back of Lawrence's car.

"My money," Lucky said.

It didn't appear that the good weather had improved the man's sour mood.

"Yes, of course, Mr. Luciano," Lawrence said, making a show of reaching through his pockets before handing over the cash. "What I owe you for this week plus last week's. Thank you again for covering for me."

"Which you realize will be the last time," Lucky said.

Lawrence was about to leave when Lucky stood in front of his driver's door, gripping the handle. Lawrence jumped back, startled yet again at the nimbleness of the man.

"Everyone in my line of work knows what kind of man you are, Mr. Henry," Lucky said.

"I don't understand." Lawrence narrowed his eyes.

"You are a gambler, Mr. Henry. And not a very good one at that."

Lawrence was about to say something when Lucky put up his hand.

"And a thief."

"Now wait just a minute—"

"Would you rather be called a murderer?"

Lawrence froze. "I-I don't know what you are talking about."

"The cops may not be that smart, but I am," Lucky said. "And you better shape up. You are becoming more of a legal liability every day. If I hear of you involved in any more of these shenanigans, I may have to start charging you a twenty-percent risk tax. Or cut ties with you all together. Is that understood, Mr. Henry?"

"I don't know who you are getting your information from," Lawrence said, keeping his voice calm and even. "But they are deeply mistaken. I am purely a businessman, and business is going well. There is no risk from me."

"There better not be," Lucky said. "Because I don't take kindly to being lied to."

He released the door handle and stepped away. Lawrence scrambled to get inside and drive away. How in the hell did anyone find out about his other life?

And how much of it did they know?

Chapter Forty-Six

Ruth removed her shoes and rubbed her feet as soon as she got into Lawrence's car. She longed to stay in one night and avoid getting all dressed up.

They had a lovely evening on a double date with Lawrence's brother, but Ruth kept getting the impression Lawrence and Charles were trying to impress the other about how much money they were spending. Charles had some woman Ruth already couldn't remember the name of, which didn't seem to matter because they didn't seem to be very compatible anyway. The brothers went through rounds of buying expensive drinks, then entrées, then dessert. Ruth tried to tally the bill from what she remembered of the shocking menu prices, but lost count.

At the end of the night, Charles insisted on paying. Lawrence practically ripped the table linens off in an effort to wrestle the bill from his brother, but he lost.

Ruth clenched her eyes shut and prepared for punches to fly, but after the waiter took the cash from the table, Charles and Lawrence shook hands and embraced warmly. She figured it was all for show and Lawrence wasn't really upset, but he was short with her as soon as they got back to the car. Ruth was exhausted over the mood swings. About the doubt that crept in any time the darkness washed over his features. They had great times, and she clung to them, but the flashes of anger peeled those times away bit by bit.

Maybe it was time to take a break from evenings out on the town. As they drove toward her parent's, she suggested a quiet evening at home for their next date.

"We can cook," she suggested.

"How provincial," he said in a dismissive tone.

"You're the one who is always talking about money," she shot back, shocking the both of them.

"Excuse me?" he said.

She smiled, not wanting to be trapped in an enclosed space with an angry man. "I just mean, wouldn't it be nice to have an evening at home? It's not like we will be going out every night when we are married," she said.

"Charles does," Lawrence said.

"Well, bully for him. I wouldn't worry so much about your brother. He seems more interested in impressing people than being an actual impressive person."

Lawrence barked a laugh, the tension ebbing out of the car and his demeanor. "That he is. All right. A night at home, let's give it a go tomorrow."

****

She arrived holding a brown paper bag with pasta, sauce, vegetables, and some crusty bread from the Italian market. Lawrence raised an eyebrow, but she pushed him aside. She placed her coat in the hall closet, feeling the heft of the envelope in the breast pocket, again having something she wasn't quite ready to give up to him yet.

"Going out to eat seems a rather better idea," he said as he carried the bags to the kitchen.

She promptly put him to work once she found the

items in the kitchen they needed. Lawrence didn't know where a single thing was. She fought a laugh as he gingerly chopped an onion as if it were a grenade filled with poisonous materials.

"It won't bite you if you really hold it with your palm. It will make the chopping easier," she said.

"And make my hand smell for a week," he retorted, going back to his inefficient method.

"Speaking of the future," she said, hoping her voice sounded light as she dropped and swirled the pasta in the boiling water. "I have been getting asked pretty often when we are getting married. Any idea on a date?"

His chopping paused and she looked over to him.

"I don't know. Isn't May a nice time of year?" he asked.

Ruth was shocked. "Yes, yes of course it is, but I imagine most places will be booked already."

He pinched together his brows. "That's over a year from now, booked already?"

She let out a small breath, realizing their miscommunication. A whole year. A year older. A year of what? Of doubt and worry? She knew it was foolish, but she just wanted to get it over with. Get to the other side with him to quell her fears that he might leave her. That he might realize she wasn't worth it after all. That he was just playing her this whole time for her money and didn't care about her at all.

"Right, May is almost upon us," he said. "I meant the following, of course. This one would be too soon."

"You want to wait over a year?" she asked, hurt.

"We don't have to. I just thought that was the season."

"It is, it can be…"

"How about New Year's Eve?"

"September is also nice," she said. And three months sooner.

"Yes, but think of it." He put the knife down, becoming animated now. "Fireworks. A lavish party. And to get married on the anniversary of our meeting."

It would be nice to be able to replace that first embarrassing meeting with a better memory.

"We could have it at my parents," he said. "It will be the talk of the town. Ruth, we simply must."

"I'm not sure if a church will marry us on a Wednesday," she said.

"No, probably not. No matter, I doubt we could get married in a church anyway."

"Why the heavens not?" Panic rose in her throat. She'd never thought to ask him if he'd been married before.

"Well, I imagine you'd rather not get married in a Protestant church, am I correct?"

It was worse.

How had she never asked him if he was Catholic? Working in retail, she didn't get to mass more than Christmas Eve service, but her parents certainly did. She felt foolish for assuming, for never bringing it up.

"You're Protestant?" she whispered.

"Baptized, but certainly not practicing."

He wasn't Catholic. Which would mean their marriage wouldn't be recognized and their children would be unable to be baptized Catholic. He looked at her with one brow raised.

"Ruth, I thought you knew."

She nodded, hoping they could let the issue drop

and give her some time to think about it. He seemed to sense her wishes and went back to chopping.

Eleanor, one of the girls from the neighborhood, married a Methodist and her kids seemed to be turning out all right. They even came to Christmas Eve mass at St. Mary's; they just didn't partake in communion. It could be okay. Her parents would throw a fit and her mother was sure to cry, but they'd manage. They were happy for her that she'd finally found someone. Someone who could take care of her so they wouldn't have to worry. That was what mattered.

They'd walk into her wedding at her new in-laws' mansion and any fears they had would slip away. They'd be impressed, as would her friends and family. No one would be talking about how the ceremony wasn't in a church; they'd be too busy eating the decadent food to notice.

By the time dinner was plated and on the table, she was feeling okay about the whole matter. Her life had turned out different than she'd imagined as a girl. What was one more shift?

Lawrence remarked on how delicious the simple pasta dish was and kissed her passionately as she stood in the doorway to leave. He placed his hand on her waist, but let it continue to travel down, not stopping like he normally did as he breathed into her ear.

"Do you need to go yet?"

She swatted his hand. "You're the one who wanted to wait until the year was over," she teased. "I suggested September."

"You will be worth the wait, my darling." And he kissed her deeply once more.

"Good night."

"Ruth." He paused and searched her eyes for a long time.

She tried to read his expression but couldn't place it. Like he was trying to read her mind.

"If it is that important to you, we can figure something out with the Catholic Church. My parents know enough people. I am sure we can get it sorted."

She was genuinely touched. He may not be religious, but still, changing someone's affiliation was no small matter. She kissed him again. Her hand was on the knob when she paused, pulled the envelope out of her coat then handed it to him.

"What's this?" he asked as he opened the top, slipped out the piece of paper, and read it. His eyes widened and he looked up at her.

"Five thousand dollars," she said. "Just in case."

"How did I get so lucky?" He pulled her into another kiss.

Chapter Forty-Seven

Lawrence couldn't believe she signed the papers. He was panicked when they started talking about religion, worried his whole plan was about to fall apart. The talk of conversion was just to make her stick around, He never imagined she'd jump in further.

He read the form a dozen times before going to bed, and woke once in the middle of the night to check it again.

Five thousand dollars.

He would never have to worry about money again. He could leave town, start a new life. Hell, he could probably stay right here and start a new life. He wondered how to swing that. Call Paul a roommate? He'd heard of women doing that without raising eyebrows.

When he woke in the morning, he went to his brother's.

"Twice in one week?" Charles asked as he let Lawrence in.

"You have always been there for me when I needed you," Lawrence said, refusing the early morning whiskey Charles offered.

Charles left his glass empty as well, concern knitting his features. "Lawrence," he said in a slow tone. "What kind of trouble have you gotten yourself into?"

"No trouble, it's about Ruth."

Charles relaxed. "I liked her. Mother and Father are in a row about her, but I think she is good for you, even without the high breeding they would prefer. Have you set a date?"

"New Year's Eve."

Charles's eyes widened. "Competing with Mother and Father's party, now you really will be out of their good graces."

"No, making it *part* of the party."

"You sly chap." Charles clapped him on the back. "They will be so pleased to parade you both around. What a good plan."

"Maybe," Lawrence said.

"And why not?"

"I have a business proposition for you."

Charles rolled his eyes. "Not this again."

"No, a *real* proposition. For one thousand dollars." Lawrence let his words hang between them.

They got the desired effect.

"Lawrence, what kind of nonsense are you speaking? Who is paying you one thousand dollars?"

"No." Lawrence shook his head. "I'll pay *you* a thousand dollars. Imagine what you can do with that money. You could turn it into something bigger, I know you. With your savvy you could quadruple it in mere months. You could get out from under Father's thumb. Open your own practice."

"He is driving me crazy these days," Charles admitted. "He insists on sitting second chair on my cases, going in on my meetings. It's like I've just graduated law school and haven't been practicing for the last five years. There was a high-profile case the firm lost recently."

"I didn't know that," Lawrence said, though of course he'd read it in the papers.

"Yes, well, it has everyone on edge, Father especially. To open my own firm…"

"And to take a woman out to dinner on your own dime."

"I always use my own dimes," Charles shot back.

Lawrence shrugged. "You know what I mean. To break away. To be a free man, imagine it. Both of us doing whatever we wish, not having to worry about Mother and Father. Never needing their approval ever again."

"What do I have to do?"

"Well, there's the rub. But maybe you wouldn't have to do it at all. I'm sure with your clients, someone has a seedy connection that can help you. I don't think it will be that difficult, nor costly."

"I don't understand."

"Ruth just took out a five-thousand-dollar insurance policy," Lawrence said.

Charles whistled. "That's a lot of money."

"A thousand of it can be yours."

"I don't understand…"

"If she were to meet an untimely end. If you mentioned to a client of yours. Maybe offered to represent them for free on another case if they did you, *us*, this favor."

The slap on Lawrence's face stung through his jaw. The hand appeared unexpectedly. He hadn't shielded himself. Charles's second blow, Lawrence did catch, holding his wrist until he relaxed enough that Lawrence trusted to let go.

"Have you lost your mind?" Charles roared.

"You pulled the trigger for me once before," Lawrence reminded him.

Charles threw his hands into the air. "We were *children,* Lawrence. Holy hell. Are you serious about this?"

Lawrence allowed his face to crumple. "I'm just not sure if I can marry her. Marry anyone." He dramatically flopped onto Charles couch.

Charles was more upset than Lawrence expected. Not that he thought his brother would jump at the chance, but he'd always been there for him. Always done any request. Even beating up boys at school so they'd leave Lawrence alone. Even putting a man in a hospital for starting a rumor about Lawrence being a pretty boy.

"Lawrence," Charles said, his voice softening. "She seems like a nice woman."

"Well, isn't that the crux of the problem?"

Silence hung between them. Lawrence had never spoken so boldly about his sexuality before, but he needed to do anything to divert the conversation and have Charles back on his side. To forget the whole matter.

"There are things that must be done out of duty," Charles said, the words sounding too much like their father's. "She's probably your best bet at doing it right, as funny as that is."

Lawrence nodded and wiped at his eyes for effect. "You're right. It's probably just jitters. You'll see, one day."

"Prayers for that woman." Charles laughed, but it seemed hollow and fake.

He escorted Lawrence to the door, again offering him a drink which he took.

"Brother," Charles said. "What you told me today, what you asked me, you can't mention that to anyone else, I don't care how spooked you get. Be glad that I'm a lawyer and can claim privilege, but you won't have that with anyone else. If they go to the police…"

"I won't. Consider the matter behind me as I leave this place. It was a stupid idea. I am in over my head in a few areas and, well, it seemed an easy way to dig out."

Charles put his hand on Lawrence's shoulder. "I can assure you, it isn't. Why don't you talk to Father? If he knew what trouble you were in, you know he'd help anyway he could."

"Yes, I will do that," Lawrence lied and promptly left the building, walking right into none other than Detective Kelly.

She made a small squeak and he noticed she threw her hand to her stomach, which was covered by a coat that didn't match the warming weather. His own overcoat was a new navy number he'd gotten from Ruth a few weeks back and while not nearly as sharp as the tan one, was at least of a lighter weight of wool.

"Mrs. Kelly," Lawrence said, reaching a hand out to steady her. "My apologies."

Her gaze seemed to linger a beat too long on his sleeve as she steadied herself and straightened her hat.

"The fault is all mine," she said.

He noted that for once, she didn't correct him calling her missus instead of detective.

He gestured behind him. "I was in a rush leaving my brother's and not paying attention. What brings you out at this late hour? Can I get you a car?"

She smiled at him, but it didn't have the same warmth most women bestowed upon a handsome gentleman offering to do a good deed. "I am fine, but thank you."

"Well, I must be off then. You take care of yourself."

He'd taken a few steps toward the road when she called out to him.

"Mr. Henry," she said, her voice faux-casual. "Looks like you are missing a button on your sleeve."

He looked down and sure enough, his right sleeve had a small tuft of empty thread where a button should be. He waved back in thanks and got into a waiting car to take him to the garment district.

When Paul answered the door, Lawrence didn't even let him get a word out.

"I have a plan to get us both out of here."

"Go on then," he said, a bemused expression on his face.

They sat at the ratty kitchen table. Lawrence's chair wobbled slightly from one too-short leg anytime he shifted. He placed his hands on the table and Paul reached across to hold them.

"Ruth just took out an insurance policy."

Paul snatched his hands back.

"Great for you."

"Great for *us*," Lawrence said. "Think about it. We can make a new life."

"Yeah, there's only one issue," Paul said.

"Which is?"

"Isn't she alive?"

"Well, that's what I've come to talk to you about."

Forty minutes later and Lawrence hailed a cab to take him back to his apartment. Paul ran the gambit of emotions. First yelling at Lawrence for having such a wild idea. Then calming down and listening to the ins and outs of it before finally agreeing to help. By the time he was getting his coat, Paul was near giddy in amped up excitement.

"We can do this, we can really pull this off," Paul said, hugging and kissing his neck.

"We can, but we must be careful," Lawrence cautioned. "It will be us after this, just you and me. We won't have to deal with the bullshit of this city anymore, but you have to follow the plan and be patient. And we can't be seen together, we can't have anyone link us. No one's seen us here before, but just in case, I can't come around here until it's over and some time has passed.

"I know it will be hard, but I'll need you to be patient. As soon as it's over, it'll take some time to get the money and get out of here. You've gotta sit tight. I will come for you, I promise. But until then, you have to act like nothing is going on. Can you do that for me?" Lawrence asked, staring hard into Paul's eyes.

"To ensure we can be together? Yes. Anything."

Chapter Forty-Eight

The train bumped and jostled Detective Kelly from side to side as it pulled into the station in Baltimore. Carlson had told her she was crazy, both for traveling alone and going on her day off.

"Waste it however you want," he said after he dropped her off at Penn Station.

She'd told Patrick something came up with work and coordinated with the girl upstairs to help him with the kids. It was the first time she'd lied to her husband in their twelve years of marriage and she felt awful about it the whole trip, but it wasn't like he could come with her. And there was no way he'd let her go. She chalked it up for the greater good. That almost helped her live with it.

She also neglected to tell Carlson the next bit of news she'd learned, which had been brewing in her mind since the previous evening: Lawrence was missing a navy button with an "A" stamped on it.

Her head swam. He was tall and blond just like the man's description and for some reason, he kept popping up. Kelly had worked this beat for six years and she almost never ran into the same people unless they were career criminals. It felt like she was standing on the roof of her apartment building trying to jump up and snatch the stars. The truth seemed right in front of her, but she couldn't quite grasp it.

When they pulled into the station three hours later, Kelly found herself disoriented. She'd been so lost in thought the whole time, it was as if she'd blinked and they'd arrived.

A detective met her at the station and after a moment of hesitation, enthusiastically greeted her.

"Detective Kelly, well I'll be. I heard there were lady cops around, but certainly wasn't expecting one to work homicides. Name's Browne. Pleased to meet you. We're real glad you traveled down here to speak with us."

"Thanks for having me," Kelly said.

Kelly had never been to Baltimore before and she found the city very different than New York. There was so much open space, she felt like she could really breathe. The streets were busy; trolley cars rolling in every direction; but it lacked the "packed like sardines" feel New York had. Their police station looked bright and new, the floors open and filled with cops moving about.

Browne brought her to a large window-filled room where one wall was covered in cork board. On it were pictures of four men and two women in four groupings. Browne explained they were the four homicides that were connected in Chicago and linked to Kelly's cases.

There was a map with four pins in it indicating the location of the murders. Details about the cases, including what was taken, were printed neatly under each grouping.

Kelly walked back and forth, amazed at the organization. She longed to jump right back on the train and do a similar thing in her commandeered conference room back in New York. She knew her boss and boss's boss would have a conniption though, so she'd have to find a way to get them on board. And then she realized it was probably a moot point anyway with what little time she had.

"This is wonderful," she remarked.

"Yeah," Browne said. "Our office girl is a real wiz with these things."

Kelly nodded, pleased there were at least some females working here even if not in the upper ranks.

The door opened and the room filled with fifteen men, most of them smoking cigarettes or gripping coffee mugs. They stopped in their tracks when they saw Kelly standing up at the white board. Browne, evidently sensing the tension in the room and wanting to dispel it, introduced her quickly to the detectives and pointed out who was involved with which cases.

"So, they sent us one of New York's finest we are always hearing about to help us," one of the men said to a round of laughter.

It wasn't the first and was probably far from the last time Kelly would hear such talk directed at her, but her smile faltered.

"She's the one who elicited the help of that Chicago scientist to help link these cases to New York," Browne said.

Like she did with Carlson, Kelly wondered what it was about Browne that made him want to help her. Was he like Carlson with a female family member also in the force, handcuffed by her sex to whatever role some boss was willing to give her?

"Yeah, we heard about that," another of the detectives said, not making eye contact with her. "We were alarmed to hear that this person has moved up to

New York. I've put a call into Philadelphia to let them know he may have made a pit stop there as well since it's on the way."

"Thank you for thinking of that," Kelly said, hoping this was the thaw she needed to make some progress with these guys.

"That's what we detectives do," he said. "Figure out what others can't."

She didn't bother to ask if they considered her an "other."

"Lieutenant Colonel Goddard believes that their Chicago cases happened after Baltimore, but you never know," Kelly said, not wanting him to have the satisfaction of thinking he'd thought of an obvious avenue and she hadn't.

"Not too far away though," the man said, unwilling to relent. "Not unreasonable to think he may have stopped at some point."

"No," Kelly admitted. "Not unreasonable. Have you heard anything back?"

Browne shook his head. "Just contacted them yesterday after you sent that telegram and phoned. They are looking into it, but it will probably take a few days. They have a lot of cases and not a lot of manpower to pull off to search through them."

Kelly turned back to the board. "And you never had any suspects?"

"Of course, we did," a large man in the back called out. "Bunches of 'em, but none panned out. It was like a ghost murdered these people. A ghost that terrorized us for a few weeks and then floated away."

"I'm determined to catch him before he floats away again," Kelly said, the image of Lawrence filling her mind's eye.

****

Four hours later and Kelly was headed back to the train station. The detectives eventually relented and walked her through what they were doing to combat the growing crime rate in Baltimore. Kelly longed to have enough clout in her own department so she could implement some of these ideas. They seemed radical, but usually that's what worked.

Browne shook her hand on the platform after escorting her back to the station.

"You all right traveling solo?" he asked.

"Just like on the way down," she said.

He gave her a sideways smile and nodded.

"Apologies, detective. Not implying that you can't take care of yourself."

His words shocked her. Who was this guy?

"No need to apologize, but yes, I am perfectly comfortable by myself." A half-truth, but close enough.

"My wife always wanted to work on the force," he blurted.

"Oh really, what stopped her?"

Browne laughed and opened his arms. "The real question is, how did no one stop you?"

"Oh, they tried. But like you said, I can take care of myself."

"I'm not going to be a detective forever. One day, one day soon, I'm going to take the lieutenant's test and there will be changes."

"I believe you," she said. "I'd like to see that."

"Is there anything else I can do for you?"

She knew it was too soon to jump into her hunch with two feet, but she had to know. "Is there any way you can knock on some doors and see if a particular individual lived in Baltimore around the time of your murders?"

Browne's eyes widened in surprise at her request. "Is there something you aren't telling us?"

"No, well, I don't think so yet, but I have a name that is cropping up and, well…" She gathered her thoughts. "This will either add fuel or extinguish it. Man of the name of Lawrence Henry."

"Gambler," Browne said without hesitation.

"Pardon?" Kelly asked, her pulse vibrating in her chest.

"Rich kid syndrome. Lived here for a short bit, but coincidence enough, I picked him up one night, poker game gone bad, turned into a brawl. I remember him because his dad bailed him out, come to think of it." Browne looked up for a moment. "Think the dad lived in New York. You don't think…"

Kelly shook her head. "Like I said, just crossing names off a list. Know how long he stayed with you? Any reason to suspect him?"

Browne laughed. "I mean, why would he need to? Sure, seemed like a dolt at cards, but with a rich daddy to cover your losses, who cares, right?"

Kelly agreed.

"You keep us informed if you get any real leads on this case?"

"Yes, of course," Kelly said. "I can't thank you enough for showing me around today. You've given me a lot to think about."

"When I'm running my own department, I'm gonna need some smart minds. You let me know if that New York City gets too big for its breeches and you wanna do some real policing."

She smiled, both as his enthusiasm and optimism for the future. "I will."

Kelly mulled over the conversation the entire ride home. Lawrence had been in Baltimore. He was missing a button. He fit the suspect's description. But the thoughts felt like a bunch of released balloons she was scrambling to grab and hold together. Something hadn't sat right with Kelly the moment she'd met the man, but plenty of guys were elitist jerks, didn't make them murderers. Right?

But she kept coming back to something being off about the man. The image of Ruth popped into her head. Sweet Ruth that looked like her little Mollie. Part of her wanted to get off the train and drive straight to Astor's to warn the woman, but say what? This man who she was seeing had some vague connection to murders? Lawrence would surely get wind of it and sue her and the department for defamation. She'd be pushed out with no shot in the world in solving the case and potentially nailing him.

Warn her just to keep her eyes open? To not trust everything Lawrence said? The information Browne gave her about the gambling issues was news to Kelly. She hadn't heard any rumors around town of a dirty gambler, but then again, who kills a room full of card players but someone on the losing end of a hand?

No, she'd have to sit tight for a little while longer. Collect more evidence. Keep her own eyes and ears open and when the time was right, she'd tell everyone what she knew.

Her mind wandered to Browne's utopia of policing. The chance to work for a department that actually embraced change instead of trying to sweep it under the rug. The idea was exhilarating. Maybe there could be a life for her on the other side of this. Nothing tied her to New York, not really. If Browne's timetable worked out, she could give birth and have time to recover and move. Hell, maybe Baltimore could never even know she'd had another child. There was no reason to tell them. No reason to make them think she was still in the business of expanding her family.

For the first time in a long time, she saw some hope down the road for them. But, of course there were matters to get through first. Growing a tiny human was one of them, but there was no way she could leave town without solving these crimes. If she got pushed out before that happened, they were surely hopeless. Carlson could probably be counted on to carry the torch for a little bit, shake down some leads every now and then, but nothing like she was going to do.

No, she needed to put all the pieces together no matter how impossible it looked. After that, the sky was the limit.

Chapter Forty-Nine

Ruth had only taken two steps down the sidewalk when she heard a car pull up and slow next to her.

"Ruth!" the driver called, and it took her a second to realize it was Lawrence.

She walked over and placed her arms on the open window. The blast of warm air from inside felt fantastic against her face. She'd been outside for mere seconds, but was already trying to figure out how she'd manage in the cold for the whole walk to the restaurant.

Lawrence put the car in park and went to open his door, but she stopped him, surprising them both by opening the passenger door and climbing in.

"A self-sufficient woman," Lawrence said, his eyebrows raised.

"I thought I was meeting you at the restaurant," she said, working the hand-crank to close the window against the air fighting its way in. "What car is this?" She gazed around at the unfamiliar vehicle.

"Mine's in the shop, so I got this as a loan. I needed to make a stop before dinner and realized I was running late, so I thought maybe you'd like to join me on my errand."

She perked up. Lawrence spoke about his work from time to time, but more the overreaching concerns, never the mundane. It was a nice change of pace.

"Okay," she said. "Where are we going?"

"To meet a potential new supplier." He kept his eyes on the road, his face expressionless.

"Supplier for what?" she asked, suspicion filling her words.

"I can't keep being under the thumb of Lucky Luciano."

"Lawrence!" Ruth cried out. "You are bringing me to meet bootleggers? Please, just drop me off at the restaurant. You can meet me there when all this funny business is done." She crossed her arms for emphasis.

"Ruth, open your eyes." His tone darkened. "First off, I have a license to sell liquor, which means I am able to buy it. Second, the longer I am under the control of that *animal*, the further and further away we are from financial freedom. I don't want to rely on my parents. I don't want you to keep working. I want to provide a wonderful life for us and our children."

Our children.

"I-I…" she stammered, unable to formulate a rebuttal. "Won't it be dangerous?"

"I wouldn't be bringing you if I thought it was." He took her hand.

They drove the rest of the way in silence to an area of town she'd never been before. Mainly because her father forbade it and said he would give her a good whooping if he ever found out she'd visited it. There were dark warehouses and the scent of water, fish, and trash started to fill the car. She lifted her hand to her nose to breathe in her jasmine perfume instead of the nauseating smell.

"Now, make sure you pay attention," Lawrence said as they neared the end of the road. "I know you are doing such a wonderful job at Astor's. It would be great if you could transfer to help at the pharmacy after we are married. Brokering these deals is part of that."

She nodded, but a lump was building in her throat. It was so very dark. She wondered why they didn't have streetlights here. The only illumination came from the two weak headlights of the car. It enabled them to see only a few feet in front of themselves, but everything to her side was in shadows. She didn't like this one bit. If this was what working at the pharmacy would be, maybe she'd stick to selling suits.

Her car door was wrenched open. She was about to scream when she realized it was Lawrence. She was so preoccupied in trying to look around, she didn't realize he had parked and got out to open her door.

"This way," he said, putting out his hand to her.

He'd left the headlights on, which threw wild shadows around them, half-blinding her. In the distance, she could make out a figure walking toward them, but couldn't distinguish any features.

Though clearly outlined in its outstretched hand was the unmistakable silhouette of a gun.

Ruth's blood turned to ice beneath her warm jacket. A scream sat like an air bubble in the middle of her throat, trapped by some unseen force. She backed up several steps, but was quickly stopped by the car.

"Lawrence," she whispered. "Lawrence, I want to leave."

But instead of returning to the driver's door or even simply standing in front of her, Lawrence moved to the side. Ruth hoped that he knew the man, that he wasn't worried because maybe this was how these transactions went down, but the deep foreboding feeling in her gut told her otherwise.

"Lawrence," she said again, but it sounded more like a plea this time.

"Who goes there?" Lawrence called to the man, but the figure didn't respond.

When the man stepped into the small orb of light created by the car, Ruth was horrified to see that he wore a mask and dark clothing. She tried to duck behind Lawrence. But he gripped her arms.

"Lawrence?"

Tears swam down her face and she looked up at him. Despite the shadows crossing his face, she could still make out the complete indifference toward her.

What in the hell was happening?

She tried to pull her arms free and get away, but he held on tighter.

The money he'd borrowed. The insistence on the insurance policy. The people after him for money. The growing uneasiness in her stomach she ignored time and time again.

No!

She pleaded with the gunman. "Please, please don't hurt me. I can get you money, I can get you things. Lawrence, please we can figure this out. I can sell everything I own. I can sell what my parents own. I won't tell anyone. I can give you all the money and you'll never have to see me again."

Lawrence responded by spinning her around. "Do it."

Ruth screamed and stomped her heel on his foot. He cried out and his grip loosened enough for her to break free. She darted away, but the other man caught her. She flailed around and pulled at his face, removing the mask. Shock ran through her as she recognized the man from the party.

"Paul?"

He let go of her, eyes wide in terror that must have mimicked her own. Ruth ran, but the darkness and fear had her so disoriented, she soon found herself on the edge of the cement and the river. She turned back. The headlights blinded her.

"Lawrence, please," she yelled out into the abyss of the night.

How had it all gone so wrong? She'd convinced herself they were happy. That her trepidations were just jitters. She should have just stayed in her simple life, traveled the world, and not been so blinded by love. Or what she thought was love.

How had she been so terribly wrong? So foolish to trust him over herself?

Two figures moved toward her, one limping slightly. She wanted to run, but didn't know where, and was too afraid to jump into the icy waters of the river some unknown distance below. Fear rooted her in place.

They blocked the light, allowing her to see again. Paul still held the gun, but his hands shook.

"Do it," Lawrence said.

Paul raised his arm toward her, but nothing happened. Her heart felt like it would explode from her chest in a desperate attempt to escape and survive. She thought how devastated her parents would be. That she wouldn't see her nieces and nephews grow up or her baby sister get married.

She shut her eyes again, the tears made it difficult to see anyway, and prayed for forgiveness. She knew praying for God to save her was futile. He wasn't in this dark alley. All she could hope for was that whatever life was next, she'd find some peace in it.

She opened her eyes to see Paul still frozen in place, his mask haphazardly pulled back down over his face. Lawrence limped toward him.

She might not be able to fully see him, but she would make Lawrence look her in the eye before he pulled the trigger.

Lawrence took the gun and moved toward her, the halo of light surrounding him letting her see his face again as he pointed the weapon toward her.

Ruth stared straight at him. She took one breath. Heard a defining bang.

Then her world exploded into darkness.

Chapter Fifty

Ruth stayed upright for several seconds before she crumpled to the ground. The smell of gun smoke was stronger in the cold air and Lawrence breathed into his jacket to get away from it. Paul stood next to him, as unmoving as he'd been the last few moments.

Lawrence stepped over Ruth's body. He threw the revolver in the river. It splashed as it broke through the surface. He considered pushing Ruth's body in as well, but figured the insurance claim would go smoother if she was found. He heard too many stories of bodies disappearing in the Hudson. He couldn't risk it.

His ears rang with the reverberation of the gunshot as he moved around. He looked at Ruth's body. Her dark eyes reminded him of those deer from his youth. His father's whippings and warnings. The hesitation beaten out of him. His chest tightened. It wasn't that he regretted the act, just needing to do it. How his seemingly privileged life was anything but. His need for scrimping and saving and surviving on the fringes of his family. Maybe in a different world they could have had a decent life together, but it became too complicated. He needed more, more than she'd ever be able to offer him and ended up having to pay the price for his sins.

And really, what was one more to the list of things he'd done to secure his place in the world?

Paul was still rooted in place, his stupid mask still askew on his face. Lawrence told him just to dress normally. They didn't want to tip Ruth off. Didn't want her to scream and possibly draw more attention to them. He knew this area would be empty at this time of night, the workday over and nefarious meetings not beginning for several hours.

When they first pulled up, Lawrence wasn't sure for a second if it really was Paul, worried maybe they'd stumbled upon something else and he'd have to scrap the whole plan. He cursed Paul's stupidity. The darkness would have done the job of concealing him enough. Now he just looked like a fool. This man he'd jeopardized his future for.

He pulled the mask all the way up and slapped Paul in the face. The cold made it feel like hitting concrete and Lawrence's hand stung. The momentary numbness that came with pulling a trigger was melting away, replaced by the overwhelming awareness of their vulnerability.

"Paul, for Christ's sake, you didn't even do anything," Lawrence said.

It was true. For a man who seemed eager to participate, when it came down to it, Paul was unable to pull the trigger. He didn't even put up a fight when Lawrence placed his hands around the weapon. Ruth probably could have taken the gun away from him if she'd tried.

Paul was the one who suggested the staged robbery. He'd even said Lawrence should remain on scene, maybe let Paul rough him up or shoot him in an easily recoverable place, but Lawrence would hear none of it. He couldn't be tied to the crime at all. If Lucky

Luciano was right and he was suspected of murder in other cases, he couldn't chance involvement in this one.

It was Lawrence's idea to come here. The place was known for backdoor deals. He could say Ruth insisted on helping him secure a more reputable seller for his pharmacy needs. He would come clean about Lucky and how they'd shaken him down and up. He told Ruth not to do it. They had dinner plans. She never showed up.

Lawrence checked his watch. His reservation was in fifteen minutes. If he left now, he could just make it.

"Paul," Lawrence said, his voice softer. "Paul, you need to get out of here. Take that stupid mask off and burn it. For that matter, burn everything you are wearing. Go right to the trash incinerator in your building and throw it all in. Then go out. Make sure a bunch of people see you tonight. Make the rounds. Get as many alibis as you can."

Paul's eyes went from glassy to focused. "Lawrence…"

Lawrence shook Paul's shoulders. "You didn't do anything, not really. Just get out of here and have a normal night. Can you do that for me?"

Paul nodded. Lawrence kissed him.

"Good. I will come for you in a few days when all this has died down. We will be fine. Soon I will get the money and we can get the hell out of dodge and start our new life together. You and me. It will all be okay."

Paul broke away from Lawrence without a word and ran into the darkness.

Lawrence returned to the car and gave it a good wiping down with a cloth he found in his pocket, making sure he hadn't left any of his personal belongings accidentally inside, other than the registration papers. The thing was a clunker. He kept it for muddy rides into the country only and was relieved when the damn thing actually started up. He'd only driven it from his parents to the garage. Rides in the country didn't happen as often as Lawrence anticipated.

As he cleaned the car, he considered trying to leave some of her prints, but decided it would be harder to explain why they weren't on the steering wheel. Plus, reasonable to think someone *would* wipe the car down. He closed Ruth's passenger door but left the driver's side open. Make it look like she got pulled from the vehicle.

With a shock he realized the cloth was Ruth's handkerchief, the one she had given him when they met at the New Year's party. It had cleaned up both the start and the end of their relationship.

He checked his watch again. He needed to leave. As the adrenaline of the last few minutes waned, the cold crept in and he tightened his coat and scarf. He walked back to where Ruth lay motionless on the ground. Snow was beginning to fall and it dusted her body. Lawrence reached down, swept the hair from her face and tucked it behind her ear, then stuffed the handkerchief in her pocket.

After one last look, he strolled away.

Chapter Fifty-One

The front desk secretary handed Detective Kelly a steaming cup of coffee as soon as she walked in. That was never a good sign.

"What now?" Her back ached from sitting on the rickety train the day before, but she couldn't risk stretching it backward and pushing her stomach out even more.

"Down by the warehouses, a woman was killed, Carlson is already there."

Kelly groaned and took a sip from the cup.

When she arrived at the warehouse district, it swarmed with people. Reporters loved early morning crimes because it gave them all day to get the story and make it to the presses. There were dozens lined up, along with a handful of photographers desperate for a glimpse.

They stamped their feet against the bitter cold. A thin layer of snow covered the spring ground, giving the place an ethereal look Kelly knew was false. Her own legs burned and she cursed the fact that, even with this cold snap, she couldn't wear pants. Why parading around in a skirt did anything to make her look more professional was beyond her. If anything, it probably made people take her less seriously.

She slipped on a patch of black ice and flung a hand out to steady herself, catching a female reporter's coat sleeve.

"Apologies," Kelly said.

The woman smiled at her. "You can give me a statement and we'll be even."

"Once I have something to say, you'll be sure to know it."

Fishing wire held a sheet in place between two buildings on the narrow alleyway against the gusts picked up by the water. Trampled snow turned into a muddied mess.

"Get back," Kelly growled as she pushed through.

One of the cops holding the front of the line looked her up and down before he nodded and allowed her to pass.

On the other side of the sheet, was a parked car with its driver's side door open. Kelly removed a glove and placed her hand on the hood. Ice cold. A man sat in the vehicle, spreading fine, black powder with a brush, looking for prints. He shook his head when Kelly made eye contact.

"Damn," Kelly whispered.

Carlson had a look of foreboding that Kelly wasn't used to seeing. He held a hand up. "I'm not sure if you really want to…"

Kelly ignored him and advanced, tightness forming at the back of her throat.

A police photographer crouched over the body, so it took a moment for Kelly to see the woman's face. Her eyes were wide open, the deep brown irises now milk white and frozen in place. Flecks of snow in her hair. Her mouth a silent "O", as if she'd been shocked at whatever happened the moment before her death.

No, not *her*.

Ruth Smith.

It was the first time in her career that she'd recognized one of the bodies. Tears sprang to her eyes and she didn't bother wiping them away. She'd just spoken to Ruth. Just the other day when …

Lawrence Henry.

She knew it. Knew it! Knew that man was involved in terrible activities, and now here was proof. There was no way the man would weasel his way out of this one. No amount of suave rich kid privilege would prevent Kelly from nailing the guy.

"It was Lawrence Henry," Kelly said.

Carlson shook his head. "Kelly, I know you are upset—"

"It's too much of a coincidence. He's the constant. They change, who it is changes, in a way, but he's connected to them all."

"No," Carlson says. "He has money. That is his only connection to the East-to-West murders. He has no connection to the bathhouse. To the prostitute."

"I didn't tell you because I was still fleshing it out, but I saw him the other day. He was missing a button."

Carlson held up his arm to show his sleeve. "So am I. So much for quality engineering."

She shook her head, refusing to be brushed off. "He was in Baltimore."

He gave a small shake of his head. "When?" Carlson asked.

"During the time of the murders there."

"Lots of people have lived in Baltimore."

"He was *with* Ruth."

Carlson placed a hand on Kelly's shoulder. "He was engaged to Ruth. Why would he kill her? What could he possibly gain?"

"I don't know, not yet, but I will." She paused, fighting through her emotions. "I should have warned her."

"Who?"

Kelly gestured behind them. "Ruth. I should have said something, I could have maybe—"

"Johanna," Carlson said.

The use of her first name shook the dread building in her.

"You know as well as I do that in no way would you have made that kind of leap on a hunch. Plus, we still don't—"

"*I'm* sure. And I'm gonna nail him."

"All right, I'm not saying that I believe you, because I don't, but why don't we go talk to the guy? Sort this all out. We need to anyway, to ask him if he saw Ruth last night. But first." Carlson took a big sigh. "We gotta go talk to her parents. They'll be moving this body soon and when they do, those reporters are going to be asking a million questions and putting things together. We gotta get to them first."

"Yeah, yeah sure," Kelly said, but her mind was elsewhere. There was no way she would let Lawrence Henry out of her grasp this time.

He placed a hand on her again and when she didn't look at him, gently took her chin in his hand.

"This isn't your fault. No matter what happens. No matter if Lawrence did or didn't do this or if we can or can't prove it. This isn't on you."

She didn't believe his words but nodded all the same and followed him out of the scene.

****

Kelly and Carlson knocked on the door of the address corresponding to Ruth's operator's license. A woman the spitting image of Ruth, but about twenty years older, answered the door.

"Did you find her?"

"Ma'am?" Carlson asked.

"I know he said he was going to call you, but I didn't expect you so quickly. I imagine that's good? You found her? I knew it was all a misunderstanding. See, I told you all this was a misunderstanding," the woman called out behind her, presumably to someone else in the apartment.

"Ma'am," Carlson repeated. "May we come in?"

The detectives introduced themselves and the apartment's occupants stared at Kelly with narrowed eyes as Carlson took off his hat. Ruth's mother, father, two sisters—one holding a small bundle wrapped in a blue blanket—two men who appeared to be in relations with the sisters, and two children spilled into the cramped living room in the wake of Kelly and Carlson. Mrs. Smith offered them coffee. They nodded their appreciation.

"I know it's cold out there with this random snap. I thought we were through with winter. Was sure spring was here to stay," Mrs. Smith said. "It must have been hard work walking the streets to find her. Please, tell me, did she go into work after all? Her father wanted to wait until the store opened, but I said, no, no she may have gone in early."

"Mrs. Smith," Kelly started, but the mother raised her hand.

"That Ruthie, always a go-getter, from a young age..." she said, as the husband placed his hand on her arm, directing her to the couch.

"Why don't you let them speak, Priscilla?" he asked gently. "Detectives, please, help us clear up this misunderstanding."

"Did you see your daughter last night?" Kelly asked.

"Briefly," her father said. "We were on our way out for the evening. Our daughter, Della, had us over for dinner." He motioned to the woman holding the small boy.

"And was she planning on staying home?" Carlson asked.

"When we left, we weren't sure, but when we arrived home there was a note on the kitchen table that she was meeting Lawrence Henry, her fiancé, for dinner," Priscilla said. "But then she didn't come home last night, which isn't like her. I know women these days are becoming more progressive and she is engaged, but it just isn't like her…"

"Mother," Della said in a warning tone.

"She is a good girl," her father echoed. "She would not stay at a man's house."

"But she didn't come home last night?" Kelly asked, trying to keep the emotion out of her voice.

Here was this family, this desperate, hopeful family, and Kelly had nothing good to tell them.

"I should have checked in her room as soon as we got home," Priscilla said and she started to cry.

Mr. Smith patted her hand and spoke softly to her.

"You couldn't have known, Mama," the other sister said.

Kelly couldn't remember her name.

"So, you realized this morning?" Carlson asked.

"Yes," Priscilla sniffled. "And Lawrence came almost as soon as we realized that. He looked frantic once we said she wasn't here. He said he was supposed to meet her for dinner, but she never showed up. Thought maybe they got their signals crossed."

"I see," Kelly said, trying to keep her voice flat and without the contempt she felt.

"But you found her, right? That's what you came to tell us?" Priscilla asked.

The hope in her eyes made it difficult for Kelly to get the next words out.

"Mrs. Smith, yes, we did find her—"

"Oh, thank the Lord!" she exclaimed.

The family jumped up and began hugging each other.

"Mrs. Smith, Mrs. Smith," Kelly said until she got their attention.

Her face must have conveyed what her words were about to, because they all froze.

"No," Della whispered.

"I am afraid we found her body this morning," Carlson said.

The wail that came out of the mother was so animalistic, Kelly fought the building urge to cover her ears.

"I am so sorry for your loss," Kelly said, but she was pretty sure no one heard her. She couldn't even imagine someone coming to her home to say one of her children was dead. She wanted to vomit at the thought.

Before they left, Carlson gave his contact information to Della's husband. Though shocked, he appeared to be the most put-together of the bunch.

"We will find whoever did this," Kelly promised.

"What does that matter now?" he responded.
Kelly didn't know how to answer him.

Chapter Fifty-Two

Lawrence checked his reflection in the rearview mirror. His eyes were red-rimmed from lack of sleep. He rubbed them vigorously to make them look worse before stepping into the police station. He strode up to a woman sitting behind a reception desk and asked to speak to an officer about a missing person.

"Missing?" she asked.

"Yes," he said, trying to keep his voice rough. "My fiancée."

The woman nodded and motioned for someone to come over. A uniformed man introduced himself as Officer Allen and motioned for Lawrence to follow him to his desk. He offered Lawrence a coffee, which he gratefully accepted. He wanted to be holding something, give his hands something to do. Have an excuse for regular pauses to take drinks. Plus, any normal, distraught person would ask for one.

Allen returned and handed the cup to Lawrence, who cradled it in his hands without drinking.

"Can you tell me what this is about?" Allen asked. "Someone is missing?"

"Yes, my fiancée. Ruth Smith."

Allen nodded and jotted some notes down. "And how long has Miss Smith been missing?"

"I'm not sure exactly, sometime last night." Lawrence looked at the floor, allowing blood to rush to his head and causing his eyes to water a little.

"You're not sure?" Allen asked.

"We were supposed to meet for dinner, but she never showed up. I called at her apartment, but no one answered. I assumed that we got our signals crossed. Maybe she had gone out with her parents. She lives with her parents in their apartment."

"Okay, so you went to her parents' apartment, where she also lives. Does anyone else live there?"

Lawrence nodded and took a sip of the weak excuse for coffee. "Her younger sister."

"Who was also not at the apartment?" Allen asked.

"No, though she is rarely there. She is getting married soon so she tends to spend much of her time with her future husband."

"I see," Allen said, writing a few more notes down.

"And have you spoken to her family?"

"Yes, I am coming from there, actually."

"And she was not with them last night?" Allen asked.

"No, no they said they thought she was with m-me…" Lawrence brought the cup to his lips, but only mimed drinking it. He couldn't swallow another sip.

"So why didn't they report her missing?" Allen sat up straighter in his chair.

"They didn't realize. They had gone out last night, they said she was still at the apartment and when they returned, they assumed she hadn't come back yet. They went to bed and realized this morning she'd never returned. I arrived soon after that and offered to talk with the police. They were very distraught. I suggested they stay in the apartment in case she came home."

Allen nodded. "Smart thinking."

Lawrence had the feeling Allen was just humoring him. The officer probably didn't think Ruth was missing at all. Maybe he wondered if she'd left with another man. Lawrence was sure they saw all types here. He figured that would work in his advantage. He could play dumb. And they were probably stupid enough to fall for it.

"Do you have any idea where she may have gone?" Allen asked.

"I know she worked during the day. She is the store manager for Astor's. She was going to run an errand for me after work. Then we were to meet for dinner."

"An errand?"

Lawrence hesitated for a moment. He hoped it would be a convincing display of remorse. "Yes, I-I own a pharmacy, and with the recent unpleasantness that has come upon my industry, I have been finding it difficult to find suppliers for some of my goods. Not everyone wants to do business with me."

"I see," Allen said.

"Ruth offered to go meet with someone she said she knew, maybe through the store? I can't remember how she said she knew this person, but she said she could speak with him, maybe convince him to do business with me, with us. She is an investor as well, you see." Lawrence added that last bit as bait.

"She invested in your pharmacy?"

"Yes, I thought it could be a good investment for her. She had been saving some money and was looking to do something with it. She said what could be better than—than our future." Lawrence closed his eyes and made a point of taking a steadying breath.

"And you have no idea who this person was that

she was meeting?"

"No, no. I wish now I had pressed her. Had insisted that I went as well, but she seemed so certain. I assumed it was someone from the store, you see. It's a high-end store, Astor's. Do you know it?"

"I do," Allen said.

"Right, so I guessed it was someone from there. Maybe someone with connections. She asked if she could borrow a car—"

"Your car?"

"Yes, well, one of my cars. I had one I didn't use very much. She said she would take that so that after work she could meet the person then join me for dinner."

"And you don't know what time she was supposed to see this person?"

"No, I just knew we were supposed to be at the restaurant at eight to eat. I waited until nine and she never showed up."

"And this wasn't odd to you?"

"Well, of course it was. That's why I went by her place, but she wasn't there and her parents weren't there. I just figured it slipped her mind we had plans. She had been very preoccupied at work and with the meeting. I figured maybe she'd forgotten."

"Well, let me get some information about her description. I can start writing up a report, and we can get looking. Mr. Henry. We *will* find your fiancée."

At that moment, two individuals burst through the door to the precinct, one with a female voice that seemed angry.

Someone needed to put her in her place.

"No, get your hands off me, I'm fine," the voice

yelled through the department noise.

Lawrence looked up to see Detective Kelly, her partner holding one arm, and two men approaching them. Kelly stopped in her tracks, wrenched her arm free, and straightened her coat.

He locked gazes with her and a shiver ran up his neck.

Chapter Fifty-Three

Detective Kelly nearly choked on her anger and frustration when Lawrence Henry looked at her and without blinking, gave the slightest smile. She was half-tempted to reach across Carlson, unholster his Model 10, and shoot the man right there. Save everyone the trouble of arresting him and having a trial. She'd be a hero.

As if Carlson could sense what went through Kelly's mind, he put a gentle hand on her arm. It was just enough to break the spell. To add clarity to the situation. Kelly strode away, the men following her muttering about "crazy woman" and "time of the month". She should shoot them, too.

"We need to take this slow, do this right," Carlson said when he'd pulled Kelly into the commandeered conference room. "Maybe bring the lieutenant into this."

"Not yet," Kelly said. "Soon, but not quite yet. I want to go talk to Mr. Henry."

"Bad idea," Carlson said.

"Hear me out, I have a relationship of sorts with him. Don't you think it would be strange if I saw him here and didn't go see him? I can be the sympathetic female ear. He won't suspect that. Plus, he's going to find out about Ruth as soon as he goes to the parents' house. If it comes from us, we not only get to control what information is given to him, but get to see his reaction. That way he can't get spooked and run."

"I don't know…"

"I won't let on that we think he has anything to do with it. Why don't you bring him into a room, Allen as well? Just say that we want somewhere private for someone of his stature, something like that. Stoke his ego. I'll give it a minute and come in and break the news. Have the lieutenant watch through the glass. You guys can get a read on him."

"All right. I don't like it, but I agree that it's better for us to see the reaction to the news. Might help us. I don't know how yet, but can't hurt."

Carlson left and Kelly paced the room. It was lined with boxes and papers, not just from her cases, but ones Goddard linked for her from Baltimore and Chicago as well. This could be it. All her work, obsession, hours from home, were finally going to pay off and be worth it. She would close this case, and even when they found out she was pregnant, they'd be so grateful they'd let her stay. She'd avenge Ruth and save herself all in the same swoop. She would make Lawrence pay.

As sick to her stomach as she was about not being able to stop Lawrence in time, she also couldn't believe her luck. To walk into the station and have her number one suspect just sitting there. That only happened in the pictures. She needed to make sure that she played this correctly. She couldn't tip Lawrence off that they knew he was involved. That they suspected him in this or any other murder. He was a flight risk if Kelly had ever seen one.

Kelly counted to ten and walked to the interview room. As she entered, Lawrence rose and took her hand, then kissed the top.

"Detective Kelly."

"Mr. Henry."

"You two know each other?" Allen asked.

Kelly gave a bright smile. "In passing. Please, continue."

"Mr. Henry here was filing a missing person's report," Allen said.

Lawrence nodded solemnly. Kelly found it almost believable. Allen sure as hell did.

"It's Ruth," Lawrence said, dropping his head into his hand for a few moments before looking up again. "I'm afraid we don't know where she is. Her family and I are very worried."

Sure you are.

Kelly brought over a chair and sat in between Lawrence and Allen.

"Mr. Henry, I am terribly sorry to be the one to have to tell you this." Kelly kept her voice low and tight, allowing the emotion she typically kept at bay out a little. Playing the acting game right back. Lawrence looked up, his features pinched.

"No," he whispered.

"We found Ruth's body this morning."

"No!"

The scream from Lawrence shocked even Kelly. Allen jumped up and automatically hovered his hand over his weapon before lowering it and himself back to his chair.

"I am so sorry. I have just informed her parents." Kelly kept her voice filled with softness and sympathy. She didn't want to play it up too much though, risk Allen thinking she was getting too emotional and suggest she leave. "She was in the warehouse district."

Lawrence looked up sharply. "Warehouse? What was she doing there?"

"Sir," Allen said tentatively. "Didn't you say she was meeting with a possible supplier?"

Lawrence looked at Allen for a beat before recognition washed over his features. "Yes, yes, but I don't think she would have met someone there. You must be mistaken. Are you sure it's Ruth? Maybe just someone who resembles her?"

Allen gazed helplessly at Kelly, but Kelly was unmoved. She couldn't wait to get her hands on Allen's report, whether the rookie cared she was a woman or not. She needed to see what web Lawrence spun to figure out how to untangle it.

"I saw her myself," Kelly said.

Her voice hitched and she swallowed hard to clear it. The pain was still real and raw. It was hard to keep that and the anger under the surface and she found herself with the strength to only support the one.

"Who did this?" Lawrence asked.

"I was hoping you could help with that," Kelly said.

"You're sure you don't know who she was meeting?" Allen asked. He leaned forward as if he could physically will the answer out of Lawrence. "You said maybe someone from the store? Had she spoken about someone with those kinds of connections before?"

"I don't think so."

"Think," Kelly said. "Or someone she squabbled with, who may want to do her harm."

"I don't know how long you've been on the force,"

Lawrence said, with a hardness to his eye. "But typically badgering a witness doesn't suddenly pull information out of them."

Kelly's face burned. "We just want to find out who did this, just like you."

"There was a Mr. Buchanan who gave her trouble from time to time. I know she talked about him, but I don't know why she would meet him somewhere."

"Buchanan, you say?" Allen asked, writing the name down.

"And...no. No, never mind," Lawrence said.

"Anything is helpful," Kelly said. "Anything you can remember, any lead that may help."

"This woman at the store, they didn't get along."

"Woman?" Allen asked, his eyebrows raised.

"Yes." Lawrence sat up straighter, as if this thought invigorated him. "Rebecca. I'm not sure what her last name is, but she is the only Rebecca that works at the store. Mrs. Astor should be able to give you her information."

"And she had a problem with this Rebecca?" Kelly asked.

"From what Ruth tells me, the woman thought she should have gotten the management job after Mr. Astor passed away."

"Was killed," Kelly said.

She couldn't help herself. She wanted to see if the correction would rattle Lawrence. It didn't appear to, but he did narrow his eyes for a moment as if he was sizing her up.

Shit. Had she blown it? Shown her hand?

He laced his fingers together and stared at her. "Yes, well, Rebecca thought she should get it."

"But you helped Ruth get the job?" Kelly asked, hoping if she asked more questions about this Rebecca character, Lawrence would relax.

"Yes."

"And can you think of anyone else?" Allen asked.

Lawrence shifted in his seat, catching Kelly's gaze a few times.

"Allen, can you give us a minute?" Kelly asked.

The young cop opened his mouth as if to protest, but dipped his head and left.

"What?" Kelly's tone had an edge, she couldn't help it. Even with Lawrence appearing suspicious of her, her patience waned.

"I can trust you, right?" Lawrence asked, his voice so low, Kelly leaned forward to hear him.

"Of course," she said automatically, her heart picking up its pace as she realized she was in a room alone with this man and without a weapon.

"Only," Lawrence glanced at the table. "Only I didn't mention it before because I was afraid. Still am, I guess." Lawrence shrugged before lifting his gaze. "Lucky."

"Luciano?" Kelly had to give it to him. This was a hell of an angle he was playing.

"Yeah, well, he came by my place a while back, roughed me up a bit."

"I see. This wouldn't happen to be around the time that boy Billy was killed?"

"So, you understand why I couldn't come to you?" Lawrence said. There was genuine remorse in his voice.

"And you think Lucky may have had something to do with Ruth?" Kelly asked.

"He was upset I tried to go with another supplier

after he made it pretty clear he was supposed to be the only game in town. I only slipped up once. He caught me and threatened Ruth, along with both our families. It was a while ago., I thought I was back in his good graces, but then I fell a little behind on my payments again. It's all sorted out now. But maybe he was trying to teach me a lesson."

Tears welled up in Lawrence's eyes. If Kelly were a gullible woman, she'd probably believe him.

"Right. Well, we will look into it. Thanks for the information."

Lawrence nodded. "May I go now? I would like to be with Ruth's family."

He put on his coat.

"Of course," Kelly said.

They stood and Kelly shook Lawrence's hand, holding on to it for a second longer than socially normal, turning his arm slightly.

"You really should get that button replaced," Kelly said.

Lawrence looked down, as if he'd forgotten it was missing and picked at the thread. "I certainly have more pressing matters."

"Of course, my manners." Kelly let go of his hand. "I am sorry for your loss, Mr. Henry. I liked Miss. Smith. We will get to the bottom of who did this to her. We will make him pay."

Kelly held his gaze until Lawrence looked away.

When Lawrence left, Kelly went to Allen. "I want someone watching that man around the clock."

"I don't take orders—"

"Cut the shit," Kelly said. "I don't want him out of our sights for one second and if I suspect that one of you looked away for just a moment to admire your dick while taking a piss…" She stood to her full height and put her nose almost at his chin. "I'll make sure you never work in this godforsaken town again. Do you understand that?"

Allen's eyes widened, the vulgarity probably shocking him more than her actual threat. But he rushed away without comment, leaving Kelly to agonize over her next move to nail Lawrence once and for all.

Chapter Fifty-Four

The afternoon had been a disaster. Some idiot let it slip to a reporter that the department had linked various homicides by using forensic evidence, and that it looked like a mass killer, Ruth being the latest victim. They even had the information about Baltimore and Chicago. That made the evening paper. The city exploded in fear and anger at being kept in the dark. As had Kelly's bosses.

"I should take your badge for this!" Captain Wade yelled, not bothering to close his office door. "You walk around here like you're better than everyone. Haughty, like a bitch."

Lieutenant Porter stood silently beside him. Kelly set her jaw. He'd gone too far, but didn't appear to feel sorry about it.

"You *should* take the badge of whatever shitter talked to the papers," Kelly said. She was angry at that person, sure, but also knew she deserved at least some of this thrashing.

She'd gone off protocol, way off. Involved other agencies and made decisions that weren't hers to make. It was a wonder she wasn't fired on the spot but they probably feared the press would get wind of that, too. A female cop potentially solves a gigantic case and they sack her? In a city that liked to think of itself as more progressive than it really was, she knew that wouldn't fly in the press.

"When all this is over," the captain said, waving his arms in the air, "we'll discuss whether you have a future within this department. I'm sure the matrons at the jail would gladly take you back. We did you a favor by giving you this job and I can take it back whenever the hell I want."

Kelly was crestfallen. How had she'd let it get so far? In hindsight she should have involved a superior right away. At least the second she got Chicago involved. Sure, she'd mentioned something to a lieutenant, but just in passing, and she knew he'd disregard her.

They most likely would have taken the case away from her. It was stupid. Her goal should have been to get it solved, no matter who got the credit. She messed up and it was possible a woman was dead because of it.

At this point, all she could hope for was they'd let her keep working the case. The limited amount of power she had was surely all that kept her inside this building and not promptly dragged out.

****

Over the next few days, her commandeered conference room became headquarters. Secretaries moved rolling blackboards into the space and Kelly began feverishly writing information. It didn't look as polished and connected at Baltimore's. Nerves made her normally neat handwriting look shaky and a few times Carlson gave her a small nod. But it was also clear he was avoiding her a bit in case anyone accused him of knowing about this whole scheme and keeping quiet about it.

As she wrote the names and brief summaries of the

cases, the silence in the room grew. By the time she got to the final blank space, the chalk reduced to nubs, all gazes were on her. She'd convinced them; she could feel it.

Lawrence played his part. Kelly had to give him that. Ruth's family gave a statement to the papers, asking the public for their help in solving the case. Kelly's boss was livid. How dare they accuse the police of not being able to do this on their own?

Kelly, on the other hand, was glad they'd spoken about it. She did need the help of the public. With the sheer number of crimes, they needed to find a witness. There was no way they could interview everyone in the city, hoping they stumbled across the one person who'd seen something. But chances were that person read the papers.

Lawrence made statements as well as putting up a cash reward to anyone who came up with information leading to a conviction. Kelly marveled at the man's cleverness. He was seasoned and it showed.

"Why would he offer up a reward if it's just going to lead to him?" Carlson asked. "It doesn't make sense. He's gotta not know who did it, Kelly. If it was him, he'd want the heat off him. This just ratcheted it up."

Which, Kelly had to admit, was true. Calls and reports were flooding in from all over the city, especially from the areas that were still held firmly down from the depression. Five hundred dollars was a lot of money. Everyone wanted it.

"So, we've been getting a lot of people *saying* they saw something, but has anyone actually given any useful leads yet?" Kelly asked.

"No."

"Exactly. He knows we don't have anything on him, and he's damn confident he thinks him cleverer than us. He doesn't think anyone saw anything. He thinks his money and his reputation are safe."

As Kelly left the station that afternoon—a quick trip home before she was on the midnight surveillance shift—she saw Lawrence in the lobby of the station, talking animatedly with the secretary.

"Mr. Henry," Kelly said as she strode up.

The wide-eyed secretary's looked like she was caught in a trap and about to gnaw a limb off to escape.

"D-detective," she stammered. "This gentleman is requesting a death certificate, but I am trying to tell him I can only release that to next of kin."

"She's correct, Mr. Henry. That information can only be released to her parents. They will need to authorize us to give you a copy or they can make one themselves," Kelly said. She noted the rising irritation in Lawrence's demeanor.

"This is ridiculous! We were engaged to be married," Lawrence said.

"If you were married, then we could release it to you, but unfortunately that's how the law works. Our hands are tied. Why don't you come back in the morning with one of her parents?"

"I am trying to save them the trouble. Plus, how do you think we can give such a substantial reward if we don't have the money to pay it?"

Kelly's senses snapped into focus. "The money?"

Lawrence sighed as if they were all fools. "The insurance money. To help pay the reward. I need the death certificate for the insurance money."

"Right," Kelly said in a tone that suggested she

was just a bit slow on the uptake. "It has been a long day, Mr. Henry. Why don't you go home and get some dinner and some sleep? It looks like you could use both. Then come back here in the morning with one of her parents or a copy of the insurance policy and we can sort this all out."

He narrowed his eyes.

Money.

The pieces slowly clicked together. She wouldn't have thought a man from a wealthy family would do such a thing, but wasn't that the perfect hiding place? Plus, her years on the force had taught her one lesson over and over. A person who feels trapped will do just about anything to get away.

"You take care, Mr. Henry," Kelly said, driving home how he should leave.

It was getting near shift change and Lawrence stepped back as a dozen or so men entered the lobby including the lieutenant.

"My apologies, detective," he said with a gleam in his eye.

A foreboding feeling entered Kelly's stomach.

"Wouldn't want to do anything to someone in your condition."

The men around her paused. She froze.

"I'd hate for anything to happen to that baby." He touched Kelly's midsection for a moment before exiting.

Kelly closed her eyes, blocking out the scene of her imploding career.

Chapter Fifty-Five

Lawrence was furious he still didn't have the death certificate. Why did it take so long for the police to get their shit together? Didn't they know how the world worked? That people needed to move on with their lives? And how could they possibly do that when the police held them up with procedures?

It was a ridiculous complication he hadn't anticipated. He was a holder on an insurance policy and Ruth's fiancé for Christ's sake.

His anger boiled up again when he thought of the way Detective Kelly spoke to him. That uptight bitch. Hadn't he just lost his future wife? Didn't that deserve a certain measure of respect? The detective didn't think so. Practically threw Lawrence out of the station. Questioned his belonging there, his right to anything of Ruth's.

Lawrence would show her. He'd get those papers, cash in on the policy, and be long gone before Detective Kelly even knew what happened. Hell, he said the pregnancy thing loud enough, and from the look on her face, it was clear she was trying to hide it. She'd probably be out on her ass by the end of the week. Served her right for questioning his authority.

No one else looked at him funny, sniffed around like she did, so there was a slim chance anyone would find out about his connection to the murders. And if—

and that was an unlikely if—they ever did put it together, they'd never be able to find him. He was a free man.

He took a deep breath and collapsed into his couch. The day had been more exhausting than he'd anticipated. Ruth's family was tedious in their grief. He kept trying to get away, but any time he mentioned leaving, her mother would go into a fresh bit of sobs and an aunt or someone would whip up some more food and try to feed them all.

Even his own parents had sent a note of their sympathy and worry for him. They asked him if they could visit the next day. Lawrence was shocked. They'd never been to his apartment before. Granted, he hadn't invited them to his parties, but still. They paid rent on it dutifully each month having never stepped foot inside.

And, Christ, once the news hit in the papers that she may be the victim of someone they were now calling the East-To-West Killer, even more attention was on them. If Lawrence had to squeeze one more tear out for an interview, he thought he'd die of dehydration. And really, where did they get this idea? How in the world had the cops connected the cases from Baltimore, Chicago, and New York? The papers had been mum on that, just saying that a connection had been found, but not how they knew.

At least in Ruth's case he'd used the poker man's stolen gun, and got rid of it right after. He was glad he'd had the sense to do that. He was about to put it back in his coat when the idea of carrying it around with him left an unpleasant feeling in his stomach. Throwing it into the river let him wash its wrongdoing off him.

Because here, in the dark, alone with his thoughts, he missed her. Damn it.

Every time he closed his eyes he saw her face. Not the terrified one. The calm one. The one that stared straight at him. That made him lock eyes with her before he pulled the trigger. The one that dared him to do it and then live with it. In the end, she hadn't begged, not like the others. Hell, she hadn't even muttered a word once she knew her fate. She'd known there was no way out of it, so she chose defiance. She stared straight at him with a mix of disappointment and resolve. It was a look he'd never seen before and that rattled him.

Her face stared back at him all day, from behind his eyelids and behind the rows of picture frames in her parents' house. They began talking details of her funeral. They included Lawrence, which made him feel odd at first until he figured it out. They expected him to pay.

Of course they did. Anytime someone without money was around someone *with* money, they expected that person to pick up the tab. It was no worry to them to say they wanted the nicest casket. The plot in the desirable tree-lined location. They would spare no expense because it wasn't their expense to worry about.

The assumption infuriated Lawrence. It was *their* daughter after all. Why shouldn't they pay for the funeral? But of course Lawrence couldn't say that. He had to play the part of the grieving fiancé. The stoic member of the family continuing on in Ruth's wake. Maybe he'd let his parents pay. It would be the polite thing for them to ask. They'd want to help, know what they could do. It would be perfect. They could chip in for once.

Without having the insurance money, there was no way he could afford it anyway. And that money was already spoken for. Lawrence had packed a bag with what few valuables he had to be ready for the money to come through. Then he'd leave town. Go west somewhere. Some place wild and isolated. Some place no one would ask questions about who he was or where he came from. He'd change his name and disappear.

He just needed the damn death certificate.

Lawrence closed his eyes again, ignoring the image of Ruth, and began to drift asleep. His body was close to being pulled under when there was a soft knock at the door. He looked at his watch. One twenty-two a.m. Who in the bloody hell was calling at this hour? If it was a reporter, he would shoot him.

He patted his pockets as he walked to the door before remembering he no longer had a weapon. That would need to be remedied quickly.

Lawrence pulled the door open, revealing a wild-eyed Paul in the hallway.

"Are you insane?" Lawrence hissed and pulled Paul into his apartment.

"I hadn't heard from you all day," Paul said. His gaze still darted around as though he was waiting for someone to jump out at him.

"Because I told you. We need to lay low for a while. I said a few days. Paul, shit." Lawrence rubbed his forehead. "Did you at least burn the clothes? Please tell me you didn't screw that up, too?"

Paul looked taken aback. "Yes, I did just as you told me."

"Except for coming here. Were you followed?"

Lawrence moved to the window to look out, but didn't see anyone in the street.

"Followed? Why, are we suspected?" Paul's voice was panicked.

"No, no." Lawrence took a deep breath and decided he needed to take another approach. "But it isn't safe for you to be here, for us to be seen together." Lawrence kept his voice soft, trying to relax Paul.

"I can't get the sound of her scream out of my head." Paul started to cry.

Lawrence held him, kissing the top of his head. "Shh. Listen, it will be okay, but I need you to go home and act as if everything is fine. I am going to the insurance company tomorrow and I will get the money. In a few days, after the funeral, we will quietly slip out of town and start a new life together, understand?" Lawrence felt Paul's head nod against his chest.

"I just needed to see you." Paul sniffled.

"I know, but it can't happen again." Lawrence lifted Paul's face and kissed him, then led him to the door. "I am serious, Paul. We can't be seen together. You have to promise me you will never come back here. I will come for you. It can't be the other way around. We can't risk this now." He kissed his fingers.

"All right."

"Goodnight," Lawrence said and shut the door softly.

The sound of his thundering heart filled his ears.

Chapter Fifty-Six

"In my office, *now.*"

Kelly didn't have to open her eyes to know who spoke. The reckoning had come. She was so close and now it was all going to be taken from her. Tears prickled her eyes, but she refused to give into them. It was a painful truth to know they'd only think even less of her.

She followed the lieutenant like a kicked dog, head bent and shoulders slouched. Scenarios ran through her mind. She had about four months left to go before the baby would be born. She couldn't be out of work that whole time. Would the prison take her back? Hell, she'd take anything they'd give her. That fact made her feel even more defeated than before.

The members of her department worked for years to break her down, and the soft words of a murderer finally got the job done.

Lieutenant Porter shut his office door, but that was for show. "Take off that foolish jacket."

He might have well used a bull-horn for how loudly he laid into her. He leaned forward and lowered his voice, the effect more chilling than the yelling. "Take off your fucking coat."

Her hands shook as she undid each button and pulled it from her shoulders. There was no sucking it in; the bulge pressed against her undershirt.

"Jesus fucking Christ. Kelly! What in the holy mother of God fuck is this horse shit!"

"Sir—"

"You better hope the ladies downstairs have a desk for you."

"Yes, sir."

He paused for a moment and looked at her. "Or I may have a better idea." He rifled through several files while he muttered to himself.

Kelly's heart rate increased and sweat built behind her knees.

"Yes," he said and waved a file at her. "This will be perfect. We can use this unfortunate turn of events in our favor. You can report right away, no time to waste."

He slid the file over and she gripped it with her fingertips, *Westin Women's Clinic* scrawled on the tab. Her heart beat even faster.

"Lieutenant—"

"You'll go in and request the procedure, let them do the full work, make them think they're gonna do the procedure, and chicken out at the last minute."

She thought she would be sick. "I don't think I can—"

"Nonsense. This is perfect. We've been trying to nab this place, especially for late-term terminations, but for whatever reason it's been hard to find someone to go undercover. This works," he said, more to the room than her.

She couldn't move. Every fiber of her being screamed that it was wrong. Told her not to leverage her baby to hurt other women. To hurt the doctors helping these women. And what if she was seen? Either her cover as a detective would be blown and the clinic would kick her out, or someone would think she was there for the procedure. Both were terrible in almost equal measures.

"I don't think—"

"This is your last shot," he said. "Be thankful there is something here you can be useful for because I have no problem letting you go. We've been good to you as a department and you abused that olive branch. You can do this, or you can leave."

She nodded, tucked the folder under her arm, and rushed out, waiting until she hit the street to burst into tears.

****

When she walked through the clinic doors, she was sure she looked the part. Red-faced from crying for the last twenty minutes, plus the rounded belly. It didn't take long for a kind nurse to hand her a clipboard.

"You can come with me and fill it out in the room if you are more comfortable."

The woman was so sweet, which just made Kelly cry harder. How had she fallen so quickly? She never imagined she'd be this close to losing her job. Would never bet she would have to sacrifice others to save her own hide. She made it halfway into the room before she froze.

"I'm sorry. I can't do this," Kelly said.

The woman gently held her forearm. "We are here to support whatever you want to do, but…" She paused for a moment, looking at Kelly's stomach. "There is only so much time this decision can be made."

Kelly nodded. "Yes, yes thank you, but I changed my mind."

She returned to the station and the lieutenant's

office. Calmly handed him the folder and told him it was just an obstetrician's office, nothing more.

"Shame," he said. "Thought we were gonna nab 'em."

She kept her face still as she shrugged and turned away.

"Kelly," Lieutenant Porter called. "That was all I had for you. You take care of yourself, but we won't be needing your services around here anymore."

She nodded, her insides too hollow to contain emotion. Five minutes later she left with a small box of her personal items and felt like she'd lost just about everything, but at least not her integrity.

Chapter Fifty-Seven

Lawrence's whole body shook in anger. He paced his apartment, taking trips out to the balcony to let the cold air calm him, but it didn't work. Paul came to his house! How dare he put them both in jeopardy! Paul couldn't follow simple instructions, and was losing his nerve one day in? How could Lawrence ensure his continued silence?

He would have to kill him.

It wasn't like anyone could tie them to each other. Lawrence was sure no one had seen the two of them together. Only Ruth really spoke to him at the party. He was always careful when he went to Paul's and they were never seen out together. Even when they happened to be at the bathhouse at the same time, they acted like acquaintances.

Their indifference in public drove Lawrence crazy in a way that required him to follow Paul back to his place. He needed to feel powerful and dominate their situation, his desire ramped up during the time in which they practically ignored one another.

But even in his frenzied state, hurrying to be alone together, Lawrence always made sure no one saw them. They took separate staircases up to Paul's apartment. The door was left slightly ajar, no knocking even to arouse suspicions. As far as anyone was concerned, they were strangers.

Yes, he could kill Paul and no one would be the wiser.

Better yet, he could stage it to look like a suicide. He could write a note in Paul's scratchy handwriting, confessing to Ruth's murder and saying that he couldn't live with what he'd done. Lawrence could plant some of her jewelry at the scene, make it even more convincing. He'd use the same weapon. If the stories in the paper were true, the police somehow connected the crimes with the firearm used. Yes, he could have a clean getaway.

Energized by his plan, Lawrence went into his closet to retrieve the revolver. It wasn't until he lifted the box and felt an unfamiliar lightness that he remembered. The gun was at the bottom of the Hudson River.

Lawrence cursed under his breath. He wondered if he could get his hand on another gun in the next day or two. Then he could just use that and leave the note.

But then it won't be traced back to Ruth.

He considered briefly killing Paul another way. He could poison his drink, but heard that cops were clueing into that as well. Slit throat? Surely some people killed themselves that way. But Lawrence wasn't sure if he could get a clean cut. And if Paul fought back, that would eliminate any thought that he could have killed himself.

He paced back and forth, trying to will an idea out of his head. But the notion of framing Paul wouldn't go away. He could still do that. Yes! He would go into the police station in the morning, explain how it had slipped his mind about Paul. He'd be apologetic. Yes, sorry, must have been the stress of the situation.

He'd explain how Paul was in love with him, which was true. How Lawrence had been oblivious for months. They'd played in poker games, plausible enough. Lawrence could admit to his gambling problem, though he was pretty sure Detective Kelly already knew. But he'd tell some truths. That way, the lies could be buried within them until one couldn't tell them apart.

He'd say that Paul came on to him a few times, but that Lawrence always declined. The last time, just a few weeks ago, Lawrence told Paul that he was engaged, that he wasn't interested. Paul flew off the handle; he'd hit Lawrence. That's actually how he'd gotten the black eye, but he was too embarrassed to say. Didn't want Ruth to know because he actually owed Paul some money. Felt like he was in over his head and was too afraid to come clean.

Then that night, Paul had come to Lawrence's apartment. Lawrence was furious and fearful, not knowing that Paul knew where he lived. Paul said he killed Ruth to get her out of the way so the two could be together. He could even say that in Paul's confession, he admitted to where the gun was disposed. The cops could drag the river and find it.

Yes, yes it was a perfect plan. He could get off scot-free and with the money…

If Paul were in jail, Lawrence wouldn't have to share anything with him. He probably wouldn't even have to leave New York. He was getting a reputation as the poor man whose fiancée was killed. He could play that up. Sympathetic people tended to loosen their purse strings. He could be rid of Paul just like Ruth and really make a life for himself. His parents would be proud.

He'd just about decided on his course of action when a knock came at the door. Light was just peeking over the buildings in the distance. Lawrence couldn't believe how stupid Paul was, to come back mere hours later.

Maybe he'd kill him right now; say it was in self-defense.

Lawrence yanked the door open, about to yell. His brother stood there.

"Did you do it?" Charles asked, his eyes wide in accusation. "Did you kill her?"

Chapter Fifty-Eight

Detective Kelly met Carlson at the edge of the Garment District and handed her old, sometimes, partner a steaming cup of coffee. The morning was already warm and since she no longer needed to hide her condition, she was dressed in a simple skirt and blouse. No jacket needed.

"I appreciate the call," Kelly said.

Carlson nodded his thanks for the coffee.

"Why didn't you tell me?" he asked, real hurt in his voice.

She shrugged, but he stared at her.

"I was desperate to solve this case. I couldn't let anything jeopardize it."

"I would have thought after all this time you would have trusted me."

"I should have," she admitted.

"How did Lawrence find out?" he asked.

"Funny enough it was his pharmacist. I'd popped into there weeks ago and she knew immediately. Women's intuition, I suppose. He happened to be there."

"Shit luck."

"Tell me about it."

She looked up at the three-story office building they stood by and knew this area of town Carlson avoided if he could. It was out of their normal jurisdiction, unless there was a lead to follow up on. Carlson neglected to tell her over the phone what he needed, just gave an address and told her to show up.

"It's killing me I'm off this case. I'm pissed and lost and, I don't know…"

"Lieutenant Porter hasn't announced it to the team yet."

Kelly whipped her head toward him, but he didn't elaborate.

"You could still get in trouble for talking to me."

He shrugged and pointed toward the building. "Followed a guy here last night after he left Lawrence's."

"Wasn't this close to that poker game murder? Think they're connected?"

"I don't know, but the guy looked less than happy when he left. Followed him on the subway and I thought the guy had me made. Looked scared shitless when we made eye contact, but I made sure to walk right by when he came in here. Hasn't come back out yet, but figure it might be worth a call to you to help me keep an eye out. Maybe having a woman's touch while I question him will help, if you're up for it."

Kelly's heart quickened. "Yes, anything to help."

"I'm not paying you for the coffee, much less your time," Carlson said.

"Nailing Lawrence Henry is the only payment I need."

"You gotta let me take point on this," he said, as if she had a choice in the matter. "I don't want you to say anything until we get in the station and get in that room. And if we get caught—"

"I'll say I ran into you outside the station. You

Kristin Durfee

tried to stop me, but I followed you in. You didn't want to compromise the interview by kicking me out, so I put you in a precarious position. This will all be on me."

Carlson nodded.

A man in a dirty suit stumbled up to them and leered at Carlson. Kelly placed her hand on his arm to keep him from shoving the stranger.

"You lost?" the man asked.

Kelly smiled brightly at him. "Oh no, we were supposed to be meeting a friend here." She gestured toward the building. "But he seems to be running late."

The man narrowed his eyes. "What you want with Paul?"

"Nothing, we just want to see him."

The man ran his tongue over his lips and looked Carlson up and down.

"What can you tell us about him?" Kelly asked, not bothering to keep up the pretense that they knew Paul.

They wanted information, plus with the way the guy wobbled on his feet, it was clear he was already a few drinks in despite the early hour. They needed to jump on anything the guy could give before he puked or passed out.

"What can you tell us about him?" Carlson repeated.

"Don't think you are his type." The man barked out a laugh. "Plus, Paul is already spoken for, from what I hear."

Carlson grabbed the man by the lapels of his filthy jacket. Kelly stepped forward and waved a dollar bill in the air. The terrified man looked from Carlson's face to the money.

"We just want some information and we'll be on

our way. Can you help us with that?" she asked.

The man nodded. Carlson loosened his grip enough for the man to break free and snatch the bill from Kelly.

"Spill," she said.

"Works some odd jobs around the city. Think he's a dealer at a few places, waiter at a few others." The guy jutted his chin at Kelly. "Seems like I'm giving you quite a bit of information for just a buck."

"We could always take you downtown," Carlson said.

"So." Kelly tried to keep her tone casual. She didn't need Carlson fucking this whole thing up because he felt his manhood threatened or some other stupid reason. "A dealer you say? Like cards?"

The man nodded, but pinched his lips. "Look, I know you're both flatfoots. I don't want any trouble. I'm not gonna name places or whatever. We're working people, just like you guys, trying to make a living."

"Of course, I'm not here to shake anyone down. And this Paul, you said he's got a special someone?"

The man laughed. "Oh, I can tell you that's not worth it. Let that dog lie, from what I hear, the guy's a bit crazy."

The wheels spun in Kelly's head, cogs clicking into place. Could it be?

"Ever see this special someone?"

"Some blond guy, don't know his name. Look, I gotta go."

"Of course, thanks for the info, and if you don't mind, not mentioning it to anyone?"

"Never seen you before in my life," the man said, his head already bent back down as he walked away.

"Holy shit," Kelly said.

"You know I don't like it when a lady curses," Carlson said. "But yeah, holy fucking shit."

Chapter Fifty-Nine

Lawrence paced back and forth through the living room, staring out the windows to the city below. He couldn't believe Charles came to confront him. Lawrence made a show of playing the bereaved fiancé. No, he never would have actually hurt her. Would never have been able to go through with it. Felt terribly guilty since she was the one who suggested meeting the new suppliers.

He also started crafting the story about Paul, not giving too much detail, but saying that there was a man who he thought he'd had bad blood with. When Charles pressed him, he said that he didn't want to talk about it, but was planning to go to the police.

Charles, while not all-together convinced, seemed placated enough, and even hugged Lawrence before he left. Terrible luck old chap, he said, clapping Lawrence on the back. Lawrence nodded his appreciation and let his brother out. He'd been pacing the entire half hour since he'd left.

No, there was no way Charles would go to the police. Even if he did think that Lawrence had something to do with Ruth's murder, his loyalty to family would prevent him from doing anything more than possibly telling his parents, which would be its own form of punishment. But even that Lawrence found unlikely. Since they were young boys they had stuck together, keeping each other's secrets. Lawrence knew about the time Charles pilfered money from their father's wallet and the time he kissed Dorothy when he was going steady with Sally-Jo. Their bond was strong. He wouldn't tell.

But there was still the problem with Paul. He could not be trusted. Lawrence decided that he would go to the police station that morning. He dressed in a smart suit and had gotten his navy Astor's coat off the rack before remembering that he would phone the insurance company this morning as well.

"Hello, Leechman's," the man said on the third ring.

"Mr. Leechman, Lawrence Henry here, I spoke with your secretary briefly yesterday."

"Ah, yes, Mr. Henry. Terribly sorry, terrible thing."

"Thank you, sir. As I am sure your secretary made you aware, I hold an insurance policy on my late fiancée, Ruth Smith."

Lawrence heard some shuffling of papers.

"Yes, I have the policy right here," Mr. Leechman said.

"I am popping by the police station today to retrieve the death certificate, but I wanted to give you a heads up so you can start proceedings."

"Proceedings?"

"For payout of the policy," Lawrence said, frustration of the man's stupidity raising his voice.

"Right, of course Mr. Henry," the man said.

"And when should payment be expected?"

"The standard thirty days."

"Thirty days?" Lawrence practically shouted as he reflexively clenched his right fist.

"That is the standard. I will have the check prepared for you. Then you can either pick it up in person or I can wire the money to any financial institution."

"I believe that sum of money would best be wired," Lawrence said.

There was a long pause on the other end.

"Mr. Henry, you are aware that the policy is not mature yet, correct?"

"Mature?" A cold prickling broke out over his body.

"Yes, well, the policy must be in effect for one calendar year to reach full maturity. Industry standard is to pay eight percent if it hasn't reached maturity, but I can authorize to pay ten, so that would be," he paused, as if double checking a calculation. "Five-hundred dollars."

The prickle feeling turned to ice. "I'm not sure I understand you," Lawrence muttered, his heart rattling against his ribs.

"Mr. Henry, I do apologize, but your maturity date is clear in your policy. The increase to ten percent it quite generous, I assure you. Relinquishing a policy—"

"I am not *relinquishing* it. My fiancée *died*," Lawrence corrected, his voice stern with rage.

"Well, yes, my apologies. I am using industry terms here, when I say relinquish, I mean claiming a policy before maturity date."

"I have a funeral to pay for," Lawrence said, and hoped that it didn't sound like he was as desperate as he was.

"I understand that. I could work with the bank to secure you a loan using the policy as collateral, but I will warn you, they typically charge double the interest. I could also call the funeral home and explain your situation. I have done that with other clients as well, set up a payment plan. You will still have to pay interest, but it will be considerably less."

"I don't need a payment plan," Lawrence said through clenched teeth. "I need you to pay out the policy that I purchased."

"At this moment," the man said, his voice suddenly bolder. "I can offer you the five hundred dollars, or you can wait the year period for the full amount, minus any interest fees to either a funeral home or bank. It is a generous offer and it is all I can do."

Lawrence slammed the phone down and grabbed his coat. That was it. He was just going to have to kill Paul. Screw it all. He'd kill him and then leave town. He was sure his parents would wire him some money. Charles, at the very least, would. He could make up some story that he was so upset at Ruth's passing, he couldn't stand to be in the city any longer and needed to get out. No one would question him. They could do this one last thing for him, give him a bit of what he deserved, and then he could disappear.

He'd gotten close to Paul's apartment, not caring who saw him, *daring* someone to see him, when a man stopped him.

"He's not here," the man said.

"What?"

"Cops picked up your boy a while ago. And if I were you," the man said, lowering his voice. "I'd get outta here so they don't do the same to you."

Chapter Sixty

Kelly and Carlson walked in silence for a block
before they ran into a pair of uniforms and gave Paul's
address and description, telling them to bring the guy
in. Carlson figured it would make the man sweat a bit to
be followed by one person, brought in by someone
different, and then questioned by someone else. Let him
get a bit rattled. Make him feel like the whole city was
looking for him, then Kelly could swoop in and offer
redemption.

Because even thought it might cost Carlson his job,
or at the very least a few months of worse cases, he was
willing to do it for Kelly. He said he believed in her and
thought she got a raw deal in the whole matter. They
paced outside the station for a few moments, coming up
with a game plan.

"So he might know something about the poker
murder, especially if he's a dealer. Probably knew who
would be there and how much cash," Carlson said.

"We could say we knew he tipped Lawrence off."

"Assuming Lawrence is in fact the person who did
it."

"We can tell him we know everything about their
relationship." Kelly murmured.

She hated having to go this route, using someone's
love life against them. She typically didn't give a shit
about what people did behind closed doors, especially if

it didn't hurt anyone, but she couldn't get the image of Ruth out of her mind. That poor woman getting tangled into whatever elaborate web Lawrence had spun. If this potential side lover was the key to unraveling it, she could justify jeopardizing one man's livelihood to avenge a woman's death.

"It's a stretch," Carlson said. "He may deny everything and really, we've got nothing on him other than I saw him leaving Lawrence's building. Shit, maybe I misread the situation. Maybe he's a cleaner or delivery boy…"

"But the guy on the street," Kelly reminded him.

She reflected on how *this* was what she loved about police work: the puzzle. Putting pieces that looked like the wrong fit from a distance, to be perfect upon closer examination. A baby wasn't going to change that. This was who she was. They'd figure it out. Go where they needed to go. This was her calling and she'd follow it to wherever someone would let her do it.

The door to the precinct opened and a man named Mitchell popped his head out. "Carlson?"

"Mmm?"

"Got him warmed up for you."

"Thanks, Mitchell. Detective Kelly is gonna join me. She worked this beat for a while and is now covering the south side."

Kelly followed the two men in, taking care to keep her head down to not draw attention to herself. They moved through to the interview rooms and paused outside a door.

"What have you found out so far?" Kelly asked, hope filling her insides and pushing out the nerves.

"Not much. Got his name." He flipped through a

small notebook. "Paul Fabric."

"Fabric?" Kelly asked, not sure if she heard correctly.

Mitchell nodded. "That's what he said, asked him to spell it twice."

"Thanks, Mitchell, We'll take it from here." Carlson clapped the man on his shoulder.

"Wait," Kelly said right before they entered. She leaned in and lowered her voice. "There should be a fat folder in the middle of the conference room table. Hopefully no one's screwed with it, has some odds and ends and photographs. Lots of photographs."

Carlson nodded. "Meet you in there in a minute and let's just hope no one sees us."

She looked both ways down the hall and slipped into the room unnoticed. Paul sat up straighter, but upon seeing her, relaxed back into his chair.

"I would kill for a coffee," he said.

She decided not to comment on the irony of his statement. "Sure, I will get you one, just have a couple questions for you."

He shifted in his seat and looked toward the door. "I'm not sure who…"

She was about to make up some lie, but Carlson saved her by walking through the door with the thick folder.

"Mr. Fabric," Carlson said. "My friend here and I have a few questions for you."

"Mr. Fabric, or do you prefer Paul?" Kelly asked.

"I prefer to leave," Paul said.

"Well, that isn't possible, at least not anytime soon," Carlson said. "But if you help me…" He dropped the folder on the desk.

The pictures spilled out a little, offering a glimpse of a bloodied leg, unblinking eyes, pools of blood. Paul's gaze darted down and back up quickly.

"I don't know what you're getting at." Paul began to get up.

Kelly reached out a hand to stop him. She took a deep breath, hating herself before she even spoke. "You know you can get up to twenty years for sodomy."

"Excuse me?" Paul asked, his body at an awkward angle, frozen and hovering over the chair.

Carlson pushed him back lightly and he fell into the wooden seat.

"Sodomy. Buggery. Sins of a carnal nature. Are you following?" Carlson took the seat across the table and shuffled the papers back in the folder.

"I don't know what you are talking about."

Paul sat back with his arms crossed, but beads of sweat formed around his hairline. He shifted and removed his jacket.

"Mr. Fabric, you know as well as I do that you could be put away for a very long time." She took the seat next to Carlson and folded her hands on the table. "I don't want to see that, and I'm sure you don't either. Help me and I promise to help you. I can get the charges brought down to a simple misdemeanor. You won't serve any time for your... lifestyle."

Paul huffed out a breath and crossed his arms again. "You don't know anything."

"I know that you are involved with Mr. Lawrence Henry, and that he killed Ruth Smith two nights ago." Were Kelly's eyes playing tricks on her, or did Paul shudder at the two names? "I know—"

"You don't know nothing." Paul's voice was an

octave higher now, tinged with anxiety.

Kelly opened the folder and began to lay out the pictures. They were gruesome, made even more so by their stark black-and-white nature. The darkness of the blood stood out better on the pale faces than in real life sometimes. Kelly was glad she'd asked Carlson to get them.

Lastly, with a flick of her wrist, she laid the photo of Ruth's splayed body over the other pictures closest to Paul. He looked down for a second then straight back up at the ceiling, moisture forming on the edges of his eyes.

"I know Lawrence had something to do with this, with all of these," Kelly said, her voice soft. "You may have even helped."

"No."

Kelly raised her hands. "Okay, but maybe you knew something."

"Maybe Lawrence confided in you during one of your…trysts. We can help you, Paul," Carlson said.

Kelly leaned forward, willing the words out of the man sitting across from them. Paul's body, rigid this whole time, lost its stiffness.

Yes.

Paul was just opening his mouth when there was a knock at the door. An officer peeked in and said Kelly was needed in the hall. She was furious at the interruption of a pivotal moment. Kelly was *sure* Paul was about to say something, maybe even to confess.

And then the fear set in. Who knew she was in here? Sure, she was getting pulled out in a professional manner to not totally screw up the interview, but this would be the end of it for her.

"I'll be right back," Kelly said and looked at Carlson, who probably guessed the same thing was happening.

He nodded and kept his seat as she left. At least he could try to salvage the interview.

When she was in the hall, she risked a look around, expecting to see an irate lieutenant or captain in the hall, but it was just the officer who came to get her. The officer pointed to the door across the hall, another interview room.

"Man here to see you," he said. "Asked for you by name. Says he's Mr. Henry's brother and he'd like to make a statement."

Chapter Sixty-One

The die was cast. Lawrence went into the police station, which was abuzz with activity, to tell his side of the story. It was imperative that he get it out; he was sure that Paul was somewhere in the building trying to lay blame on him. He couldn't be trusted, but there was no way Lawrence could get to him now and kill him. Even if both of them somehow left the station, it would be too suspicious now.

Lawrence removed his jacket, draped it over his arm, and straightened his tie. He needed to look polished and professional. No one would believe Paul. Lawrence was sure of that. He kept bad company and lived in a nefarious section of town. But to gain any points he could, Lawrence wanted to look the part of someone who was trustworthy, important, and could be relied upon.

There was no one sitting at the long desk like the previous times he'd been in the station. Men and a few women briskly walked back and forth, files and papers in their hands. There was a large commotion by the door as four uniformed officers dragged a man, kicking and screaming, into the station and down a long hallway to Lawrence's right. A loud banging noise was followed by quiet.

An officer walked by and Lawrence grabbed him by the arm. He startled and reached for his gun, turning to Lawrence wide-eyed.

"I am looking for a detective. I need to make a statement," Lawrence said, his hands palms out and half-raised. The officer relaxed.

"Busy morning, going to be a while. Take a seat." He gestured to a row of occupied chairs.

"Don't you know who I am?" Lawrence pulled himself up to his full height. "I am the fiancé of the murdered Ms. Ruth Smith."

People began to look their direction. The officer, realizing that everyone was paying attention to them, motioned for Lawrence to follow him.

"Yes, of course," the officer said.

He brought him down the same hall the kicking and screaming man had been dragged through. There was no sign of him.

"In here, please," the officer said, gesturing to an empty room. "Someone will be with you shortly."

"Don't keep me waiting," Lawrence called through the open door. "I know who did it. I know who killed her."

A twitchy young detective walked in and introduced himself as Salinski.

"O'Malley said your name's Henry?" Salinski looked down at the small notebook in his hand as he took a seat.

"Mr. Lawrence Henry."

"Apologies." The man had an accent that lengthened some of his letters and shortened others.

"Salinski, what's that, Russian?" Lawrence asked.

"Polish."

"Polish," Lawrence echoed. "Many officers in your family?"

"Naw, mostly farmers and shoemakers. You said you wanted to speak with someone?"

His sudden shift annoyed Lawrence, who was hoping to use this familiarizing conversation to build Salinski's trust in him.

"Yes," Lawrence said, sitting up straighter and making a show of collecting himself. "My fiancé, I am sure you have heard, Ms. Ruth Smith, was—was killed the other night." He took a dramatic pause, waiting for Salinski to lean forward just a millimeter before continuing.

After a beat, he indulged Lawrence.

"I have been wracking my brain ever since the detectives talked to me, but I just realized some information that I didn't give them before."

"Oh yeah?" Salinski opened his notebook. "What's that?"

"This is difficult for me to admit," Lawrence said, looking down at his hands. "But I believe there is a man who is in love with me." He looked up, and registering the shock on Salinski's face, pressed forward. "Yes, well, it's a funny thing, I actually had no idea. I think the chap worked a party at my parents' a while back. That's how he first saw me. Then he started hanging around my place, trying to get an invite inside, which I always declined. Mind you, this isn't something I am particularly proud of, but I have been known to gamble from time to time."

"Go on," Salinski said, now not taking his gaze off his notebook as he feverishly wrote.

"Yes, well, I guess this gentleman was also at one of my poker games. He made a lewd comment to me, which I promptly deflected and said I wasn't interested.

I tried to be kind about it, being in unknown company and all, but I think I offended him. He started to double his efforts and must have gotten word that I was engaged to Ruth. I, I believe he is the one who killed her. He came to my apartment late last night, confessed and said he loved me and asked me to run away with him. Naturally, I told him to get out, that he was a sick man that needed help."

"And you didn't think to phone the station right away?" Salinski asked.

Lawrence shook his head. "No, I see now that I should have, but it really shook me up, plus I wasn't sure if I believed him at first. Then I went back and looked through some of the old records of the parties and realized that he did, in fact, work a party a while back. That part of his story checked out, which made me wonder what else could. Plus, it is the only explanation that made sense to me. If he worked the parties, he probably knew where the alcohol came from." Lawrence paused.

"We can deal with that later," Salinski said in a reassuring tone.

"Yes, well, he must have contacted Ruth, set up the meeting under the guise to sell her spirits for my pharmacy, and, well, you must know the rest."

Salinski nodded, a somber expression on his face.

"I should have taken him seriously all those months ago. Maybe this wouldn't have happened..." Lawrence placed his head in his hands, and breathed deeply.

"You couldn't have known," Salinski reassured him. "Someone making a proposition like that, I'm sure anyone would have done the same in your position.

You couldn't have known what he was going to do."

Lawrence sniffled once. "I suppose, but it doesn't help me feeling awful about it."

"I'll get this statement typed up and bring it back for you to sign in just a few minutes. Can I get you something to drink?"

"Oh, yes, a coffee would be wonderful," Lawrence said, sniffling again. "Cream, no sugar."

Salinski left and Lawrence sat back, pleased with his performance.

Chapter Sixty-Two

Detective Kelly's mind was filled with a jumble of reverberating words. This was it. She'd finally nailed him. Charles Henry the Third spilled his guilty guts. Between tears and gulps, he relayed how his brother told him about a scheme to kill Ruth for her insurance money.

It was all falling into place.

Between his statement and Paul's, Kelly was sure a jury would convict, but if only she could get the murder weapon too. Let Goddard wrap the whole thing in a damn bow for a jury to string Lawrence up.

She rushed to the typists before someone could stop her, hands filled with hastily scribbled notes. As she entered the room, she searched for Josey. The young woman wouldn't question Kelly being there and was also the best at deciphering her poor handwriting. Then Kelly ran right into someone else.

"Hey, watch it!" she cried, her excitement turning to frustration at the temporary impediment to her task.

"My apologies, ma'am," the man said.

It took Kelly a few seconds to realize he was Detective Salinski, one of their newer hires that Carlson had been mentoring.

"Detective Kelly! I thought—"

She waved her hand. "Salinski." Kelly tried to move around him, but the man stayed rooted, blocking her path. "Josey," Kelly called, then handed her a stack of paper. "Need these right away, please," she added.

"Detective!" Salinski waved his own notes. "I was under the impression…" He turned a bright shade of pink. "Well, it's lucky I ran into you! You won't believe it. I got a man here claiming to know who killed that broad down by the warehouses."

Kelly's attention whipped to him. Could she be this lucky? Having even another person corroborating the brother's story would be too good to be true. Maybe she should march back into Captain Wade's office and demand her job back.

Salinski nodded, taking Kelly's silence as disbelief. "Yeah, the fiancé."

"They said it's the fiancé?" Kelly asked, her heart racing again.

Salinski wrinkled his nose for a moment. "No, the fiancé is *here*. Says he knows who did it, a man named Paul," he said, double checking his notes. Salinski flagged down another typist and gave the papers to her with similar instructions to please rush.

The woman smiled, like she planned to ignore his request.

"Paul?" Kelly asked.

"Yes, said this guy," Salinski paused and leaned closer to Kelly. "Was in love with him. Killed that lady so they could be together. I knew the city was a wild place, but I've never…"

Kelly mulled this information over, wondering how to exploit this information in the limited time she'd still have access to the building. She spotted Carlson across the room. His eyes were wide as he took in the sight before him. Evidently wondering why she was out in the open instead of hiding in the shadows like he probably expected. She smiled, realizing like most things in life, if act like you know what you're doing, people tend to leave you alone.

She brushed right past Carlson and he followed her into an empty interview room.

"We gotta be careful," he whispered. "Only a matter of time before we're found out and my ass is on the line."

His previous bravado of including her had dissipated a bit. He probably realized how much trouble he'd be in and, with a new baby at home, how damn much he needed the job. She tried not to be resentful that he was welcomed right back to work without a second thought at who would take care of his new son, but her? Just the mere fact that a baby would emerge from her practiced body meant she could no longer do the job.

She pushed the thought away. There wasn't room in her mind for such ruminations at this moment.

Salinski poked his head in, clearly excited to share with his mentor what he'd learned. "Detective Carlson—"

"Great job, Salinski," Kelly said. She grabbed the papers Carlson still clutched from Paul's interview and handed them over. "Why don't you pass these notes along too and make sure all these reports get typed up on the double? Carlson and I are going to pay Mr. Henry a visit. Did he ask for a cup of coffee?"

Salinski's eyes widened in fear. "Yes, yes, ma'am, I am sorry, I completely—"

Kelly waved his comment away. "Don't worry, you did the right thing coming to tell someone. We will get him that cup and have a talk with him. As soon as those papers are typed, I want you to bring them to me."

"All of them?"

"Yes. Can you do that for us?"

"Yes, ma'am," Salinski said, standing a little taller.

When he'd left, Carlson looked at her with one eyebrow cocked. "Mr. Henry?"

"Holy shit," she said, not toning down her language. Not like she worked here anymore anyway. "This is wild. I just got out of an interview with Charles Henry the Third, who stated Lawrence propositioned him to kill Ruth."

"No," Carlson said, shock making his eyes bulge cartoonishly.

"Oh, that's not even the half of it. Apparently Lawrence is fucking *here*. Just gave Salinski a sob story about how some man named Paul was in love with him and killed Ruth so they could be together."

"Holy shit," Carlson said, then apologized.

"So, we need to figure out how to play this. Let him hang himself or do we tell him Paul and his brother are here and giving their own statements?"

Kelly really didn't know. She could see both failing and both succeeding, but which would work on Lawrence? Put his back to the wall or let him dig his own grave?

"Let me get this straight," Carlson said, rubbing his left eye with the palm of his hand. "You've got Lawrence's brother in a room saying that Lawrence asked him a few days ago to kill Ruth and split the insurance money. Then you've got Lawrence here saying that Paul is in love with him, and killed Ruth so the two of them could be together. And we've got Paul who is teetering between cooperating with us or getting nailed for buggery. That about sum it up?"

"Yup. We gotta act fast. With all three of these guys here, it's won't go unnoticed for long and I can't let this one slip out of our hands. I just can't."

Carlson nodded. "Okay, Paul hasn't given an official statement yet. Let's pay Lawrence a visit first and see if we can't get him cooperating a bit more. Then we speak with Paul, let him know that the supposed love of his life has just thrown him under the bus, tell him that we have another witness that claims Lawrence was the mastermind, and ask Paul if he'd like to make a statement. Pretty sure that will open him up. Guy doesn't strike me as someone who'd like to see what life is like on the inside."

"Thanks, really."

After a few moments of silence, Carlson said, "Looks like you were right."

"You sound surprised," Kelly teased.

"I didn't see the connection, but you did."

"You would have gotten there eventually."

"Maybe," Carlson admitted.

"Well, we're here now, you in for taking this guy down, once and for all?"

He grinned. "You bet your sweet ass."

Chapter Sixty-Three

Lawrence vibrated with the desire to get up and move. He wasn't sure how long the detective had been gone, but it felt like ages. He shifted a few times in his seat, crossing and uncrossing his legs, but didn't get up. He needed to keep the air of calmness. Pacing would ruin that.

Just when he couldn't take it any longer, the door opened. Lawrence was surprised to see Detectives Kelly and Carlson enter with three cups of coffee. He was certain Kelly would have been sacked, or at the very least, reassigned given her condition. His senses sharpened at the abnormality.

"Cream, no sugar, correct?" Kelly asked, placing a cup in front of Lawrence.

"Detective Kelly, I wasn't expecting to see you again," he said as he blew on the steaming cup. "What happened to Detective Salinski?"

"Waiting for your statement to be typed up, but he mentioned you asked for a drink and we didn't want to keep you waiting. He'll be with us in a bit," Kelly said as she took a seat.

Her partner stood by the door, arms crossed, as if he was blocking it. From Lawrence leaving or someone coming in, he wasn't sure.

He raised the cup in mock cheers before taking a sip. "Much appreciated, especially with you in your *condition.*"

He peered at the partner and Kelly, but neither made a comment to what he'd said. Something was definitely up and he couldn't quite place what it was. They sat in silence, sipping their coffee, when a soft knock sounded on the door. Carlson opened it a crack, but Lawrence couldn't see who was behind it. He was pretty sure he heard Salinski's voice, but the detective didn't enter the room. Someone's hand gave papers to Carlson, who closed the door. He presented them to Kelly.

"What brings you in today?" Kelly asked.

"Well, surely you must know. Are those the papers? Have you spoken to Detective Salinski?" he asked, while reaching forward.

Kelly covered them and dragged them a few inches back. "He mentioned something about why you were here, but we'd like to hear it from you," Kelly said.

Her voice was void of all the normal pleasantries she gave him. Maybe she was pissed about the whole ratting her out thing. Understandable, but he didn't appreciate being spoken to that way by a woman, even one he'd slighted.

"Then don't you have some work to do? I thought you were the detectives assigned to my fiancé's murder. Or at least, you were…"

"We are," Carlson said, breaking his silence.

Lawrence narrowed his eyes, losing his patience. He reached for the papers again, but Kelly's grip tightened on them.

"So, I hear that you asked for a copy of the death certificate," Kelly said.

Her tone was casual, but something about it made

the hairs on the back of Lawrence's neck stand.

"I did," Lawrence said, choosing his words carefully.

"Nice of you to want to get it for the family," Carlson said.

"Yes, well, I also needed it, for insurance purposes."

"Insurance?" Kelly asked, though it wasn't really a question. "That's pretty quick, asking for a certificate before the funeral even."

"Well, how do you expect said funeral to be paid for?" Lawrence asked, his temper rising. "Everyone expects me to be made of money, but it's tied up in investments or property. Those things take time to unload, and it's not like Ruth's family is scrambling to help out." He knew he shouldn't be allowing his cool demeanor to falter, but the stress of the last few days were eating away at his resolve.

Carlson moved away from the door and sat down next to Kelly, leaning slightly back. "People always expect the rich to foot the bill."

"Exactly!" Lawrence exclaimed. "As if we don't have our own troubles as well. Worse, we have double the troubles because we are worrying about ourselves as well as our employees."

"So, you took out an insurance policy to safeguard, as any reasonable person would," Carlson continued.

Lawrence felt relieved Carlson understood the story he wove. He gave a side glance to Kelly, who didn't seem to be on the same page as her partner, but how could she be? Typical woman. Thinks being taken care of magically happens. That money appears whenever you need it and not realizing how much her husband burdens himself with.

"Well, Ruth actually took out the policy, but named me as the beneficiary."

"That was nice of her," Kelly said, no warmth to her voice.

"Yeah, we were business partners. I'd written her into my will since we were set to be married and our assets were already connected by her investment in my pharmacy. It only made sense for her to take out a policy. That way, if something happened to her, it would protect her family. They won't be liable for any hit the business may take by the lack of her continued investment."

"Makes total sense," Carlson said.

"Right, you get it. I am sure this is all stuff your husband takes care of," he said to Kelly who gave him a tight smile. "It's not your fault. You just don't know how the world works."

Lawrence wished Kelly would leave. It was clear the woman didn't like him. Plus, now she seemed suspicious of him. Carlson, on the other hand, obviously knew something about business and the workings of the upper class. He was clearly the man Lawrence should be speaking to.

"So, you'll get the payout, and be able to cover the funeral, plus business expenses?" Carlson asked.

"That was the plan for it," Lawrence said. He wasn't too keen on letting them know about the clause that didn't let him collect right away. It wasn't important to admit his oversight.

"How much was the policy for, if you don't mind me asking?" Kelly asked.

"Five thousand," Lawrence said flatly.

Kelly whistled. "That's a lot of money."

"You should be glad you don't have to worry about knowing such things. Funerals and businesses are expensive," Lawrence said. "Speaking of which, I really need to get back to both. Is that my statement?" he asked, pointing to the paper. "May I sign it and get on my way?"

"In a moment," Kelly said, her hands over the typed pages. "I'm not sure if you are aware, but we have a Mr. Paul Fabric here. Brought him in a bit ago."

Lawrence slapped the table and smiled. The first piece of good news he'd had all day. "So, you all got there as well. Great news."

"Yes?" Kelly asked.

"Of course, I knew you would solve it. He is the one who killed Ruth, I'm sure of it. You must've read my statement. Again, I am ready to sign it so I can be on my way—"

"Your brother is also here," Kelly said.

The words hung in the air for a few seconds before Lawrence's brain fully processed. Charles? Here? But why? Why would they be…

No.

Kelly rose and brought the papers with her. Carlson gave Lawrence a smug look before also standing.

"We know it was you," Kelly whispered before leaving the room.

Chapter Sixty-Four

When Kelly and Carlson walked out of that interview room, the dreaded, inevitable firestorm greeted them. Salinski, having no idea of Kelly's status, or lack thereof, had brought half the homicide department into the hall.

It was only a matter of time before the lieutenant popped his head out to see what the commotion was. He reddened, then grabbed Kelly by the upper arm, and dragged her out of the building, a protesting Carlson in their wake.

But the die was cast at that point, she knew. The statements were made, the arrests imminent. The fact that she was no longer on the payroll meant little. Carlson could testify and she could still be brought in. The courts didn't really care and the jury would be riveted, no matter what her status was.

****

To say the trial of Lawrence Henry was a media and social frenzy would have been the understatement of the year. His photograph, printed next to one of Ruth looking lovely in a floral dress, graced the front pages of the paper the weeks leading up to and including the trial. Kelly, now eight months pregnant and practically the width of a city sidewalk, could barely walk down the street before someone would stop her to ask questions about the case.

"Is it true that he killed all those people?" a woman at the grocers asked.

"I hear he may have killed someone in Baltimore," another chimed in.

"No, Chicago," the butcher said from behind the counter.

"Both," the woman said.

They'd stare back at Kelly, wide-eyed and expectant, as if she would give them details the reporters couldn't even get their hands on. Carlson admitted to her the other day when he'd called about the case, that the state was having a hard enough time trying to find an unbiased jury. There was even talk about going across the river into New Jersey to try to find jurors who hadn't heard of the East-to-West Murders.

While Lawrence was only being charged in Ruth's death, the moniker stuck. The press found out that a necklace recovered in Ruth's bedroom was believed to have be stolen from a woman murdered on New Year's. Kelly phoned Carlson, but he informed her it was actually some mass-produced piece of costume jewelry and they couldn't be sure it was Mrs. Chanler's.

She hung up with renewed disappointment. It was a miracle Carlson still took her calls. Her "charade" as the captain called it, got him suspended for a week. Since he was the only one left on the payroll with much of a part in the case, they had to let him back in.

Most days she puttered around the house while the kids were in school and took over the cooking from Patrick, who appeared as lost as her at their new arrangement. The city was wearing on them both and they stayed up late into the night discussing their future.

They had a bit of money saved and didn't have to make a decision right away, but with another member soon to join their family, they needed to figure something out.

She figured she was stuck in town at least for another week or two until she testified. Then after she had the baby, move on to whatever was next. The attorney had prepped her, but really, her testimony of putting the pieces together paled in comparison to the star witnesses: Paul and Charles the Third.

As part of his plea bargain, Paul had told them everything, including where the murder weapon was tossed into the river. It was dragged, and while three weapons were found, none matched the bullet pulled from Ruth's brain. The revolver found at the scene of the poker murders wasn't registered to Lawrence, or anyone for that matter, and there was no record of its purchase, so that series of murders couldn't be connected to him, either.

Their evidence wasn't ideal, even Kelly had to admit that. A confessed sodomizer wasn't the best witness, but details were corroborated by Lawrence's upstanding citizen brother, Charles. With the insurance policy, which the issuer was set to testify about Lawrence's eagerness to cash out and outrage at its lack of maturity, compounded into some pretty damning evidence.

Lawrence, however, refused any kind of a plea deal. Kelly had even talked the state attorney into offering life in prison, taking the death penalty off the table, if Lawrence would admit to all the killings but he flat out refused. All he talked about was how Paul was the real guilty one.

Carlson even told her that on one particular day,

when he went to re-interview him for the umpteenth time, Lawrence even suggested that maybe his brother was in cahoots with Paul. Maybe *they* were in love and trying to push Lawrence out. If Lawrence died, Charles may be the beneficiary of Ruth's life insurance policy. Kelly was pretty sure it didn't work that way, but Carlson said Lawrence was convinced this was a reasonable defense.

"He tried to spin some crazy bull that they were the ones who were together." Carlson laughed and waved his hands. "Blew me off when I reminded him about the statements we have of him being in a relationship with Paul. How no one ever saw his brother in town, or Paul anywhere near Charles's place. I about throttled him for wasting my time, but he wouldn't budge. Even told him I could maybe spare him from the chair if he cooperated."

Kelly pinched the bridge of her nose. "And still nothing? That's a huge offer."

"*Nada*. Kept spewing that crap about his brother really being behind it. Wanting the insurance money for himself so he could get out from their father's shadow, which sounds ridiculous. No jury is going to buy it even with Paul being a bit of an unlikable character."

Kelly started to peel the paper from the coffee cup and drop it in her lap. "That man is so wrapped up in his own fantasy." She puffed a laugh. "I wouldn't be surprised if he actually believed his own lies. Let's just hope a jury doesn't."

****

After giving her testimony, Kelly sat in the court room every day. A parade of witnesses, some even Kelly didn't recognize, helped piece together the fragments of what happened to Ruth. The insurance adjuster was probably the most convincing as he relayed the anger Lawrence displayed at not having access to the money.

Kelly herself was surprised by a piece of incriminating evidence from one of Ruth's sisters. Della said Ruth confided in her that she'd met Lawrence at a New Year's party and embarrassed herself by spilling a drink on him. In the haste of cleaning him up, she accidentally left an heirloom handkerchief with him. Their mother would be furious, Ruth worried. But when the police returned Ruth's belongings to them, the handkerchief was there, tucked in her coat pocket. Della knew Lawrence hadn't given it back because Ruth would have told her sister. The jury looked riveted through the testimony, but again, Lawrence appeared as if the words had no effect on him.

At the end of the trial, against his lawyer's wishes, Lawrence took the stand. He rambled for almost an hour about different conspiracy theories. Neither lawyer even asked him any questions. By the end of his performance, it wasn't clear what side he was helping anyway and it was apparent the state and defense were too rattled to see how the scales would tip, so they left it alone. It only took the jury two days to find him guilty on all charges. Lawrence looked stunned and Kelly fought back tears of relief.

"You're letting them get away with it!" Lawrence screamed as the guard pulled him away.

Kelly noted that Lawrence's mother, who'd sat stoic and silent during each day of the trial, promptly got to her feet and rushed out of the courtroom, her eyes welling with tears. His father, dry-eyed, rushed to catch up. Several families of apparent victims cheered, though their loved ones weren't technically included in the verdict, it must have seemed like a victory for them all the same.

Kelly waited the courtroom to clear. She told Carlson she'd meet him for a celebratory coffee in the morning. The bailiff raised his eyebrows at Kelly.

"I'll make sure to shut the lights off," Kelly said.

The man nodded as if he understood she needed some quiet time to process in this room before moving on with the rest of her life.

She sat for the better part of the afternoon, filling her lungs with the smell of polished wood and cigarette smoke that lingered in the space long after the occupants left. Rubbing her belly and ignoring the tightness building in her midsection. Soon, the baby would come, but now she would celebrate. This was the biggest case she'd ever worked. The most doubt that had even been thrown at her, and she'd overcome.

She stuck to her guns. She worked hard, compiled evidence, turned over each and every stone, and it paid off. It actually paid off. She lost everything in the process, but it was worth it. She got justice for Ruth.

As for the rest of her life, she'd simply have to figure that out.

She pushed on her back as she stood, worried her water would break in the courtroom and put on her coat. There was no point in trying to button it; it hadn't closed for months, Storm clouds moved outside the window, bringing an early summer cold front. She stuck her hands in the pockets to close the coat a little, then felt a rough piece of paper and pulled it out.

It was the business card of the Baltimore Police Department science lab.

Chapter Sixty-Five

New York, December 1936

Detective Kelly trailed Warden Lawes down the hall. She struggled a bit to hold the large banker box filled with papers and photographs. Lawes was too busy pointing out items of interest and talking about the various programs to notice. Once he'd heard Kelly had been a jail matron, he couldn't wait to regale her with tales of the storied institution.

In all the years she'd worked for the police force in New York, Kelly had never been to the famed Sing Sing prison. Though part of her wanted to know everything about the place, she also wanted to get out as quickly as possible. While reforms had transformed the prison from its days in the early part of the century, it still remained a fortress of stone, concrete, and metal holding some of the worst criminals of the day.

Kelly was surprised when she'd gotten the call from her old lieutenant asking her to come back to town. She'd been in Chicago for almost five years. Patrick and she packed the family up when Franny was only three months old. Other than the occasional call from Carlson, she heard nothing from her former colleagues.

Her old boss seemed just as surprised he was calling as she was in receiving it. He made small talk he pretended to give a shit about, but Kelly didn't have time for such things anymore. The cases on her desk piled higher every day. She was mentally and physically exhausted each night, but also happier than she'd been in years. It wasn't until she heard Lieutenant Porter's voice, she realized he had no hold over her and how much better off she was. She'd cut him off and asked him what he wanted.

"Lawrence Henry wants to speak with you."

If he said more after that, she couldn't remember. The next two days were a blur of packing and traveling and now here she was. She'd kissed her family goodbye, told an understanding Goddard where she was going, and got on a train.

For the entire ride she played over those last few months in New York. She'd never forget Lawrence Henry. The name would follow her for the rest of her career and probably life. The state knew the saga was about to come to an end as the execution time neared, but they wanted closure. Wanted to see if he'd talk, give a deathbed confession of sorts. Carlson had tried, without success. Lawrence apparently asked after Kelly from time to time. They were desperate.

The city seemed to sprout like a pop-up book as the train neared. The New Deal was only a few years old, but the construction which surrounded her made it look like a depression was decades in the past. She wondered what the city would look like in ten, twenty more years and if, after this visit, she'd ever see it again.

They had no family here and had settled surprisingly well into the move to the Midwest. Chicago had its problems, sure, but as a family they felt like they could breathe better. The parks and zoo were constant stops, her kids delighting in the primate house. Even Patrick seemed happier in this place. Chicago was easier to get around than New York and, thankfully, the food just as good.

She'd been torn about accepting the job. For the first time in her life two places wanted her, a miracle as so many people were becoming unemployed. She'd gone to Baltimore for an interview, but ultimately couldn't get the work Goddard did out of her head. Stories were popping in all over the country of firearms evidence solving previously unsolvable cases. She wanted, no, she *needed* to be involved in that.

Goddard was more than happy to have her and utilized her investigative and interview skills to help them move through the backlog of cases. Chicago's increasing gun crime seemed to have no end. The work was mentally taxing, but so rewarding she never missed the city she'd previously called home for so many years.

Stepping out of Grand Central Terminal was a shock to the system. All the Midwest hospitality she'd gotten used to was nowhere to be seen. A gentleman in a suit bumped into her and instead of apologizing, growled "Leave the commute times for the men, little lady. You can shop whenever."

When she saw Carlson standing next to a marked car, she breathed a sigh of relief and surprised them both by giving him a kiss on the cheek and a hug. The drive up to Ossining was without fanfare. Kelly caught glimpses of the Hudson River as Carlson chatted away. He asked her how Chicago was and filled her in on the station gossip. Kelly hadn't realized that she'd missed her old partner until she saw him, promising herself that before she left, she'd try to convince Carlson to move.

Carlson stayed back in the warden's office so Kelly could meet with Lawrence alone. No one told Lawrence that Kelly was coming, just that someone wanted to meet with him. After weeks of asking, they figured he'd never think Kelly would actually come. Everyone hoped the shock would rattle him enough that his façade would crack, letting some truth spill out. Kelly wasn't so sure, but she felt he owed it to the other victims to try.

Lawrence had been moved to another area of the prison where those awaiting execution were held. He'd be fed his last meal, a requested dinner of steak and lobster Lawes said, and sleep in a bed one last time before being roused at five in the morning. His parents would get to say goodbye. No other visitors requested time, other than media outlets which Lawrence refused. Then he'd get marched to the gallows and hanged at ten-twenty-seven a.m.

"Gallows?" Kelly asked, startled.

Lawes shrugged. "He insisted. I thought the electric chair was the only way to go, but he requested special exemption from the governor's office and they allowed it. Damndest thing too, had to build it. Took ours down years ago. And asked us to paint it yellow." Lawes chuckled as if it was his wife asking for an unreasonable paint color for their kitchen.

"Yellow?"

"Bright yellow," Lawes confirmed. "Ask him about it, I'm as curious as the next guy to know why."

They paused before a door with two guards standing on either side of it.

"He's already in there, boss," one of them said.

Lawes put his hand on the small of Kelly's back. Here she was, summoned by the powers that be because they thought she was the only one who could get what they wanted, and they still treated her like some little girl. She stepped away from his touch.

"Good luck to you, ma'am," Lawes said. If her movement upset him, he didn't show it. "These gentlemen will show you back out once you are done or if you need any help in there."

"Thank you, Warden," Kelly said.

When the guards opened the door and stepped aside, Lawrence's mouth fell open as Kelly entered.

"Detective Kelly!" He half-stood before the guards rushed forward to push him back. "Easy, okay, easy boys. Just trying to greet an old friend. Easy."

"I've got this, officers. Thank you." Kelly dropped the box on the small stainless-steel table. Biting back her feelings, Kelly reached out her hand and allowed Lawrence to kiss it. She fought the urge of wrenching it away by reminding herself she was here for a purpose, not to settle a score.

"Well, I'll be," Lawrence said. "How's the new addition to the family?"

"Good." She didn't like him talking about her personal life. She took the lid off the box and began to organize its contents as well as her thoughts. "Been some time."

"I hear you are in Chicago now. You know, I spent some time there."

Kelly's gaze snapped up to meet Lawrence's devilish half-grin. Her shiver had nothing to do with the temperature of the room. For all the times they'd met in the past, it wasn't until this moment, Kelly truly realized what Lawrence was: a completely psychotic killer.

She laid out the pictures. "Baltimore," she said, flipping three photographs. "Miami." Flipping another. "Chicago. New Jersey. New York."

The table was covered with photographs of lifeless bodies. Lawrence glanced at them, but showed no emotion. Time to change tactics.

"Yellow," Kelly said.

Lawrence's brow furrowed. "Yellow?"

"Why did you want it painted yellow?"

"Ah! Well, so everyone can see it from miles away, of course. Brown, you see, blends in. Brown is without imagination, but yellow!"

It was clear he wanted Kelly to approve. Wanted *anyone* to approve, and in that look, he showed his weakness. Every man had a tell, and Lawrence had just given his up.

"Seems a bit much for your accomplishments," Kelly said flatly.

"Pardon?" Lawrence asked, the smile dropping off his face.

"Well, one murder? I'm not sure if someone who has killed one person really deserves for everyone to see him. Know what I mean?"

"I'm afraid I don't. May I ask how many people you have killed, Detective Kelly?" An edge entered Lawrence's voice.

"Just in New York?" She let the question hang, allowing its implications to sink in. "Look, I'm just saying, it's not that I don't think it's a bold move. I do. Hell, I think asking for the hanging itself is a bold move, but anyone can kill one person for insurance money. Happens all the time. Happens more than you would think." Kelly glanced down as if noticing the pictures for the first time. When she looked up, she noticed Lawrence studying them.

"Now," Kelly continued. "Five murders, ten, hell, twenty? Twenty definitely warrants yellow gallows. Maybe even with lights." She nodded as if affirming this thought. "And more than that, I think it would warrant more public attention. That many murders? A man like that, they'd probably talk about forever."

"You think?" Lawrence asked, failing to hide the disinterest in his voice.

Kelly knew she had him.

"Oh, sure. 'Bugs' Moran, Ma Barker, Al Capone. Everyone knows them. They made actual contributions. People feared them, were correct to fear them. They were brilliant in their own way. Bet we'll be talking about them long after you and I are dead. Well…"

They sat in silence for several minutes before Kelly decided this was it. She needed to see if the seed she planted would sprout, if Lawrence's ego was bigger than his desire of self-preservation and dislike of a woman's goading.

She returned the photographs to the box, then stood and held out her hand. No dainty fingers. No invite for a kiss. All business.

"Mr. Henry, I am sorry we are meeting again under such circumstances, but I hope everything goes smoothly."

Lawrence took her hand, but didn't let go. Kelly started to pull back, but Lawrence held on tighter. She thought about calling the guards as the panic rose in her stomach.

Had it been a mistake to call him out like that?

Then she relaxed. Stared into his eyes. Dared him to talk.

"Let me tell you a story," he said.

Author's Note

This story was loosely based on the 1894 killing of Catherine (Kitty) M. Ging by Harry T. Hayward. Mr. Hayward was an heir to a wealthy family, but had a gambling problem and frequently sought money from various people.

Ms. Ging was a self-employed and talented 29-year-old seamstress. The two began dating, Hayward quickly borrowing more and more sums of money before finally taking out a life insurance policy on her. Ms. Ging was described as an intelligent woman, but no doubt her "advanced" age played a role in being swept up and wooed by a rich swindler.

Hayward tried to get his brother, and a person from his own building involved in her murder, even offering to split some of the insurance money, but both refused. One night, Hayward picked Ging up in a carriage and took her to the waterfront, then shot her in the head and left her body to be found by workers the next morning.

Hayward "assisted" the investigation, bringing false leads and stories of Ging's "money troubles" to the cops, while also bragging around town about the insurance money he would receive.

Finally, both the brother, and man from the building turned on Hayward and he was convicted of her murder in 1895.

Hayward was sentence to death by hanging, and ever the showman, requested the gallows be painted red so they'd be more visible. A journalist cousin interviewed Hayward before his death, the latter revealing he'd killed two other people he owed money to, though it was never proven he was involved in any additional murders.

If you are interested in learning more about this fascinating and tragic case, I encourage you to check out the wonderful podcast by Most Notorious!: A True Crime History Podcast.

Two historical figures also make appearances in this book, Charles "Lucky" Luciano and Lt. Col. Calvin Goddard. Lucky Luciano ran a crime syndicate in the early 1930s in New York, at one point starting a governing body for organized crime nation-wide called "The Commission." His use in this story is completely fictitious.

Goddard is considered by many as the "father of forensic firearms examination". He was involved in many prominent cases in the 1920s, including the St. Valentine's Day Massacre in Chicago involving the Bugs Moran crime family. This work specifically led to his moving from New York to Chicago to establish the Bureau of Forensic Ballistics, as well as the American Journal of Police Sciences.

He revolutionized using a microscope to compare objects. To this day, many of his techniques are still used by firearms examiners all over the world. His use in this story is also completely fictitious; however the science and procedure are historically accurate.

While female detectives were starting to be accepted in police departments starting as early as 1890, it wouldn't be until 1967 that a female firearms examiner would join the profession (in the Chicago area actually). I am extremely lucky to have trained under Susan Komar when I went through my forensic firearms training. I owe her and all the women scientists who came before me a great deal.

A word about the author...

Kristin Durfee lives in Central Florida and when not enjoying the sun with her husband, son, and two quirky dogs, you can usually find her on a run, horseback ride, or wandering around a theme park. *Shot* is her first novel for adults.

****

www.kristindurfee.com

****

If you enjoyed this story, leaving a review at your favorite book retailer or reader website would be much appreciated. Thank you!